To my beautiful mother, Tena, I wish you could have read my book. I love and miss you every day.

AMERICAN OBSESSION

MEGAN SENA

ARCHWAY
PUBLISHING

Archway Publishing books may be ordered
through booksellers or by contacting:

Archway Publishing
1663 Liberty Drive
Bloomington, IN 47403
www.archwaypublishing.com
844-669-3957

ISBN: 978-1-6657-5325-8 (sc)
ISBN: 978-1-6657-5324-1 (e)

Library of Congress Control Number: 2023921801

Print information available on the last page.

Archway Publishing rev. date: 11/29/2023

CHAPTER 1

LIV

THE DOORBELL IS GOING TO go off any minute.

I've been hastily curling my long dark brown hair into something manageable for ten minutes now. It's just not working. Too much hair spray still litters my hair from last the night's show. I was so busy all day that I didn't have time to wash it. Now it's a losing battle. Screw it! It's going in a messy bun.

Thankfully, my makeup went on fast, and I already knew what I was wearing: a white spaghetti strap cami dress with some burgundy and dusty pink flowers on it. It comes down to about mid-thigh, and I plan on pairing it with a distressed light wash jean jacket and my favorite tan wedges. Simple, comfy, and perfect for my date tonight. It's a nice July night in the low 80's.

It's my first date with Kevin. I was completely caught off guard last week when I went to the bank to make a deposit into our bands account. Kevin was standing next to the teller, and then proceeded to ask me in a quiet voice, "Olivia, can I take you out for dinner some time?"

It was the last thing I was expecting, and the way the young teller next to him smiled at me with big, enthusiastic eyes I didn't dare say no. I got the feeling she was more excited about the idea than I was.

I have to say in all the times I've been in the bank I don't think I've ever talked to him. Maybe he's a new banker there. Maybe I just have tunnel vision, who the hell knows.

I looked him up on Facebook. Kevin Baker. He grew up in a place about two hours from where he is now in Pine Lake, Minnesota. He seems to be way into sports from the little I could see on his page without being his friend.

I finish assembling my mop of hair into a messy bun on the top of my head. A quick glance at my vividly white teeth in the mirror to make sure there are no foreign objects, and I am good to go.

I flick the switch off in my master bathroom, the sage green walls darkening as the lights fade out. I head into the bright white walk-in closet, looking myself over in the floor length mirror one more time, then turn off the light. I make it about three steps when I hear the chirp of my doorbell. He's here, I timed this perfectly for once, usually I'm scrambling until the last second.

Making it out of my bedroom, down the hall and to the entry way, I let out a deep breath before I open the heavy wood front door of my house. Not going to lie, I'm just not sure I'm that interested in this guy, even though in all fairness I know nothing about him.

Putting on an enthused face, I open the door. For a moment, I can't seem to remember his name. *Kevin. Kevin. Kevin.* I remind myself a few times. Although, if I haven't remembered it already then at some point tonight, he's probably going to get called Karl, or Kelly, or something.

His blonde hair is slicked to the side and from the looks of it, he spent more time on his hair than I did on mine. He has bright blue eyes, and a nice smile. I wonder if he was in a frat. He looks like a frat guy that you would see in the movies. Tucked in white polo shirt, khaki pants, and a copious amount of hair gel. In my head, I joke that his date clothes and work clothes are one in the same. He probably has pajamas to match. The voice in my head says *knock it off Liv.*

"Hey Kevin, come on in," I silently applaud myself for getting his name right. He's holding a small bouquet of flowers. Yellow tulips, daisies, and a few red and pink roses are sprayed together in a pretty bundle.

"Hi Olivia. Here, these are for you." He awkwardly holds the flowers out to me as he comes in the door.

"They're beautiful, thank you," I tell him with a smile. Then, I turn and head into the kitchen, grabbing a vase from one of the bottom cabinets. I fill it up with water from the sink and place the flowers inside it. That was sweet of him.

I'm not good with flowers as they usually die the second I look away from them. They've probably already started their slow painful death just by being in my house.

"What's the plan for tonight?" I ask, peeking my head around the corner as I get done arranging them in the vase of water.

"I was thinking Antonio's for dinner, if that's alright with you," he says nervously as he glances around my open living and dining room from the entry way.

"Sounds great." Antonio's is always delicious, and hopefully it will be good company as well. *He'll either be the one, or just another one* I think to myself. We shall see.

The band I'm in has a show scheduled most Fridays over the summer, but not tonight. Our drummer has other plans, so we ended up doing Thursday and Saturday shows this week, so it worked out good for Kevin and me to go out tonight. We don't get too many weekend nights off in the busy season but when we do, it's always a nice reprieve.

I gather up my phone and keys from the kitchen counter and stick them in my small black purse. Locking the door behind us, we walk in silence down the sidewalk to his car. A white Altima. I feel like this car fits him. I always think it's funny when people's cars fits their personalities, sort of like when pets look like their owners.

He opens the car door for me like a gentleman. I slide into the smooth leather seat as he walks around the front and gets in on the driver's side.

We sit in awkward silence almost the entire ten-minute drive to Antonio's. Is he normally this quiet, or is he nervous? I make a little small talk but not much gets reciprocated, so I don't push it. Some new age pop music is on the radio, playing a song I've never heard, and judging from the fact that I can't pick out a single word of what they are saying, I don't think I want to hear it again.

Antonio's is a restaurant sitting on the outskirts of Pine Lake, on the edge of the golf course. There is a bar side and a dining room side. There are Edison style string lights hanging above the patio on the dining side, illuminating the evening sky as we drive up. I hope that's where we sit, so we can enjoy the warm evening weather.

We walk up the lit path to the front door and a young man in all black opens it for us and greets us. His eyes take a rather too long survey of my body and I shoot him my notorious, "don't push me" look. Kevin catches on and immediately his cheeks flush.

For once, I'd like to date a guy that would go on the defense for me in these situations. Give him his best "piss off dude" look and get all territorial. And then go back to being charming. Why is that too much to ask? Where are those guys hiding?

Luckily the host can get us out on the patio. It's an ideal summer evening to be sitting out here. Clear sky, light breeze, not too hot. Apparently, everyone else had the same idea, the patio is packed. We take our seats at a small metal table set for two at the edge of the deck.

I order the shrimp carbonara and a glass of Moscato. Kevin gets spaghetti and a Coke. I don't know what it is about this guy, but he just seems a little uptight. Hopefully he's just nervous and not always like this. Maybe he doesn't drink. I remind myself again to stop judging and have fun.

I sip on my wine as we wait on the waiter for the order we have placed. I catch multiple glances in my direction from other customers on the patio. I do my best to ignore them and focus on my own table. This happens a lot. They know who I am, I get that. But sometimes it makes me want to stand up and announce it in a bold, cheeky way. *Hey, yep seen you looking! I'm Olivia, or Liv, and I'm the chick in that band you've all seen – American Obsession. Want a picture? Maybe an autograph? Should I come sign your baby's forehead?*

Sometimes I just want to be that kind of smart ass. I'm used to this happening but don't always particularly enjoy it.

It makes me happy that our band is successful, but sometimes it gets odd knowing that people are staring at you when all you crave is everyone minding his or her own business. It's one thing when it's on stage, that's to be expected, but right now I'm trying to hold my own on this awkward date, and I don't need strangers making it weirder than it already is.

Kevin senses the other patrons staring as well. He clears his throat, and I can tell he wants to say something.

"So, are you originally from Pine Lake or did you move here for the band? I'm a big fan of AO by the way."

Ah, he knows about the band. I'm not surprised. Hell, he's probably looked at our bank account and been to every show.

Sometimes I wonder if I get asked out because of the popularity of the band that I'm in, or if guys really do want to go out with me because of who I am.

I guess I wouldn't be surprised if guys ask me out in interest, it just seems like some guys get wrapped up in the fact that I'm on stage all the time. Then there are guys who are only interested in my looks; those ones are never worth keeping around.

I work out often – okay, I work out *obsessively*, so I'm in great shape, not to mention the amount of sweating I do on stage at our shows every week, it keeps me damn fit.

I'm average height, 5'7", and petite. My hair is a darker ashy brown and long. It goes down to about where my bra rests on my back. I have a few layers in it, nothing too crazy. I don't have that rocker chick hair that some people would expect, or gobs of tattoos. Just one string of flowers and leaves that runs on my back, kind of curling around down my right side under my arm. I have my ears and left nostril pierced, just a tiny stud in my nose. I doubt most people even notice it until they get very close.

I usually dress the part of typical rocker chick for shows but when I'm off stage I'm just like everyone else. I'm just me, dressing like many other people of my economy status, doing what the average person does.

I'm a perfectionist when it comes to my appearance. I guess I need to be since I'm almost always under everyone's microscope, which is overwhelming and feels like it's all the time. Some of that also came from my mom. She was a cosmetologist and fixated over my looks when I was growing up, which I was irritated with as a child, but came to appreciate once I became a teenager.

I realize that I've been spacing out with my own thoughts for a hot minute. I hope my date hasn't been asking me anything. If he has been, I sure as hell wasn't listening. I look over at him and he's looking around the patio mindlessly. I don't think I missed anything.

Finally, our dishes arrive, thank goodness. We dig in, which is like a comforting safety blanket during our date, it hopefully won't be as awkward now. I order a second glass of Moscato, perhaps a little extra wine will make me want to talk to this guy more.

I'm just about to open my mouth to speak when there comes a heavy hand on my right shoulder.

I turn around and instantly wish I could melt into my chair. It's Mark. I went out with him two weeks ago. One of the worst dates ever. Mark was, no- is, very arrogant, and just assumed that if he took me out for dinner and drinks, he would get lucky. Well, sorry not sorry Mark, that wasn't going to happen. He had made a couple snide comments to me that night about me not asking him in after he brought me home.

"Hey, you haven't returned my calls, *or* my texts," he says with way too much arrogance, his hand still on my shoulder.

"Sorry, been busy, which is kind of the story of my life," I say, brushing aside his hand, trying to think of anything to combat him.

"Clearly you aren't too busy to go out with this guy," he shoves a finger in Kevin's direction.

I give him my "don't push me" glare with my eyes squared at him. Second time tonight that I've had to use that look. All I can manage to choke out is a clipped, "don't be rude."

"Whatever. Call me if you wanna hang," and he turns and walks away. It's too bad he's such a creep. He's a great looking guy, and he's almost done with law school. I like a guy with goals and a lot going for him, but not a guy with too big of an ego.

I look over at my date who has a mouthful of spaghetti and a petrified look on his face.

"Sorry about that guy, he was a bad date I had hoped to not run in to again." He just nods and keeps on chewing. He never says a word about it, as if he couldn't care less now that Mark has walked away.

We finish our food with too little being said between us. After we pay our tab, we get up and start heading inside, past the bar, toward the front door.

It's a Friday night and the place is packed. The bar area patrons are loud, most likely enjoying a liquid dinner. A young girl at a high-top table of five shouts, "hey" above the crowd and waves her hand in my direction as we pass by. Shit, another person who wants a picture, I guarantee it. She gets off her stool and makes her way over to me, a big smile plastered on her face. I can smell the booze on her breath as she gets closer to me.

"No way, you are Oliva, from AO! We are in town for a girls' weekend; we are going to your show tomorrow!" She exclaims a little too loudly. Next thing I know, her four girlfriends are all over me as well, asking Kevin to take a picture of us.

I nod my head in agreement to take a picture with them, and they all gather around me. "Take a couple!" she exclaims while he fumbles with her phone. By the time they get done telling me what "big fans" they are, two guys have also walked up to us. "Hey, I'm Jake. I love going to your shows." He says with a smile. "Yeah, you are so hot, we love watching you," says the other guy. Then, like clockwork, they bust out a cell phone and request a picture. After this one I'm dashing out of here, before things get out of hand.

Kevin reluctantly takes the phone and waits for us to get in place. The guy who claimed I am "so hot" has his hand almost directly on my ass. What a snake!

After he snaps a picture, I give a half-hearted smile with a little wave and get away from them. I imagine they would have bought me drinks and talked my ear off all night. That would have been a big change from the almost silent date I just endured with Kevin. At least, Kevin's not trying to take selfies with me.

Kevin drives us back to my place. We are rounding the hilly curve of my paved driveway, past the tall mature oaks, and my house, and the garage, comes into view. There is a black car sitting in my driveway. It's Erik's.

"Whose car is that?" Kevin asks me uncomfortably. That's a legit question for a date to ask.

"That's Erik, the lead singer of AO." I'm sure he knows who that is, but I feel compelled to tell him out of courtesy.

"Does he live with you? Why is he here?" Again, valid questions.

"He has his own place, but he's over here a lot. We're very close, he's like a brother to me," I tell him, trying to smooth it over so he doesn't feel bad.

"Oh, okay," and I can tell he's uncomfortable.

Despite the awkwardness, he still walks me up to my front door. We are standing on the cement patio by the front door, facing each other. His hands are buried in his khaki pants pockets, and mine are holding my small purse in front of me.

"I had a nice time with you tonight, thank you for taking me out, and thank you for the flowers. Sorry about that guy Mark and the people that wanted pictures," I tell him with a sincere smile.

"I'm glad you came out with me, maybe we can go out again?" He makes it come out as a statement and a question all in one. I'm choosing to not answer it and take it as a statement.

"Well, good night," I say slowly just as the front door opens partially and Erik pops his head out with a mischievous smile.

Kevin panics as he leans over and gives me an awkward peck on the cheek, then turns and says, "good night" before starting to walk back to his car.

I look at Erik who is grinning and mocking me like an idiot making kissy faces at me. "You're such a shit," I tell him as I shove him back into the door, following behind him.

CHAPTER 2

LIV

"SO, WHO'S YOUR NEW STUD muffin?" Erik says mockingly as if he is the queen of gossip. He props his chin on his hands, leaning his elbows on the entry way table, like he's one of my girlfriends waiting for a juicy story. He has a playful smile on his face, accentuating his deep dimples. He has a smile that can light up a room, but right now I could smack him for being an ass.

"Kevin," I say quickly. "He works at the bank where our bands account is. I'm pretty sure he only said like three sentences to me tonight, it was a quiet date. I don't do well with people that are too quiet like that. I'm not sure we'll go out again. Ugh, now we're going to have to switch banks. Every time I go in there now it's going to be weird." I slap my hand against my forehead dramatically then take my shoes off, sliding them aside.

He smiles again and it reaches his deep brown eyes, as he runs his hand through his dirty blonde hair. It contains about one tenth as much gel as Kevin's did.

"Well, you deserve someone who can keep up with you, and he doesn't seem the type." I nod lightly in agreement but also note that Erik had only seen him for about ten seconds.

Erik looks at the time on his phone. "So, it's only 8:50...your bar still stocked? It's Friday night and I need a beer."

"Did you come all the way over here just to steal the beer from my fridge? What's wrong with yours?" I say mockingly, but he has already turned to go to the basement bar. Not that I really care; this isn't the first time, and it won't be the last.

Sometimes it's just Erik over here, and sometimes it's the whole band – Erik, Joe, Waylon, and Darren. We have an open-door policy with one another. Pretty sure I've never locked the doors of my house; I think they would freak out if they couldn't get in.

I'm putting my jacket away as I hear Erik snapping off the cap on a beer bottle. Grabbing my phone from my purse I head down the carpeted stairs to him.

The bar is on the far side of my rec room in the basement. The stairs come right down to the edge of the room, and as I'm on the last step, I jeer Erik. "You drink me out of house and home already?" His tall, muscular frame is already perched on one of the four barstools at the table in the center of the bar.

It's not much of a bar really, just a bar top table, four black stools, and a full-size fridge that I apparently always need to keep stocked. About a half dozen liquor bottles adorn the shelf on one of the walls, and the rest of the walls are covered in odds and ends and random bar signage. My favorite is the antique sign that reads, "Kindly Control Yourself" that I got from my grandpa's collection of old stuff.

Across from the bar, the rec room has a dark brown leather sectional sofa, and an oversized chaise lounge. The chaise is my spot, none of the guys dare sit there because they know they will catch holy hell if they do. The sofas face a large flat screen, and on the other side of the room is a pool table. I never use it, but they enjoy it when they are over. I'm terrible at pool, even though the guys have been teaching me how to play for quite some time. It's just not my thing.

"Have a glass of wine and drink with me. Here, I'll pour you one," Erik says. He gets up and starts pouring me a tall glass of Moscato from the open bottle in the fridge.

"Fine, just one." I look apprehensively at the way over full glass of wine that he's pouring for me.

"I'm thinking I should spend the night here so we can get messed up. I want to enjoy our night off," he shoots me a wink and his charming smile.

"What about that girl you have been out with – LeeAnn? She seems nice, maybe you should go drink her beer." I say with my usual clip of sarcasm.

"I'm not seeing LeeAnn anymore," he says, without a hint of remorse.

"Why not? I thought you liked her."

"She was okay, but all she wants to talk about is the band and shows, and blah blah blah…. she was just another wanna-be groupie type. I broke it off with her this morning."

"Oh," I say as I collect my thoughts. I guess I never seen that side of her. Not that they dated long enough for me to get to know her well.

Erik has quite the following of women that seem to fixate over him. I guess you can't blame them because he is handsome, and extremely talented. When he's up on stage doing what he loves, he is so carefree. I'll never tell him, but there is a sexiness that radiates off him.

He has struggled with dating for a while, only finding women who want him because he is on a stage and in a spotlight, not so much for his real personality. He has no shortage of dates, just a shortage of women he finds he can connect to. It's sad, he is one of the most loyal and honest people I know.

His family moved here when he was in second grade. I was his first friend, we hit it off instantly when he first showed up at school. We have been inseparable since then.

Almost immediately after high school his parents moved away. His dad took on a new job and had to relocate but Erik decided to stay here in Pine Lake and get his own apartment.

His parents have always been very supportive of him and the band, and there is nothing more that Erik dreams of than landing a record deal someday. I just wish he find that right person in life to follow him on his journey getting there.

I can relate with him in so many ways – I've had my fair share of crazy fans who follow me around like lost puppies, looking for me to take them in. I've also dated guys that seem to only be interested in me because of our band's popularity, or because of my looks and they just want to get in my pants. I suppose Mr. Right is out there somewhere. Apparently I need to kiss a lot of frogs before I'm allowed to find him.

"Fine, one enormous glass of wine for me I guess." His lips quiver up into a wicked smile as I take the glass, as if I'm the prey and he's got me backed into a corner.

CHAPTER 3

LIV

I'M DIZZY FROM THE EVENTS of the previous evening. We stayed up way too late, talking for hours, and he cleaned me out of beer...again. I shake my head in disbelief at myself while pulling on my black leggings and pink tank top. I need a good run to clear my head and shake off this hangover. If I don't start my day with a run, I feel like absolute hell.

Erik has already left. I know some of our nights together, he wishes things would happen between us. I can see it in his eyes occasionally, and I do my best to brush it off and act like I don't notice it.

We dated in high school, which eventually we figured out was a mistake. If we fought, it created tension in the band, and we never wanted our group to have to pick sides when it came to us. We broke it off mutually and have been closer as friends than we ever were as a couple. Don't get me wrong, we had a great connection, and the sex was good, but if our relationship would have ended badly it could have destroyed the band. It wasn't worth the chance.

Now, in our mid-twenties, he's drunkenly and stupidly brought up a "friends with benefits" physical reunion of sorts a few times. Usually, it happens after he's broken up with someone and he's frustrated. Unfortunately for him, it never pans out and I plan on keeping it that way. I don't feel the same, I see us hooking up as a liability.

I take my two daily pills with some water and head out the front door. Even in the early morning hour, the hot July sun is already beating down on me and last night's wine is already seeping out of my pores. I'm going to run this hangover right out of my body. Luckily my run is mindless, last night floating out of my mind. I go my same course as usual. Down my winding driveway that curves through the trees, and past the other four houses that make up our small development just on the edge of the town. It's a nice quiet area, close to everything but still has lots of privacy. My neighbors are great. All older couples that have lived here for a while and keep to themselves.

I turn left and run along Highway 128. Almost all my morning runs go along this route, about two miles in each direction. Every day I run; I wouldn't want to start my day any other way.

I make it to an old dead oak tree that hangs close to the road, that is my marker to stop. I stop and rest for a minute and catch my breath.

I turn on my heel and start back in the other direction. Back up 128 to Crescent Hill Road, where I am the last house. Going back is always worse; it's a winding and uphill battle.

As I get up to my yard, I spot a familiar vehicle. My best friend Lexie's car. She's waiting outside on the front porch as I jog up the driveway, and dramatically collapse in the grass in front of her.

Lexie stops by as she pleases, just like the AO boys do. It makes me happy people want to come over and hang out and they feel comfortable just showing up.

"I see you were out for your morning five miles of torture," her dark chocolate brown eyes giving me an eye roll.

"Actually, it's about four miles. But sometimes when I'm having a good day, I go farther."

"Yuck, you are a crazy person."

Lexie is not the ambitious type when it comes to running or working out. I'm the opposite. I love it and hate the days that I can't go for a run, which are few and far in-between. I keep telling her she should run with me; she's always complaining about her weight. I don't think she's overweight, but she seems to think so.

"I just sweat out like three quarters of a bottle of Moscato. Erik and I tied one on last night," I say with a groan at the end.

"Was it another night of a lame attempt to get you in bed?" She flicks her blonde hair over her shoulder and eyes me suspiciously.

"No, luckily, he was just in the mood to chat. Apparently, him and LeeAnn broke up. Now he's free to be all yours." I give her a wink.

Lexie's cheeks flush with embarrassment at my comment. We both know she thinks he's hot but will never make a move. She doesn't even bother to jab me back.

"What does your day look like? I have time to hang out if you want," she says. She's over here often on the weekends, as neither of us work and can go do things together, unless I have a show and band things to do. She is the office manager at a chiropractic office in town and has been there for a few years now. She is probably one of the most dependable and reliable people I know.

"I need to be at the radio station by 1:30, AO is doing a live air interview at 2:00. Then we have our show tonight at Garden Park. Why, what did you have in mind?"

"I don't know, I just didn't have plans. Maybe tomorrow we can round people up and have a girls' night?" There is a hopefulness in her voice, she must be bored.

Hell yes, I am always up for girls' night. We both simultaneously do our, "girls' night, girls' night, woo-woo," jingle in our girly voices and laugh.

CHAPTER 4

LIV

I STAND OUTSIDE THE RADIO station building and wait for the rest of the band to show up. One by one they appear.

The first one to pull up is Erik in his black 1963 Chevy Impala, I swear, that car just fits him to a "T". He has this James Dean look to him, usually in a basic white T-shirt and jeans, and lightly gelled hair. It's a little longer on the top then on the sides. He just looks like he belongs in 1963, right along with his car, which is his baby. All he needs to complete the look is a pack of cigarettes rolled up into the sleeve of his shirt, like one of the T-Birds from Grease.

"What's up James Dean?" I say with a smirk.

"I think you think that will offend me, but it doesn't." He says, walking up, slapping me in the ass and giving me a smirk. I just roll my eyes.

We both look over and see Darren roll in, his Maxima barely making a sound.

Darren is one of my best friends, like a brother. Although all these boys are like my brothers. Darren is my go-to for advice on guys – being that he likes them too, we get to go out on the town and scope out the local talent together.

His skinny frame slides out of his car and heads our direction, his dark hair gelled and styled to perfection, tousled, and twirled dramatically on the top, brown eyes covered in dark sunglasses. He has a black and white Ramones T-shirt on.

Rolling in behind him is our bassist, Waylon. He's big and bulky and mostly covered in tattoos. He climbs down out of his dark blue F-250 and joins us in the parking lot.

Waylon is not the kind of guy you mess with. He had a rough upbringing. When he was in junior high school his parents divorced, and they basically left him to fend for himself. They were both into drugs and didn't give him the time of day, much less take care of him or themselves. He cut ties with them and hasn't spoken to either of them since. He takes no shit from anyone but also has the biggest heart of anyone I've met, if you stay on his good side. He's 6'3", with long wavy dark brown hair and a beard. He is covered in tattoos and has a deep growl of a voice. I call him "Way" for short.

"Way, again with that shirt...do you ever wash it? Also, you realize we are going to be on the radio, and nobody will be able to see it, right?" For his birthday, I got him a black T-shirt that says: "I slap that bass"; the "b" is crossed out with a red line, so it says "ass". He's had it about a month and I've seen him wear it like fifteen times already.

"It's my favorite. I need about five more of these, so I don't have to do laundry so often," he says, walking up to me and points to the shirt with a smile.

"Just waiting on Joe," Erik says. Joe is our drummer and our always fashionably late member of the band.

"Probably working on his last puff-puff-pass," Darren says as he pulls off his sunglasses, a smirk on his face.

Joe Dannon is our resident pot head. Rarely drinks, but usually smells like weed. We hear the whir of a car and Joe's little Ford Fiesta wizzes into the parking lot, coming to a stop in front of us. His bald head and thin but muscular frame steps out of the car and he's chewing on a piece of gum.

"I'm here, I know, shut up, I'm always the last one," we smile and nod in agreement and head into the radio station together.

Once inside, the receptionist directs us to a room with a long table with multiple chairs, headsets, and microphones at each spot. It smells like Clorox and leather. A short scruffy dark-haired man comes in from an adjacent door, I recognize the booming voice immediately, although the face is new.

"Hi, I'm James Fuller, with KQ98 Radio, welcome American Obsession!"

We are given the rundown of how our interview will go. We were already told the questions he plans on asking, so this shouldn't be hard.

He seems excited for us to be here. I've listened to him many times on the radio, although now more XM gets played in my car than FM, but I'm not going to tell him that.

James: "How did American Obsession get started?"

Erik: "Music was always intriguing to me, and Liv and I learned at a young age we shared that passion. We've been best friends ever since I moved to Pine Lake."

Liv: "Both of us started guitar lessons in fourth grade and found every excuse to play together after that. We took turns going from Erik's house to mine, which was necessary since our parents weren't amused at the noise we made."

Erik: "In sixth grade we decided we wanted to start a band. We asked other kids if they wanted to play with us. Not understanding how much we wanted to play, nobody really took us seriously. Finally, we came across Joe. He was just starting out in the school band, trying out percussion."

Liv: "I remember the day we asked him to play with us, it was over lunch, and he happily agreed. We met up after school that same day at Joe's house. We were thrilled he was willing to consider it and didn't make fun of us."

Joe: "We played together almost nine months, before our bassist Waylon joined our group. He was kind of unruly, and most of the kids were scared of him but we weren't. He wasn't into playing music at that time, but we really liked him, so we convinced him to take lessons that summer. He took a liking to it and has been with us ever since."

Waylon: "Our last addition was Darren, and by the time he joined the band, we were halfway through seventh grade."

James: "How did the band get its name, *American Obsession?*"

Erik: "Oh, we quickly realized early on that guys would obsess over Liv, so we nicknamed her *Obsession Olivia.* For the first few years we didn't have a band name, we were just kids playing together. Then one day when we were giving Liv hell about guys, and Darren blurted out, "she's like an American Obsession." We decided it might make a good band name and it just stuck."

Joe: "Yeah and now every time Erik rips his shirt off at a show, it's the women obsessing over him, so it works in more ways than one."

James: "Where did you practice at?"

Waylon: "We spent countless hours, days, and weeks playing in the shed behind Joe's mom's house. After his mom and dads divorce, Joe's dad's tools no longer occupied the space, so we gladly took it over. We furnished it with some couches that were left for dead on the side of the road, some garage sale tables, and the most random collection of band posters, wall art, and broken neon signs. Its trashy but we love it. When we were ninth graders, we all assumed the band was going to be a huge success, so we wrote ourselves a "contract". It still hangs on the wall in there. We still practice in the shed at Joe's house to this day."

James: "You mentioned a contract – what do you mean by that?"

Darren: "We made rules: no changing members, we are either all in or we are all out; we don't keep anything from each other, no secrets, ever; and any money made was divided equally between us all, even though at the time we had yet to have a paying gig.

We put it in a cheap $2.00 frame and hung it on the wall in the shed, all our sloppy signatures scribbled on the page. In the years that passed after we used it as a scapegoat, calling it silly and juvenile, but the unspoken fact is that we put a lot of stock into the rules that our teenage selves created."

James: "Wow, what a great story!"

Erik: "Some of the band members didn't have good upbringings. So, for us to be together as a group made us better people. We've grown together, through all our ups and downs: the fights, and the best moments. We have shared it all together. We never realized at the time that those days would mold us into the people we feel we were truly meant to be, the American Obsession band."

James: "Have you been approached by any record labels?"

Waylon: "No, but we also haven't gone public with our own music. Covers only at this point."

James: "So are you implying you have written your own music?"

Erik: "There's a chance."

Liv: "Let's just be frank here, we are working on our own music."

James: "So, right now you are staying around this area – do you hope to make it big some day?"

Joe: "We cover about a three-state area right now, doing shows at lots of different venues. We sell out pretty much every time we do a public show."

Darren: "It would be awesome to make it big. Maybe one of these days we will catch a break."

CHAPTER 5

JAY

"A SATURDAY NIGHT AT GARDEN Park when American Obsession is playing is always awesome, you are going to love this," my older brother Brandon rambles on in the car as he drives us through Pine Lake. He was hell bent on getting me out tonight.

"I've seen them so many times in concert I can't even count. Manda loves them too." His wife Amanda is in the front seat nodding her head, a big smile on her face.

"Jay, you will love them. And honestly, I'm so happy you came out with us. Now let's get you drunk and laid!" I can tell she's already had a few drinks, normally she's much more reserved than this. Her blonde head is bobbing to the rock music playing over the radio.

Brandon is giving her a sideways glance as if she's a lunatic. I am for sure having some drinks tonight; it's been a while since I've been out. Thinking about it, this will be my first night out since moving to Pine Lake.

Brandon and Amanda, along with my parents and most of my extended family live about thirty minutes away in Greensboro, which is where I grew up. Pine Lake has a population of about 70,000, which is about twice the size of my hometown. I hope the move to a slightly bigger city will be a good change for me.

It was time for a change, everyone was telling me, even my therapist. I knew it had been a lot of years of being in a funk, and apparently, I've reached my limit and need to move on.

"Maybe you can find someone that will be willing to go back to your new loft with you," Brandon says with a raised eyebrow and a glance at me in the rearview mirror.

"I doubt it, no girl is going to want to come back to some guys loft mid-renovation."

"Just go have a good time tonight," Brandon adds with a reassuring smile.

Garden Park is absolutely packed. We park what feels like seven miles away. At this rate we could have just walked from my place, which is about two blocks off Broadway, about a ten-minute drive away. People are pouring out of cars, dressed up and ready to party, filing through the parking lot to get to the front door of the event center.

We get to three sets of double doors at the entry way. This place is huge. It takes me a minute to look around and take it all in as I walk through the door. A two-story concert and show venue, with a bar on the main level and another upstairs. The dance floor area is massive, with some bar height tables and chairs around the perimeter. The walls are combinations of red and black, with huge bar signs and TV's on them. The upstairs bar is visible beyond a black metal railing, tables spread along the edge of the terrace, with views of the space below. There is a stage inside to the right where a black curtain is drawn, the band presumably behind it, getting ready for the show.

We get past security where they check our ID's and give us wrist bands. First thing I'm doing is heading to the bar to see what they have for whiskey. Brandon and Amanda are in front of me, getting in the line of people waiting for drinks. I would imagine this is the kind of place where you grab two at a time because the lines can get ridiculous.

As we walk to the busy bar, I hear the first few pounding beats of a bass drum and the wail of an electric guitar. I look over to see the stage curtain get pulled to the sides, exposing a five-person band. The venue lights dim, and the bands lights come to life. There is a spotlight is on the singer. She's the most gorgeous woman I've ever seen. Long dark hair, clad in tight black leather pants, black boots, and a white T-shirt. She is absolutely owning the stage, singing the lyrics to her own rendition of Queen's, "We Will Rock You." The crowd in front of her is mesmerized and so am I.

I can't take my eyes off her. The fog machine is billowing out smoke and its seeping around her as she commands the crowd's attention. Red, green, white, and blue lights change in and out of color, creating a glow around her figure. Forget the other four guys on stage, she might as well be the only person up there.

The song ends and I realize I have unknowingly gravitated towards the stage, about halfway into the crowd. The guitar strums of Sweet Home Alabama are now playing in the background, and they introduce themselves as American Obsession. That seems like a fitting name for how I'm feeling right now. I'm pretty sure I'm going to be at every show from here on out.

The rest of the song picks up, and wow, she is smooth with that guitar. I don't know much about music, but witnessing this I can tell she's a natural.

"Hey, thought you were seeking out the nearest whiskey," my brother slaps me on the back.

I barely look away from her. Brandon and Amanda made it to the bar and have red plastic cups of beer in their hands.

"Manda, looks like he's already hooked, only took one song," my brother says, mocking me.

"I knew it, you are going to have so much fun. Let's get closer so we can dance. I want to *feel* the music!" I never see her like this. It's kind of a fun change. Usually, her large eyes and round features are in listening mode instead of talking and partying mode. I've been waiting for her to come out of her shell. She and my brother have been married for seven months now, but we haven't been out this much together.

Brandon and Amanda start sneaking their way through the crowd, with me close in tow. "We want to get up front, right in front of her," I yell to him above the crowd. He looks back and shoots me a crooked smile with raised eyebrows. He listens though, and after a few minutes, and many dirty looks and elbow jabs later, here we are...right where I want to be, right in front of her.

Guns 'N Roses' "Paradise City" is slowly starting. Her guitar kicks into high gear and this might be the greatest thing I've ever seen. I'm pretty sure Brandon and Amanda are secretly laughing at me, but I don't care.

The band plays through their set list, and I have yet to get a drink, much less leave my place at the stage. I've never felt so compelled to catch every second of something like this before. I'm absolutely mesmerized by her. I've had a couple girlfriends but have never felt an instant fascination to someone like this.

I've been a recluse of sorts over the years, but I feel like tonight something has awoken inside me and come whirring to life. My goal in life for so many years has been to just survive my days and not feel so depressed, but now I have a new goal – to see her shows, figure her out, to know her.

She sets her guitar on one of the stands behind her. A skinny dark-haired band member picks up another guitar. He has been switching back and forth between keyboard and guitar throughout the set.

He stands back farther than she does and a little to her left, at least from my perspective.

The drums have had a slow steady beat in between the songs, and I wonder what they are going to sing next.

She grabs the microphone off its stand and turns back and shoots the drummer and keyboard-guitar guy a look, I'm guessing to make sure they are good to go.

They start the next song simultaneously. Dear God, it's Halestorm's, "I Get Off."

Microphone in hand, she approaches the front and center stage. She sounds so much like Lzzy Hale. The music really ticks up and she is screaming her heart out.

As she starts the second verse, she slowly moves around the stage. She goes to the right, away from my side, entertaining the crowd, then starts back towards my side. This is exhilarating. The crowd is really into it, singing and dancing along.

She moves closer, and now she's right in front of me. I could almost reach out and touch her. The song slows and she slowly bends her knees and gets closer to the floor.

She has her eyes intermittently closed while she sings, and as she opens them, they move and focus right on me. I can't breathe. She is still staring; and I can't stop either.

After a few moments, she raises back up and launches right back into the next lyrics of the song. She doesn't move away though, she stays right where she is on stage, finishes the song, and maybe I'm hallucinating but I'm pretty sure she glances at me a couple more times.

That's it. Last song. I need more.

The band members wave and give their goodbye's. They aren't even off the stage yet and the crowd is chanting "one more song".

They stay backstage for a minute, and sure enough, reappear with smiles. As if they didn't see this coming, I bet it happens at every show.

The drummer, who whipped his shirt off long ago, starts into a leading beat. The male lead singer, who is front stage with her, takes his shirt off too. He turns enough that I can see his back is covered in tattoos. I hope to hell he and she don't date. The women in the crowd are going ballistic. He just smiles, clearly, he knows the effect he has on them.

Her electric guitar starts in the first chords of Hinder's "Up All Night". The song launches and the crowd is in a frenzy, soaking up the last of the excitement from the band for the night. These guys can play a range of different things and just rock all of them.

As the song fades out and the fog machine kicks out the last of its breath, I can see shadows of the band members. They are all ripping pieces of paper off the floor from their spots. They group up near the drums and the drummer pulls out a Sharpie. They each take turns with it on their papers.

The crowd around me is slowly dissolving, the level of drunkenness much higher than at the start of the show. Surprisingly though there are a lot of people still hovering at the front of the stage, watching the band in anticipation, even though the show is done.

All the fog has dissipated now, and I can see the band clearly. They filter out over the stage to the remaining crowd, handing their papers to them. *What's going on?*

I look up, stunned to see she's walking toward me, paper in hand. She's staring right at me. *What do I do?* She gets in front of me, crouches down, and with a flirty smile, hands the paper to me.

It's the set list, and she signed it. By the time I look back up, she's walking away, heading backstage. Fuck, I could have at least said "hi."

Amanda squeals next to me, "oh my God, you got the set list and a smile!"

Brandon grabs it and looks it over, "too bad she didn't put her phone number on there for you."

No shit. I feel like running after her, but I'm pretty sure security would get to me first.

I look at the set list. She signed it "Olivia" with a little heart. A little heart! I can feel the excitement building in my stomach. Who knows, she probably does that every time, although deep down I hope she's only ever done it for me.

CHAPTER 6

JAY

THE THREE OF US HEAD back to my mess of a loft after the show. I'm so wound up; I feel like I'm never going to be able to sleep. Brandon and Amanda are pretty buzzed off the tap beers they've been putting down all night.

It worked out in Brandon's favor that I was so distracted tonight. I didn't end up drinking at all, so I was the lucky one that got to drive us home with the drunk masses leaving the show.

Brandon and I are sitting at the newly purchased barstools at my kitchen counter, which is covered in things that still need to be unpacked. I have the lights in the loft turned down, only the kitchen and bathroom lights are on, along with the glow of the streetlights pouring in from outside through the large windows.

"What do you know about...the band?" I hesitated too long on the last part of the question.

Brandon sees right through it. "You mean what do I know about that girl, the one you never took your eyes off of."

It was a statement not a question, and he nailed it. "Yeah," I say self-consciously.

"Wow, I've never seen you worked up over a girl before, this is new." He looks happy for me, his brown eyes have a twinkle in them as he says it, a smile appearing on his face. Him and I look a lot alike, similar smiles, eyes, nose. His hair is darker than mine, and he is a little bigger than I am, He's put on some pounds since he met Amanda. She must be feeding him well.

"Yeah, yeah," I reply dryly.

"No, it's good though, it's good to see you come out of your shell after all these years. You need this."

He's not wrong, I do need to come out of my shell. I've barely dated anyone; I've never had the desire to try to care for someone new. I've had a hard enough time caring for myself.

"Let's use the internet to our advantage on this," he says as he grabs my laptop on the other end of the kitchen counter. "We can do some snooping and drink a little whiskey. Manda already passed out." He tilts his chin in the direction of where they are crashing: an air mattress with a twisted heap of blankets and pillows on it, and an Amanda cocooned in there somewhere.

"Sweet, let's do this." I log on to my laptop while Brandon filters through the semi-unpacked kitchen, looking for glasses. Finding them in one of the cupboards, he fills them with ice and the whiskey that's sitting on the counter.

"Cheers," he says as we clink our glasses together. Both of us are whiskey drinkers. We acquired a taste for it because of our dad, Warren. He loves his whiskey and there was always a cache of it in the house. As we became teenagers, we grew accustomed to stealing some here and there. Both of us have had a taste for it ever since.

Taking a sip, I Google "American Obsession band", and get a whole multitude of things. But sure enough, a couple links down from the top, I see their website. I can tell because there is a thumbnail photo of the band next to it.

Brandon and I skim over their website. Upcoming show dates, merchandise, meet the band.... all things I've been looking for.

I click on "Meet the Band". A new page opens, and I see the members pictures with their names and titles by each one. I read through with anticipation.

Erik Pierson – Lead Vocals/Guitar
Olivia Dunne – Vocals/Lead Guitar

Darren King – Keyboard/Guitar/Brass
Waylon Norden – Bass Guitar
Joe Dannon – Drums

"Olivia Dunne," I say out loud.

"Well, now we have her name, let's see what we can dig up on her elsewhere," Brandon says.

Opening Facebook, I type in her name. Sure enough, she comes right up. Her profile picture is beautiful, a close-up of her smiling into the camera.

Her smile is radiant and perfect, and she has cute little dimples. I couldn't tell as much at the show, but her eyes are a piercing blue color. I click on it and make it bigger, and Brandon chuckles and shakes his head. She has golden flecks in her eyes and her long lashes have me mesmerized.

I close it and start my search on her page, Brandon watching me. "You probably won't find much because you aren't friends with her," Brandon states.

I click on her "About" info. It says she is a mortgage underwriter at Mid-Central Mortgage. It also lists the band as a profession. Looks like she went to Pine Lake Community College and I'm guessing she has lived here her whole life from what I can see. I can't see her phone number or email address, but I can see her birthday is September 13th. It doesn't say anything under "Relationship", and I can't see any of the posts on her page. Shit. I lean back in exasperation on the couch.

"Don't give in that easy," Brandon says. "Let's see if you guys have any mutual friends. If you do you can ask them if she's single." He starts clicking around.

Luckily enough we have a few mutual friends. I'm making it my new personal goal in life to know this girl.

CHAPTER 7

LIV

LEXIE AND I ARE IN the kitchen whipping up some margaritas. It's a gorgeous Sunday, perfect for a hang out with the girls, so I volunteered my place since I have a nice big backyard that we can spread out on.

Of course, when she called a few of our friends, they were all-in on girls' night. It's more of a girls' afternoon, which will roll into the evening if all goes well. So, we're starting at my house with margaritas on the back patio.

"What is this?" Lexie asks, and I turn around and see she has a red envelope in her hands.

"Yeah, I seen that. Wasn't sure what the red envelope was all about. I just grabbed it out of the mailbox this morning."

"Can I open it?

"Go for it. You can read it out loud to me while I finish these up," I say as I dump cheap tequila into the blender.

She pulls out the white printer paper and holds it out in front of her. She starts reading out loud.

My dearest Olivia,

You know what one of my favorite things about you is? Your voice. It is utterly sexy. It's like honey, warm, thick, and flowing over me in a sensual caress. When you are on stage, I'm entranced by you. I'm sure I'm not the only person sending fan mail to you. Maybe you don't read the other ones. It would make me happy if you didn't, and you only read mine from now on. I know you will read mine. How you ask? Well, because that's how it's meant to be. We are meant to be. You may not realize that now, but I will show you.

See you soon,
X

"Who the fuck is this from? Liv you have a stalker," she says, appalled.

I grab the typed letter and read it over for myself. This is disturbing. I've had fan mail before, but this one is just overboard.

I pick up the blood red envelope that it came in, there is no postmark or stamp on it. This person must have personally dropped it in my mailbox yesterday or this morning. The thought makes me uncomfortable.

Looks like I will be keeping my metal baseball bat next to my bed at night, and locking my doors now, which I normally never do. I live in a nice part of town, so I've never had issues before, but clearly this person knows exactly where I live, which is a problem.

"This might sound weird," Lexie adds, "but you really need to keep this. Just in case. You never know, you may need it one day."

"I'll be sure to start a box of creepy stalker letters…"

We are interrupted by Jenna, one of our friends. "Hello, it's hot and we need some mar-ga-ri-tas!" She accentuates every part of the word. I had completely gotten sidetracked by the disturbing letter. Her red hair is up in a bun and her short frame is leaning into the house with a smile on her face, accentuating her freckled cheeks.

Lexie tucks the letter by her side, which is good. I don't need the other girls asking any questions on the situation, especially when I don't have any answers.

Jenna is still standing in the threshold of the patio door, waiting for us. I hand her two of the margaritas. Lexie and I will get the rest. A smile spreads across her face and she turns and heads outside toward the patio table and chairs.

Lexie and I went to high school with Jenna, she graduated a year ahead of us. She had moved away for a while during college, but recently moved back to Pine Lake with her boyfriend Bo, and they both work at the high school. She teaches Math, and he is the Phy-Ed teacher. They are both so down-to-earth and easy to hang out with. I'm hoping soon Bo pops the question. We've been hanging out with her more and more lately.

Lexie grabs the last two margaritas and I open the door for her. Jenna was right, it is hot out here. Luckily, my patio table has an umbrella so there is a little reprieve from the hot afternoon sun and lack of a breeze.

"You need a pool back here," our other friend, Tina says.

"I would so love that. Do you want to help fund it?" I say laughing.

"Seriously, how awesome would that be? Maybe you should get one in time for my bachelorette party," Tina adds with a goofy smile.

Now she's really on a roll, and Lexie and Jenna agree with her, nodding their heads. I admit, it would be nice, and Tina's bachelorette party is coming up soon. She said she doesn't want to fly anywhere, so we decided to do something local. And a pool in my backyard would be a perfect addition to her party, seeing that everyone is staying at my house.

Tina is getting married at the local winery just on the edge of town. She is marrying Tim, who is just starting out on his own, doing investments. We were introduced to her through Jenna.

Tina is one of the office administrators at the school and we all quickly became friends a couple of years ago. Her personality is sweet, and I've never seen a bad side of her. Seeing her and Tim together, always makes me laugh; she is barely 5' 0", and Tim is 6' 1". That gap in their heights makes them adorable. Tim is a sweetheart too; they are perfect for each other.

Tina has been obsessed on saving as much money as she can for the wedding. According to her, the winery was quite expensive to book, so she's been trying to pinch pennies everywhere else.

My yard would be a perfect place to have a pool – no neighbors watching out the windows or cars driving by. Her bachelorette party is in two weeks. I wonder if an above ground pool could be done in that short amount of time. I know nothing about pools. Their wedding is two weeks after that, in mid-August. This just might be doable.

"We'd have a little less than two weeks to get the pool in, if we want to do it in time for your party," the wheels in my head are really going now. The girls give me surprised looks. I am considering it, not sure if they realize that or if they think I'm messing with them.

There is a nice flat spot back here, so one of those above ground pools might work. And in all honesty, I can afford it. I have my job at Mid-Central, and the money I make from AO, and I'm conservative about my spending. I don't have a mortgage; I inherited my house from my parents after they passed away.

My parents passed when I was twenty. I was living in an apartment on the east side of Pine Lake and attending the local community college. I received a phone call on my cell about 11:00 PM on Friday, May 15. It had been the Sheriff, informing me that my parents were in an accident, and that I needed to come to the station immediately. Shock set in instantly. I didn't call anyone I was in such a panic; I left home and went straight there. It was an absolute blur of chaos and emotion. I broke down when Sheriff Hayden told me that a drunk driver blew through a stop sign and smashed into my parents' car while they were on their way home. They were dead on site, along with the drunk driver.

That was six years ago already.

After they passed, I ran out my lease on my apartment and moved into their house, now my house. My uncle Rick had helped me with financials, paperwork, funeral planning, and well, everything. Even to this day, he is the person I call when I have a dumb question on something.

I was so young, I hadn't paid much attention to how they ran things, and I never foresaw them not being there. Now I'm twenty-six, and still figuring out what the hell I'm doing, although I'll give myself a little credit, I've learned quite a bit over the past six years.

I'd give anything to have them back. I made two crosses as a memorial for the intersection where they were killed. Every year on their anniversary, I put flowers there. I'm always decorating their gravestones with flowers and plants, especially on their birthdays and holidays. Sometimes I go out to the Pine Lake Cemetery where they are buried and just sit there and talk to them, staring at their headstones, wishing for them to come back.

There is nothing in life that doesn't remind me of my parents, and all the things that I will never be able to do or say to them again. Some days aren't so bad, but some days I can cry until there is nothing left in me, just wishing I could hear their voices or tell them what I'm up to. I wonder what they would think of the pool idea.

"Earth to Liv," Tina says.

"Sorry guys, I totally spaced out there," I say apologetically, shifting in my seat.

Jenna raises her glass, and the rest of us follow. "Cheers to great friends!"

"And cheers to me getting a pool, well, hopefully anyway," I say with excitement and a smile. We clink glasses and the girls all cheer, and we chat and drink the afternoon away.

CHAPTER 8

JAY

IT'S BEEN ALMOST A WEEK since I've seen Olivia at the concert at Garden Park. I have thought about her fanatically every day.

I've wanted to reach out to some of our mutual friends but haven't had the guts to, yet. I'm too shy, stepping out of my comfort zone is not something I do easily. Two of them I don't know well, they are more like acquaintances, and one is Tim, a friend of our families, good friends with my brother.

I've been spending my days getting my place ready. Well, it's two places technically. I purchased an old, neglected brick building a couple of blocks off Broadway in downtown Pine Lake.

The main floor is where I'm going to put my photography business, *JJ Photography*. Jay Jones Photography was just too long of a name.

I don't have as big of a renovation budget as I'd like, but it will save me money leaving the exposed interior brick walls and ceiling the way they are. A fresh spray of black paint on the exposed ceiling really made it look a lot better. I had the hardwood floors buffed, and they aren't too bad looking. I'm hoping clients think its trendy and that the scuffs add character to the place. There is a bathroom and small office at the back, along with a storage room that I divided into two rooms, one will be my dark room and the other will be storage. Simple and basic; nothing flashy. That's all I want.

On the side of the exterior of the building is a door and an enclosed set of stairs, leading up to a loft. Years ago, someone used it as an apartment, because there is a kitchen and bathroom in it, thankfully. At least if I clean it up and live there, I will only be paying one mortgage a month, instead of two.

What drew me to this building, besides the low price and the huge glass windows on the main floor, are the windows in the loft. On the second floor there are half-moon shape windows with intricate wood designs in them. Not only are they gorgeous but also huge, and I keep thinking it would be a perfect backdrop for photos.

A large metal sliding barn door is at the landing at the top of the steps and opens into one large expanse of a room. This will be my living room, dining room, and kitchen. All exposed brick, and exposed ceilings. I love the industrial look of it, which also helps my wallet out a ton. There are a couple large posts on the other side of the room. I'm going to have to find a way to use them to partition that off. That will be my bedroom with some room on the side for storage, and the bathroom.

It's 1:00 in the afternoon and my brother Brandon, Tim, and Jordan are supposed to be here soon to help me unload my furniture. I've already unloaded what I really need to function, but the rest of it is still in the U-Haul.

I stand up at the island in my kitchen and pull up Olivia's Facebook page. I see a link to the American Obsession page, so I open it and start following them. Maybe she posts things on there and I can find out more about her.

Scrolling through the band's page I notice they don't have many pictures, which disappoints me. Mostly, uploads are things fans have tagged them in. However, they do keep the page up to date with upcoming shows, which I plan on attending anytime I'm able.

I'm completely zoned out when there is a knock on my door. I look up as the door slides open, its Brandon. His large frame slides inside, closing the door behind him.

"Hey, thanks for coming to help me," I say, closing my laptop. He's early, we can get a start on things.

"No problem. What are you doing, stalking the girl in the band again?" He says laughing, his dark eyes glinting with laughter. I know he's joking but it kind of burns me because he's right. I roll my eyes at him in response.

"The place is looking great. I peeked through the windows downstairs, that cleaned up nice. From mouse infested shithole to photography studio, you did a good job."

"Thanks." He knows how much I appreciate and need his support, and I know he'll always be there for me.

"Who else is helping?" He asks.

"Jordan and Tim."

Jordan is an old friend who is also from Greensboro, but now lives on the outskirts of Pine Lake out in the country. He works at a local mechanic shop, if somethings broke, he's the guy to fix it.

Then there's Tim. Tim has always been closer to Brandon than he is to me, so Brandon asked him if he could come over. I suggested it, having found out that he is a friend of Olivia's on Facebook. Tim's a great guy and immediately he said he would help with anything I need.

I'm invited to his wedding in a few weeks, so I'll end up going with Brandon and Amanda and my parents.

Tim and Brandon graduated from high school together. I didn't realize they were that close when we were in school, although a lot of those days were a blur for me.

We manage to get quite a few boxes brought up to the loft. I'm already hating these stairs, but I'm stuck with them now.

Eventually Tim and Jordan roll up and start helping us unpack. Of course, it's a hot as hell July day when we decide to do this, and it doesn't take long before we are all covered in sweat. Things go by quickly though; I don't have too much to unload.

We're finally done and settle in on the newly moved black Chesterfield style sofa. I love this couch; it looks like it belongs in a cigar shop or something. It has the deep button tufting and scrolled arms and nail head accents. This couch makes me feel distinguished. It was a hand-me-down from my grandparents that my parents didn't need, so I took it. Tim and Brandon are sitting on it, and Jordan and I take spots on the floor and lean back against it.

"Thank you, guys. Beers are on me," I say with a tired smile, catching my breath.

We sit and rest for a few minutes, then make our way down to the street and walk the couple blocks to Broadway. There are plenty of bars on this street, which is convenient for us.

We get to the intersection and Brandon looks around in both directions. "Where do you want to go?" He asks and I shake my head at him; I have no idea.

"I really haven't been out since I moved here a couple weeks ago, I'm open to suggestions."

"We could go to B&B's, maybe shoot some pool while we're at it," Jordan says. We all nod in agreement and let Jordan lead the way.

"What is B&B's exactly?" I ask.

Tim chimes in, "Billiards & Beer. It's two stories, pool tables only downstairs for anyone under twenty-one, and more pool tables and a bar upstairs. Cool place."

We get to B&B's, and it reminds me of the style of my new building, except it's all black on the outside. Black brick and black trim, and a gold sign saying "B&B's, Billiards & Beer".

We head in and up the massive twisting metal staircase to the second floor. Cold beer is what we need right now.

The upstairs is one large room with brick walls and hardwood floors. It has a long bar going most of the way down the side of it, and pool tables scattered throughout. We belly up and order our first round. Usually I'm a whiskey guy, but today I'm in need of a cold beer to cool me down.

We get our drinks and head toward an open pool table in the far corner. It's mid-afternoon and it's quiet in here. Other than us, it's just a couple middle-aged men sitting at the bar.

After grabbing my pool cue from the rack, I look up at the wall and to my amazement, there is a large black and white photograph of American Obsession hanging there in a thick black frame. I go around the table to get a closer look.

Olivia and the lead singer Erik are both sitting on a pool table at B&B's, this table to be exact, and the rest of the band is scattered behind them. They all signed it in silver Sharpie.

Once again lost in my thoughts, my brother chimes in. "Oh look, there's Jay's wanna be girlfriend." He's laughing like a hyena, so I take the opportunity to jab him with my pool cue.

"Shut up dude." I shoot him an embarrassed sideways look and I can hear Jordan and Tim chuckling behind me.

Tim rounds the table and stands next to me. Leaning in close, he says, "so you have a thing for Liv?"

"Yeah, I mean I've only seen her once, but wow." I can feel the embarrassment build in my cheeks.

"Well, if you want, I can put in a good word for you." He says, and now I'm really interested in this conversation.

"You know her? How do you know her? You would seriously do that for me?" *And now, I sound like a lunatic.*

"Yeah, I know her. Not gonna lie, I don't know a guy that doesn't have the hots for her – although, she's picky. But I'll give her credit; she's not out dating every weirdo that asks her out. Liv and my fiancé Tina are good friends. Next weekend Liv is throwing Tina a bachelorette party." My interest is piqued.

"Apparently, the girls got drunk last weekend and Liv decided to put in a pool at her house for the party. When those girls get together you never know what's going to happen," he rolls his eyes.

In my head I'm already thinking of ways I can get invited to this bachelorette pool party. *Come on Jay, be realistic and get your head out of the gutter.*

"I'll tell you what...if you aren't busy next Saturday, I'm dropping Tina off at Liv's for the party. You can come with me if you want, and you just might get a chance to talk to her," he says with a friendly smile and a twinkle in his eye.

"Yes, absolutely, count me in. You have my number, just text me that day." Now I need to try to play it cool, like that didn't just make my year.

"Oh, and another thing. She and the rest of AO come here some Tuesday nights. The guys have been trying to teach her how to play pool, and they'll sit and have drinks and hang out."

And there Tim goes again with these gold nuggets of info. I lean in closer to him and half whisper, "thank you man, you just made my day."

Now, I know where I will be on Tuesday and Saturday. I wonder where she'll be the other days of the week.

CHAPTER 9

LIV

IT'S FINALLY SATURDAY. THIS WEEK went by so slow, probably because I've been tirelessly counting down the days and hours until Tina's bachelorette party. Luckily, I work from home, so there are things I can clean and do in my spare time, so I'm not behind on getting anything ready.

The girls should be at my house any minute now. It's almost 2:00 in the afternoon. Luckily Lexie got here this morning, just after I got done with my morning run, took my pills, had a banana for breakfast, and took a shower.

We picked up the house, made sure the backyard was picked up, took the cover off the new pool, and prepped all the food and snacks for tonight.

It's been almost two weeks since our girls' night when I decided to put in a pool. It's been hectic, but we got it done just in time. Thankfully, I could pay the company to set it up and teach me how to take care of it. I would have had no idea on my own if they hadn't helped me.

"Ok, so we have all the food done, we are just waiting on Tim to drop off Tina and the booze, and then we are good to go. Right?" Lexie says, biting down on her lip.

"Don't bite your lip, you'll fuck up your lipstick," I say poking her in the cheek and she smiles.

"And yes, I told the girls to get here at 2:00, and Tina to get here about 2:15, that way everyone is here when she walks in. I hope she enjoys this," I add with a smile.

Lexie walks over to the basket on the kitchen counter with my mail in it.

"Is this the same stalker letter from last week or a new one?"

"New one. Haven't opened it yet. I'd rather light it on fire," I say aggressively.

Lexie tears the red envelope open and scans over the page quickly before she begins reading out loud.

My dearest Olivia,

My heart is racing. There are so many things I want to say to you about how I feel – but putting it on paper doesn't do it justice. I could be perfect for you, always giving you the best things, always giving you everything you want. And you will only be with me. It's the way things are meant to be.

See you soon,
X

Lexie reads it aloud, with a disgusted look on her face the whole time, and I have goosebumps. It's fucking creepy. I wonder if I should tell the police about them. I don't have time to dwell on this right now, because one by one cars start rolling in.

The first one here is Annie, a petite blonde-haired girl that Tina met at the salon she goes to. I don't know much about her, but I'll try to get to know her better tonight. Tina says she is great, quiet at first, but fun once you get to know her. She's just a little younger than we are and has been dating a guy named

Robin since she was in high school. Apparently, they have a small apartment together on the south side of town.

The next one in is Jenna, who apologizes profusely about being late; even though she isn't. She's got the black satin bachelorette sashes in her arms, along with her overnight bag. All the girls are spending the night here, we don't need anybody trying to drive wasted.

"Here," she says, handing the sashes over to me. I look at the pile, they are all there, including a one white satin that has an inscription "Bride", in pink.

"Awesome, these are perfect," I smile at her and give her a hug. I hope everyone has a good time tonight, especially Tina.

Another car pulls in and two girls get out. One is Sabrina, Tina's cousin, and the other is Tina's younger sister Tara, who is the maid of honor.

Lexie and I have met Tara before, we went out for drinks with her and Tina one night. She was as quiet as a church mouse. I wonder how she is going to pull off doing a maid of honor speech at the wedding.

Sabrina is the opposite of Tara. 'Loud and ready for anything' sums her up perfectly. Her ashy gray-brown hair is long and straight. She has dark smoky makeup on her eyes, and some tattoos on her forearms.

The last car pulls up and it is Evelyn, Tim's sister. Tall like Tim, similar blonde hair, large eyes, and crooked smile, she seems nice. This should be a great group of girls, hopefully nobody gets catty when the drinks start flowing.

I give each of the girls a glass of champagne and pour an extra one for Tina. She should be here any minute. First thing we'll do is cheers to our bride-to-be.

The girls are all roaming around the house quickly, getting their bags put away. Luckily, I have a big rec room in the basement, and I was able to find enough room to fit everyone either down there on some air mattresses, or in my two spare bedrooms.

I peek out the window as Tim's truck pulls up.

I'm heading out the front door and down the sidewalk when I see someone get out of the backseat. I slow in my steps, staring straight ahead, surprised. It's the guy I saw at our Garden Park show last Saturday. I gave him my set list. And like a stupid teenage girl with a crush, I put a heart by my name.

His face has been in my dreams every night this week.

Oh God, is he here to mock me and my stupid heart signature? My heart is beating out of my chest. *Alright Liv let's get our shit together.*

Putting one foot in front of the other I walk up to the truck and give Tina a big hug. We squeal with excitement at the fun we are going to have tonight.

Tim heads around the back of the truck with Tina's bag and picks up three packs of seltzers. I gave him money to pick up booze, I wanted Tina to pick out her favorites.

"Hey Liv," he says cheerfully, and gives me a half attempt at a hug with him arms full, his large frame towering over me.

"I recruited help, this is Jay Jones, a buddy of mine," he says nonchalantly, tipping his head toward his friend.

My eyes meet Jay's, and I can't look away. They are the most captivating hazel eyes I've ever seen. I noticed him at the show, and decided early in the night that he was getting my set list. I just didn't have the guts to put my phone number on it.

"Hello Jay Jones. You know, your name sounds like it's out of a superhero movie, like, "Peter Parker" or "Wade Wilson." I instantly regret that comment. Is that really the first thing I can think of to say to this guy?

He's still starting at me, and my stupid superhero comment made him smile and laugh. And not just laugh a little, laugh hard. His smile broadens and I can see it's beautiful, and oh my God, does he have adorable dimples in his tan smooth skin.

Damn, he is really hot. He looks like he could be one of those guys in a cologne commercial or something. Square jaw, hazel eyes, longer light brown hair tousled and styled to the side in a messy 'do. He's got a little bit of stubble on his face, it looks so good, especially with his thick lips. He looks cut too, and I can see part of a half sleeve sticking out the bottom of his T-shirt on his right arm.

"It's nice to meet you Olivia," and I'm still not peeling my eyes from his.

I feel like my legs have turned to stone. I'm scared to move. I've never been nervous quite like this around a guy before. Usually I have no issues flirting, or flat out telling someone to go away.

Tim clears his throat, and it breaks me out of my trance. I look over at Tina and she is giving me that shit-eating-grin look behind Jay's back. Apparently, I've made it obvious I have the hots for this guy. I should walk away now before I embarrass myself more.

"Well, let's get this stuff unloaded so you girls can *get* loaded," Tim says with a chuckle.

Jay starts going around the back of the truck, so I follow him. As he walks, I can see the muscles in his arms, chest, and back rippling through his tight black shirt.

There are bottles of wine in a cardboard box, and a case of beer in the back. Jay grabs all of it.

"I can get something," I say, trying to take the box of wine from him.

"No ma'am, if you can get the door, I've got this." I blush and I'm not even sure why.

Usually, if someone calls me "ma'am" I'm put off, I absolutely hate being called that. He makes it sound good though and I don't mind it. How the hell does that work?

Jay follows me into my house and into the kitchen, and we start loading copious amounts of alcohol into the fridge. From the kitchen we can hear the girls surrounding Tina and they are chatting about how awesome the night will be.

I'm here in my own kitchen, nervous as hell, afraid to speak to the hot ass man standing next to me, especially after my stupid superhero comment. We keep catching each other's eyes, and I hope he's not just looking at me because he thinks I'm crazy.

"Alright, that's it. Thank you for helping us," I say with a smile as we get the last of it in the fridge. What I really want to say is, "I'm so glad I get to see you again, please take your shirt off for me."

He finally speaks up. "I was at your show for the first-time last Saturday. It was awesome."

I'm going to play stupid here and pretend like he didn't distract me that entire show. "Good, I'm glad you had fun. Hopefully we will see you again at more shows. Obviously tonight we couldn't schedule one because of the bachelorette party." Seems platonic enough, that statement can't get me in to trouble.

He stands straighter with his hands buried in his pockets, staring at his feet. "Yeah, you gave me your set list, I think I'm a fan for life," he says looking back up at me with a crooked grin. Oh wow, my heart just melted into my stomach.

Tim's head pops around the corner of the kitchen. "Hey guys, sorry to interrupt, but we should get going so these pretty ladies can get their party started." He's looking at us back and forth with a funny smirk on his face like he's up to something.

I'm excited for the party but disappointed all at the same time, it means Jay is going to leave. I walk them both to the front door, and Tina rushes up to Tim, jumping up and wrapping her arms around his neck and giving him a long kiss.

"Love you, I'll see you tomorrow," she says warmly.

"Love you too, have fun and be safe. You take good care of my fiancé tonight, Liv, get her real good and drunk," he says with a smile.

Jay is standing next to me. I can hardly focus on the conversation when he is this close.

He turns and faces me. "It was nice to meet you. Hopefully I can see you again soon," he says, sending butterflies dancing in my stomach. His stare is intense, as if he is trying to see inside of me.

"Nice to meet you too," I say with a smile. He makes me so nervous. Or excited.

I think it's both.

CHAPTER 10

LIV

"CHEERS LADIES!" SABRINA YELLS OUT as we all clink our champagne glasses together.

All the girls have settled into their spots in the house. Bags, clothes, makeup, and curling irons seem to be scattered everywhere.

Its mid-afternoon and we have made our way into the backyard. The early August sun has warmed up the water in the pool. It's a gorgeous Saturday afternoon and we are taking advantage of the weather, and my new pool. We decided on margaritas for our pool party. Strong ones.

Lexie, Annie, and I are in the pool with our drinks, and Tina, Sabrina, Tara, and Evelyn decide to get some sun laying on their towels before getting in.

"I still think you need one of those huge unicorn floaties, you could sit in here all day. Imagine how tan you'd be," Lexie says with a laugh.

"Yeah, but it would take up my whole pool. Not to mention I'd probably end up flipping off the side of it and breaking my neck," I say, laughing with her.

Suddenly, Annie is focused on something in the trees behind the house. I can see her eyebrows furrow like she's squinting behind her sunglasses.

"Hey, Liv, just act natural okay, but just over there, straight back by those three big trees, I can see something shiny and reflective once in a while, like a camera maybe," she is saying this almost in a whisper, trying nonchalantly to act like she isn't talking about it. "I'd swear to you I thought I saw something move over there. Don't look and make it obvious, but it's freaking me out," I can hear the concern in Annie's low whispers.

Lexie and I share a look of apprehension.

"Let's just kind of move around the pool casually, like we normally would. We all have sunglasses on, so sneak glances when you can," I say, trying to sound like I'm in control but internally I'm starting to freak out too.

We move about the pool, I take a couple sips of my drink, tilting my head so I can sneak looks in the direction of the trees. I pick out the three large oaks in the rows of thick trees behind my house.

It takes me until the fifth look before I finally see it. She was right, I can see a reflection of something. Glass? Metal? It's barely visible in the thick trees and brush.

"Have you noticed it yet?" I ask Lexie.

"No, I can't pick it out," she says, stealing another look.

"Oh my God, I see it," she exclaims and points at it.

All three of us look up at the same time, and the shiny reflection moves and disappears quickly, a dark shadow flitting through the trees with it.

"What the fuck was that?" I exclaim loudly.

They are both scrambling out of the pool. Tina, Sabrina, Tara, and Evelyn snap out of their conversation and look at us.

"What's going on?" Tina asks nervously as she stands up.

"I think there was someone in the trees with a camera or something," Annie says, panic in her voice. She's out of the pool grabbing her towel.

"Let's get in the house," I say, and I hurry out of the pool behind Lexie. We all run to the back patio door and quickly scramble inside.

"Do we call the police?" Lexie asks, cell phone in hand.

"Should I go out there and look?" I ask, and all the girls respond together, a simultaneous, "no".

"I'm calling Tim, he told me to call if we needed anything, we'll have him come over. It will make me feel better," Tina says, scrolling through her phone quickly.

Tina moves to the living room; I can hear her on the phone with Tim. I breeze past her and lock the front door, then the patio door, and over through the kitchen and utility room to lock the door to the garage.

"He'll be here in a few minutes. Maybe we should call the police." I'm wondering the same thing, but I don't say it. We will see what he says when he gets here.

About ten minutes later I hear his truck pull up. He comes screeching to a halt in the driveway. I walk over to the front door and flip the lock so he can get in. A few seconds later, an exasperated Tim runs through the door.

"Is everyone okay?" Tim asks right away, all the girls gathering around by the front door. Tina wraps her arms around his waist.

"We think we saw someone in the woods behind the house," Tina tells him.

I turn and head towards my bedroom closet and dig out a pair of jean shorts and a T-shirt.

I slip into my flip flops that are by the front door and turn and head back towards the patio door.

"What are you doing, Liv," Tim asks me with trepidation.

"I'm going out there to see what the hell is going on," I tell him, mustering up as much courage as I can.

"Absolutely not," Tim says, moving towards me.

"My house, my rules," I retort back with my "don't push me" look.

"Like hell, if someone is out there, nothing good will come of that."

He is right. I go back to my room and grab my metal baseball bat. I'm not putting up with this. What if it is the red envelope stalker? I'm ready to put an end to this madness.

I emerge from my room with the bat, Tim tipping his head back and rolling his eyes.

"I'm not going to be able to stop you, am I?" I shake my head for a no-you-can't and I'm already walking toward the patio door.

"Fine, we go together, and we stay right next to each other. You have your cell phone?" He's talking to me like he's an overprotective dad.

I nod my head in affirmative.

"Do you have another bat?"

"Yeah, I have one in the garage," I say as I hand him mine and jog across the house to the garage.

I dig it out and head back in, the bat gripped in my hands. "Alright, let's go," I say with as much courage as I can muster.

Tim and I head back out to the backyard through the patio door. The rest of the girls stay inside the house.

"Where exactly did you see this light and the shadow," he asks, looking around for signs.

"See the three big oaks there?" I say, pointing straight ahead. He nods.

We start cautiously walking back across the yard. It's big so it takes us a minute to cross it, not that we are in a real hurry either.

"Jay didn't come back with you," I say flatly.

"No, he said he had things to do. And, if I didn't know any better, I'd think you are disappointed about that," he glances over at me with a raised eyebrow. I brush the comment off.

We approach the edge of the trees, armed with our bats. I remove my sunglasses and hang them on my shirt collar.

The trees are dense back here, and over the years it has become a tangled mess of brush. My dad used to dump brush back here if a tree in the yard fell or died. I haven't been back here in a while; I didn't realize how overgrown it had gotten.

Tim and I are moving slowly, picking the easiest path to walk on, dodging brush and branches as we go. I'm following Tim, but I'm constantly looking behind me, fearful someone may be sneaking up behind us.

"Stop!" Tim lurches to a halt. "Look, there are footprints here in the dirt," he says, pointing down at the ground. I can see them clearly.

I'm appalled. I have an overwhelming feeling of being violated and I wonder if this has happened before.

We continue forward slowly, finding more and more footprints. Clearly this *has* happened before, there are multiple prints, all going in different directions.

"I wonder if someone was back here with a camera. I bet someone was and that was the glare Annie had seen, and the person was hiding behind this brush pile so you couldn't see him or her," he seems more concerned now.

My mind is racing. What if it is the red envelope stalker? Should I tell Tim about that? No, he has enough on his plate right now.

"Let's go back to the house." Being out here is making my skin crawl, I'm so freaked out the hair on my arms is standing up, as if I've been struck by lightning.

"Good idea. You go first, I'll follow you," he says, and we start making our way out of the trees.

The second we get out into the yard; I realize how much we picked up the pace on our way back to the house. I keep checking behind us as we walk. I can see the girls watching us carefully as we make our way back to the patio door. Tina slides it open for us, closes it, and locks it.

"Well, what happened," she asks nervously.

"We found footprints. Lots of them. Whoever it was has been out there before," as Tim says this, I can feel a chill run through my body. I put my arms around myself and squeeze. This can't be happening.

"Are you ladies okay to drive? I'm thinking we pack things up and move the party to our house," Tim says.

"Yeah, we're fine. Let's get busy – everyone let's gather up your stuff, and make sure we grab the air mattresses too," I say, my head swimming.

"I'm so sorry," I say, giving Tina a hug.

"Liv, don't apologize, as long as we're all safe that's all that matters," she says with a reassuring smile. "In the meantime, though, you might want to start shopping for security cameras," and she's exactly right.

CHAPTER 11

JAY

I MAKE MY WAY UP the torturous steps to my loft. Leaning back against the wall, I kick my shoes off. My legs are tired, and I'm covered in sweat. I hate running.

I turn on the radio in the living room for some music, and head into the shower.

I can't stop thinking about Olivia. I need to figure out more excuses to be around her, with she preferably wanting me around too.

As I shower, I question where the girls will go tonight for the bachelorette party. I know they were starting at Olivia's, but then they were going to go bar hopping. It would be nice to be out too, to hopefully talk to her before some asshole tries to bring her home.

I wrap a towel around my waist and grab my phone and decide to text Tim.

> Jay: Hey. Just thought I'd see if you want to bar hop with me tonight, since the girls are predisposed.
>
> Tim: Sorry man, I can't. The girls found some creep watching them through the trees while they were in the pool. We just moved the party to our house. I'm gonna stay sober tonight in case something weird happens.

The blood drains from my face. Fuck. The real question is...
did they figure out who it is?

> Jay: What the fuck? Did they figure out who it is?
> Are they still going to go out tonight?
> Tim: Still going out. I'm thinking I will just drive
> them where they want to go, and then make
> sure they get back safely to our house.
> Jay: Good idea. Want me to drive too? I don't
> think they will all fit in your truck.
> Tim: That would be awesome. Thank you.

This is perfect. I will get to see Olivia again. I'm just a little
nauseous now over what the girls saw.

I text Tim a few more times and get more details, he tells me
to come over right away if possible.

Now I'm pulling up in their driveway. All the lights are on
in the house, and it looks abuzz.

A whole group of girls step out, Tim is following in tow,
locking the front door behind them. I lean against the passenger
door of my truck, secretly hoping Olivia gets in my vehicle and
not Tim's.

All the girls are wearing black dresses and heels, all done up.
They start coming down the sidewalk, I finally catch a good
look of Olivia. She's wearing a black dress that is a little longer
in the back than in the front, it's nice and tight, with a slit that
goes up her left leg. The top is a deep cut halter and judging by
the amount of cleavage that is showing, she doesn't have a bra on,
and it's making my imagination run wild. Dear God. I feel like
the wind just got knocked out of me.

She's tan, and her gold heels make her legs look even longer
than they already are. Her brunette hair is in loose curls, and as

she gets closer, I can see she has some pinkish red lip gloss on. My God, I would give up anything to get a chance to kiss her.

She walks up to my truck, eyes locked on mine, smiling. "I call dibs on the front seat of Jay's truck," she says, still looking at me.

Yes, yes, yes. I can't help but smile, she wants to ride with me. I feel like I just won the lottery.

I turn around and open the passenger door to my Silverado. As she walks by me, she gives me a flirty smile. She gets in and I close the door after her, then head around the front of the truck to my side.

I think there are seven girls total in the group, the only other one I know is Tina, and she got in with Tim. I have three more in my backseat, and Tim has the others, I have no idea what their names are. The only one I care about is sitting next to me, checking her makeup over in the visor mirror.

I start the truck and follow Tim.

I steal a glance at Olivia, and I see that when she is sitting, that slit runs dangerously far up her leg, and luckily, it's on my side of the truck so I can see it easily. I turn the A/C up higher, thinking about it is making me sweat.

The three girls in the back have struck up a conversation and its going strong.

"Thank you for driving us tonight," Olivia says, looking at me.

"You're welcome," I say, looking back at her, holding her gaze for an extra second. "You know that dress should come with a warning," I tell her.

"A *warning*? About what?" She asks, confused.

"You are going to give some poor guy a heart attack tonight wearing that," I say, and she bursts out laughing.

The car ride isn't long, and we are working on finding parking spots downtown, when she leans a little closer to me. "So, what are you and Tim going to do tonight? Are you going out with us?"

"No, Tim says Tina needs her own night out, although I feel differently. If it was up to me, I'd be your bodyguard and wouldn't take my eyes off you," I say, and I'm instantly embarrassed that I said it out loud. I watch her chew on her bottom lip a little and she's holding back a smile.

The girls start piling out of the back and Olivia opens her door. I hurry out of the truck and try to get there before she gets out. She beat me, she's already out.

"I was going to get that for you," I say, trying hilariously to look like I'm hurt.

She blushes. "Thanks, you can get it later. I get shotgun in Jay's truck on the way home." She calls the last sentence out to the group of girls.

I start laughing. Apparently, she wants to ride with me again, so I haven't screwed anything up so far. Thank God I had a few sips of whiskey before I picked them up, so I was a little loose and not so nervous.

"Catch you later," she says, catching my eye before turning to walk to the bar with the girls.

"Bye," I say weakly as she walks away.

Tim claps me on the back. "Well, you wanna go play some pool or something?"

"Hell yeah, let's stay close in case they need us," I say, watching their figures get smaller and smaller as they disappear into the glow of neon signs and crowds of people on Broadway.

We head to B&B's and grab the pool table nearest the window that faces the street.

Through the course of the night, we each have a couple beers, but that's the extent of it. The bar is filling up, and I know people want our table, especially since we don't have drinks in front of us now, but we aren't ready to give it up quite yet. They will just have to wait.

We keep the occasional eye on the street, in case the girls are outside. We did see them one time, heading to the south down the sidewalk.

"Tina said their goal was to stay out until bar close, guess we'll see how *that* goes," he says with a smirk and a chuckle.

It's 12:15 now and I'm getting stir crazy. It bugs me that Olivia is out in that damn dress, and every asshole is probably ogling her up and down, trying their hardest to take her home.

"Should we call them, if we wait too long it will be almost bar close and we won't get let in to find them," I tell Tim over the noise of the crowd.

"Good plan. Let's pay our tab and get out of here. I can only beat you in pool so many times in one night," he says with a smile.

After we pay, Tim gets on the phone with his sister. Evelyn, I think her name is. She tells us they are a couple buildings down, at the Whiskey Whistle.

He hangs up the phone with her, turning to me. "I figured they would end up at the Whistle, just wanted to make sure before we walked down there."

A few minutes later we make our way to the entrance of the bar. Two large men in black are bouncing at the door, the neon orange sign lit up above their heads. I can hear the roar of the crowd from outside and The Weeknd's "Blinding Lights" is playing over the speakers.

"No more people in," the bouncer on the left says in a firm voice.

"We are picking up the bachelorette party of seven girls. Are you sure we can't get in to find them? We need to get them home." Tim says, the bouncer nods and lets us pass.

The bar is absolutely packed. Like a typical historic downtown building, it has brick walls, wood floors, and an old tin ceiling. Black and white pictures and bar signage cover the walls. In the back there is a stage with a dance floor, and a mechanical bull off to the left.

There are two sides to the bar. We scan the left side where the entrance is, not finding them. We go through the large opening into the right side, and sure enough, I see a little bunch of black dresses, dancing to the pounding bass of the music. But I can't see Olivia.

Nervously, I keep scanning the room. A woman, probably mid-thirties, grabs my arm and runs her hand up and down it. I can smell the alcohol on her breath as she leans into me.

"Hey you. You wanna dance?" Her alcohol saturated breath covering me like a fog.

"No thanks," I tell her quickly, turning and looking back around the room. Her hand is still squeezing my arm, so I remove it for her.

I look across the room and mid-way back I see her. Her eyes are burning into mine, a grin on her face. There are four guys around her, and she is leaning up against a high-top table, her elbow resting on it casually. It's obvious they are all drooling all over her, clearly fighting for her attention, and she isn't looking at any of them. She's looking at me.

As I approach her, a big smile spreads across her face. She pushes through the four of them and sweetly says, "excuse me guys," and they all deflate a little, their egos broken as they stare at her ass while she walks away from them.

"Just in the nick of time, Mr. Jones." She says, adding "there was way too much testosterone over there."

Tim is getting the other girls rounded up and ready. It looks like as much fun as trying to herd cats.

"We're getting ready to go. Do you need to pay your tab," I ask her.

"No, I haven't paid for a drink all night. The testosterone has taken care of all my drinks," and she swoops her arm behind her, laughing.

"Looks like your dress was worth every penny then," I say, raising my eyebrows.

Tim rolls by us, all the girls in tow.

"Hang on, I have to pee!" Tara exclaims.

"Me too," says Tina.

"We'll be right back, meet you guys outside," and off they go through the thick crowd.

I turn to follow the group toward the front. Turning back a few seconds later, I check to make sure Olivia is behind me. She's not. A tall guy with a baseball cap on is talking to her. How is that possible? I looked away for a few seconds.

I turn back around to grab her, pushing past the tall guy, touching Olivia's arm.

"Hey man, watch it," he says to me.

"We need to go. Are you coming?" I'm not going to waste my time acknowledging him, I'm only looking at her.

"Hey, I was talking to her. Maybe you should move on." And now I'm pissed off.

"She's with me asshole, so back off. Olivia, let's go," I say looking at her. I have a light hold on her arm, and she reaches out to grab my free hand with a smile on her face, without saying a word to the guy.

We keep moving toward the door. The crowd is swelling and it's a struggle to get through without losing each other.

Olivia let go of my hand, and has drifted a few feet behind me, and it feels too far away. I keep looking back and can just watch the wave of men check her out as she walks by.

Finally, we reach the front door and meet back up on the sidewalk. One of the girls looks like she could fall asleep, the rest of them chatting nonstop. *How can there be that much to talk about all the time?*

"Liv, how many phone numbers did you get tonight?" One of the girls says, slurring a little.

"Jay, this is my best friend Lexie," she says pointing to her as she walks closer to us.

"Don't avoid the question. How many?" She says it again, more persistent.

"A few," Olivia says blushingly, looking away trying to avoid her gaze.

"Bullshit. How many for real?" She's really hounding her now.

"Fine. Eight guys gave me their numbers," she says coolly.

Jesus. She does need a bodyguard, and it should be me.

The other girls egg her on, cheering wildly. Sabrina says she got one, and the girls are staring at Olivia like she is their idol. Then there's me, just flat out irritated about it.

Finally, Tina and Tara show up, and we walk back to the little parking lot where we left our trucks. As we get closer to my truck, Olivia shoots me a crooked smile. "Shotgun, bitches!" She calls out a second later, still looking at me, and I start laughing.

I use my key fob and unlock the door, but I wait until I'm right next to the passenger door. I open the door for her, giving her a flirtatious smile. She smiles back, and I notice as she gets in, she has no modesty now when it comes to the slit in her dress.

Closing the door behind her I blow out a deep breath. I wonder if she notices the effect that she has on me. She's a smart girl, I'm sure she does.

I get in and check the backseat. All three girls are in and fading fast from the looks of it. Olivia is looking out her window, seemingly unaffected by however much she drank tonight.

I pull out of my parking spot, and start heading down Broadway, following Tim. It's quiet, the only sound is Morgan Wallen's "Last Night" coming out of my radio.

"So, how long will you wait until you call your eight new guys?" I ask, although I can hear a little tone in my voice that I didn't mean to direct at her.

She looks over at me with an arched eyebrow.

"Who says I kept any of their numbers," she says coolly and turns back to the window.

"Why wouldn't you keep them?" I ask, surprised.

"I'm not really interested in any of them. Maybe I'm looking for something specific," she says, looking back at me.

"Ah. And what specifics might that be?"

"Not sure, I guess I'll know when I find it," she says with a devious smile.

"How many numbers did you get tonight," she asks.

"What? Seriously? You think girls gave me their numbers?" I say, astonished she would even think that.

"Why does that seem so crazy? You are a good-looking guy; I don't see why a girl wouldn't want you to have her number. I saw that woman grab your arm at the Whistle, I bet you could have gotten hers." She says, looking at me with a sly smile, raising her eyebrows.

"Um, I don't know," I stammer out. Until this point I wasn't interested in dating, my life goal was making it through each day without being too depressed. But after meeting Olivia I've been turned upside-down. I keep driving with her next by my side, unsure of what to say to her.

We arrive back to Tim and Tina's. The girls are moving much slower getting out of the trucks than they did getting in earlier. Olivia seems like the only coherent one. Maybe she refuses to drink all those drinks that the guys at the bar buy her. Or maybe she just has a better tolerance than the rest of them.

Oliva is following behind the last of the girls, holding a couple of their purses for them, as they go up the steps to the front door.

"Thanks for the ride. Drive safe," she says, giving me a million-dollar smile. That one is going to haunt me in my sleep tonight.

I push off the side of the truck where I'm leaning and take a couple uneasy steps forward toward her, and she freezes.

"Um, good night, Olivia," is all I can manage to get out.

She holds her stance for a couple seconds in hesitation, then turns and heads towards the house, looking back at me once before she reaches the door.

I haven't taken my eyes off her.

CHAPTER 12

LIV

LAST WEEK'S BACHELORETTE PARTY IS still reeling in my mind. I have a whole bag of mixed emotions on it.

First off, I'm terrified to be home alone now, given that someone was spying on us, trespassing on my property.

Second, I really hope Tina had a great night, even though it started off shaky.

And third, I can't stop thinking about Jay. He is so charismatic, and my mind keeps drifting off to him. It's a good distraction, at least so I think. I was really hoping when he dropped us off at Tim and Tina's that he would ask me out, but sadly he didn't.

I finish washing my hands in the bathroom sink in the AO shed and give myself a glance in the mirror.

Erik suggested that AO get together around 1:00 to work on the songs we have been writing. After that, we'd pack up and head out early to tonight's show.

It's in St. James, a town about an hour and a half south of Pine Lake. We've played there before, it's a nice outdoor pavilion, and we were asked to play for their town's festival days.

We started working on our newest song, but I couldn't focus. I broke down and told the guys what happened with the creeper behind my house.

I feel better now that they know, since they are my biggest support group, but now I'm getting bombarded with questions, suggestions, and offers of them moving in with me.

I come out of the bathroom and all eyes are on me. They clearly aren't going to let this conversation go.

"I think we should take turns staying at your house Liv," Darren says.

"Yeah, it wouldn't be hard for any of us. We could rotate days no big deal. We're used to being over there all the time anyway," Joe says with a nonchalant smile.

So, they are all on board with this, well, I'm not.

"Absolutely not. I'm a big girl and can deal with this myself. I'll just avoid using the pool and going outside until I figure out who it is," I say, making a lame attempt to counter them. I flop down on the couch, exasperated.

"So, you are never going to mow lawn, walk from a car to the house, or do anything outside," Erik's tone is sarcastic and dramatic, but he does have a point. But still, I'll be fine.

"Listen, let's not do anything crazy here. Let's just see how it plays out," after that comment they are all giving me sketchy looks.

"We will talk it over and figure something out. Let's finish up with practice and get packed up for our show." Waylon says with a deep-voiced finality that none of us argue with.

We scatter about the room to our instruments. I pick up my guitar off the old, tattered gold couch. That poor gold couch: it's seen better days, especially since we picked it up off the side of the road years ago. A furniture upgrade has never been high on our priority list since we moved in here.

Joe's mom has remarried and moved out, leaving the house and property to Joe. It's not much, but Joe likes it, and we're glad for that so we can keep our practice spot. Joe is a desk clerk at Peterson Lumber in town, so his coworkers have been able to give him some how-to's on fixing the place up. It looks better now than it ever did when his parents lived here.

After working on our last song, we start packing up our equipment for tonight's show. I can't keep my other secret about the letters in any longer, even if it is going to make them more worried than they already are.

"Guys, I have something else to tell you," I say, and they all stop dead in their tracks, giving me uneasy looks.

"I've been getting letters lately too. They come in red envelopes, and this guy keeps talking about how we are supposed to be together....", I'm unable to get the rest out before I'm interrupted.

"How many have you gotten? When did this start Liv?" Erik sets his guitar case down and gets right up close to me, grabbing my arms.

"Um, I've gotten two, just in the last couple weeks," now I'm regretting telling them.

"I'm staying with you tonight after the show, and you aren't going to argue with me on that," Erik says, the rest of them nod in agreement.

"Fine," I say. They win.

— — —

We take two vehicles to our shows. We, along with all our equipment won't fit into just one. It barely fits in two vehicles – my Tahoe and Waylon's truck. One of these days, we need to buy something as a band that can fit everything.

It's a process to unload all our equipment to get set up, but we have a routine that we've done for a long time now, so there are hardly ever any issues.

I hook up my mic on its stand and head back to the side of the stage. My cell phone dings in my back pocket. It's a Facebook notification. I pull it up and see Jay's face. He sent me a friend request.

"Who's that hunk? And what's with the big ass smile on your face? Do you have a boy-toy and haven't told me yet?" Darren is quizzing me from over my shoulder. I tell him about all the guys I date, and he does the same with me.

"He's a guy I met recently. I saw him at the last Garden Park show and gave him my set list. Turns out he's friends with Tim Brennan, so I've gotten to see him since then, but we haven't been on any dates," I'm trying to fill him in without wasting much time and getting behind schedule.

"Well damn, he is super fine, you should definitely go out with him," he's still staring at his profile picture.

"Oh, trust me I want to, hopefully one of these days he asks me out," I say eagerly. I'm glad he added me on Facebook.

One thing I don't have is any shame; if I like someone I'll openly flirt, but on the same hand if I don't like someone, I have no problem telling them I'm not interested. Hopefully, Jay has noticed already that I'm interested, I haven't exactly been shy about it.

We get back to setting things up after I've confirmed his friend request. I want to look at his profile, but I don't have time. I'll do it later after we get home.

The crowd starts rolling in, liquid libations in hand. We've moved off the stage, so we are out of sight. Joe, Erik, and Waylon are backstage, and Darren and I are on the side, inspecting the crowd.

We have a lot of fans that follow us from town to town if the shows aren't too far away from Pine Lake. But in all honesty, the only fan I want to see right now is Jay. He said he would come to more shows, and I hope this is one of them.

Finally, I spot him. He's alone, lingering at the front in the thick crowd, on my side of the stage.

"You are grinning like a schoolgirl again," Darren says from beside me.

"He's here," I say with excitement and point to him.

"He looks even better in person. If he ends up being gay, I call dibs," he says raising his eyebrows and smiling.

We stare out into the crowd and pick out people we know, we do this a lot just for fun.

"I see Debbie, Sara, and Laura right there," as he points over to the left. I know of them but don't know them well, which is true for a lot of our fans. They come to a lot of our shows.

"Lydia and Conner," I say pointing. "There's Molly," I point to her standing in the crowd center stage. We wave but she doesn't see us. Molly is Joe's girlfriend; they've been dating for about a year. They make a great couple; they've been talking about her moving in with him soon. Joe met her when he went in to get a tattoo, she inked him, and they hit it off. He ended up asking her out, and they've been together ever since. She's so pretty, black hair, tall, pierced eyebrow, and a full sleeve on her left arm. Joe is absolutely smitten with her, and she comes to as many shows as she can.

"There's that group of girls that always show up in about half the amount of clothing they *should* be wearing," he says, and we both roll our eyes.

"There's John DeMarcus. He comes to a lot of our shows," I say.

"Which one?" Darren asks.

"He's there, kind of over by Jay, on our side of the stage. Older guy, mid-height, brown hair with a little gray in it. John and my dad were acquaintances, and maybe kind of friends, before my dad passed. He's a pharmacist in town."

"Oh my God, there's that guy I've been crushing on," Darren smiles, and points back toward the left side. "Matt, and from what I hear through the grapevine he might be interested," he does a cute little shimmy and smiles.

"Let's hope so," I say and give him a nudge and a wink.

The event coordinator comes back and gives us the green light to start. "We're ready," Erik tells him walking up, looking around at the rest of us for confirmation.

Darren has instructed him to hit a button on his DJ panel to start our entrance music. After he climbs the stairs up to the stage, he hits the button and Audioslave's "Cochise" starts playing. "Let's give a big St. James welcome to American Obsession," he says into my microphone, and the crowd starts roaring.

The five of us filter up the stage stairs, waving as we make our entrances, each of us taking our places and instruments in hand.

I decided to wear sunglasses tonight so that I can keep sneaking looks at Jay without him noticing. I just can't help it. Sure enough, there he is, that adorable smile on his face.

We start into our set, which is a collaboration of songs we normally play, which includes Joan Jett's "I love Rock & Roll, Dorothy's "Black Sheep", Green Day's "Basket Case", and Whitesnake's "Here I Go Again." This crowd is just eating us up, anything we play they are loving.

As we wrap up, we play Halestorm's "The Steeple" as our final. "Thank you all very much, and goodnight!" Erik says into the microphone.

We all know this won't be the last song. The second we start heading off stage the crowd starts in with the usual "one more song" chant. Each of us grab a few sips of water and take a couple seconds to rest before heading back up the steps.

The crowd is roaring as we re-enter. This time instead of taking my guitar, I grab my mic off the stand and head to center stage. Erik will take over lead guitar for me on this one.

I start the first drawn out hums of Dorothy's "Rest in Peace" and a hush has fallen on the crowd. This is one of my favorite songs, it's the ultimate break up song, and I love doing it as the encore.

Moving around the stage, I sing through the song, feeling the beats in my chest until the last notes. I call out, "we are American Obsession, thank you for coming, goodnight," and turn to exit the stage.

The crowd starts to disperse once we've said goodnight. I'm not handing out my set list tonight, I have an agenda.

"I'll be right back, I need to go find someone," I tell Erik once we've gotten to side stage.

I want to find Jay. I walk out past the security guard at the fence to get to where the crowd is still mingling. I look around through the darkness and the mass of people, hoping he hasn't left yet. Finally, turning to my right I see him walking by, craning his head back toward where I just came from.

"Hey there. Looking for someone?" I say with a smile as I walk up to him.

"Hey. Great show tonight, you guys really nailed it." He shoves his hands deep into his pockets and gives me a shy smile.

"Thanks. I saw you sent me a Facebook request. It popped up right before we went on stage."

I'm startled by a hand on my right shoulder. I look back and see Molly.

"Hey Liv. Just a heads-up, Joe is going to ride home with me, so you guys aren't so crowded on the way back," Molly says, leaning over to me.

"Sounds good Molly, see you later," I call to her as she starts to head backstage. I turn back to Jay, who smiles at me nervously.

"Well, I need to get back to it, I guess. Thanks for coming tonight," I tell him with a smile.

"There's nowhere else I'd rather be," and he flashes me a charismatic smile and his cheeks redden. It makes me blush too.

We start to haul our equipment back to our vehicles, meticulously packing it back in. As I make my first trip to my Tahoe, I see something disturbing. A red envelope, sticking out of the top of a bunch of red roses, sitting on the hood of my SUV.

I rip the envelope off the flowers, tearing it open.

My dearest Olivia,

My dear girl you are so amazing. I love watching you on stage.

See you soon,
X

My skin is crawling. Apparently, my stalker came to the show tonight. I look around nervously, unsure of who I can trust anymore.

CHAPTER 13

JAY

IT'S THE FIRST MONDAY IN August. I have my monthly appointment with my therapist, Dr. Stangel.

I've been seeing him since I was sixteen. His office is back in Greensboro, so now when I go back for my appointments, I make a stop and visit my parents.

I realize I zoned out while sitting on his couch.

"I'm sorry Dr. Stangel, I didn't mean to be rude. My mind was elsewhere for a minute there."

"That's alright Jay. Why don't you tell me what's on your mind today." He is very reassuring, but I'm a little uncomfortable telling him how I feel about Olivia, I've never talked to him about someone I like before.

"Well, I met a girl. And not just any girl, she is amazing. I feel like she has lit my heart on fire, I think about her a lot." I start off a little unsteady but manage to blurt it out in an awkward sentence.

"Well, that's great. How long have you two been dating?"

"Um, we aren't. I've met her a couple of times now, and I've been to her concerts recently. Her name is Olivia Dunne, she's the lead guitarist and singer for the American Obsession band." I look up at him, he is studying me warily over his dark rimmed glasses.

"Okay, so you aren't dating. So, this is the beginning stages of getting to know her. That's...exciting. I will say, though, given that you have gone through a great trauma, just be mindful that you are not rushing things and getting too wrapped up in someone early on just in case it doesn't work out."

I don't like anything he said there. In my mind that just doesn't fit. I start fidgeting with my fingers. His comment made me uneasy, and I want to change the subject.

"Okay, Jay let's look at it this way. As you know with trauma, there is no way of just 'getting over it'. The stages of grief mark universal stages in learning to accept loss, which you are familiar with. Healing from trauma can also mean finding new strength and joy in life. To heal doesn't mean you cover up trauma with a Band-Aid to present things as normal, just to feel healed. It's to enjoy your new life. Just make sure she is not that Band-Aid for you. Take things slow. I would hate to see you get too wrapped up in this and if it doesn't work out, you end up with loss again and must start your stages over."

Holy hell, my mind is swimming. That was a lot to take in.

"Thank you Dr. Stangel. I get it. But I just want to add that I am living proof that a shattered heart can beat again. And I'm going to prove it to Olivia, you, and myself."

CHAPTER 14

LIV

THE WEEK HAS GONE BY in a flurry.

After telling the guys last Sunday about the creeper in the trees and the red stalker letters, they have been watching me like a hawk.

Sunday night, Erik came to stay with me. We didn't stay up late, as we both had to work in the morning. Lucky for me I get to work from home, so even though I didn't get great sleep, I didn't have to go to an office, so no one would see my bloodshot eyes.

Erik is the store manager at Staccato, our local music store. I couldn't think of a better place for him to work, music is his life. Darren also works there doing everything from lessons to helping with instrument repair.

Monday night, Way stayed with me. It worked out well for him since bar he bartends and bounces at, "Rumors", is closed on Mondays, so we didn't have to worry about his schedule.

He's a night owl, and I tried to stay up as late as I could with him but fizzled out like a wimp around 11:00. My garbage sleep from the previous night didn't help matters either.

Tuesday night was Darren's night to stay with me. We decided to not stay at my house and ended up at B&B's to play pool.

We called Erik, Waylon, and Joe to meet up with us. I was surprised to spot Jay in there. He was sitting with Tim and another guy I didn't know at one of the high-top tables on the other side of the large room.

Darren kept nudging me and making kissy faces, every time he would notice Jay staring in my direction. A couple times I caught his eye. I felt the urge to walk over and say hello but wasn't sure if I should. I was worried that I came on a little strong with my flirting the previous times I seen him. To my disappointment, he never walked over. Maybe he isn't interested in me. Maybe I just seemed clingy to him.

Darren and I had gotten back to my place around 9:30 that night. Jay was on my mind, and I could still feel the pang of disappointment that he didn't feel the urge to talk to me. I was hoping he would stroll over with his sexy smile and ask me out.

On Wednesday Erik was back and stayed with me. We both fell asleep on the living room couch watching a movie. We ate three bags of popcorn. It was mostly Erik; he's obsessed with popcorn.

Thursday was Joe's turn, and I was so preoccupied with getting things ready for Tina and Tim's wedding that I had neglected to really hang out with him. I felt bad, although I think he was fine, he had a few beers in my basement bar and ended up falling asleep on the couch watching TV. I even let him have the chaise lounge, which is a rare move for me.

Friday came around and I was busy with the rehearsal and dinner for the wedding. I had sent a group text to the boys letting them know that Lexie was coming over after things wrapped up. We would be getting ready for the wedding Saturday, so they had a night off from babysitting.

It was the perfect girly hang out that I needed all week.

CHAPTER 15

LIV

IT'S SATURDAY MORNING, THE DAY of Tim and Tina's wedding. As the sun rose, I lay in bed and quietly wished for them to have the most amazing day ever.

I get up early, feeling refreshed after our laid-back girl's night. I peek in the spare bedroom down the hall from my room and find Lexie snoring away, her hair a mess, wrapped up tightly in the gray comforter.

I close the door and creep back down the hallway. I want to go for my morning run, and don't want to wake her. Slipping on my running gear, I unlock the front door and begin to stretch on my front porch.

I get into a steady pace going down my winding driveway. I turn left and run along Highway 128.

Before I can reach my stopping point at the old dead oak tree, I hear a car behind me. I turn and look, and a silver Cadillac slows in the road, coming up next to me. I stop, unsure of who it is.

The car pulls over to the edge of the road and the passenger window rolls down. I hesitantly walk to the window and see that it's John. I remember seeing him at the concert in St. James.

"Hello Olivia, out for your morning run?" He says it cheerfully, but something about it seems off to me.

"Yep," I say, regretting that I stopped running.

"Will I see you at the wedding later?"

I hadn't realized he was invited. I wonder how he knows them.

"Yeah, I'm in the wedding, so I better be there," I say with a chuckle.

"Make sure you save me a dance," he says with a wink, and slowly starts to pull away.

That was odd, I think to myself. He's still driving away slowly when I get back into my run.

Heading back toward my house I stop at the end of the development at my mailbox. I've come to dread opening this thing. Opening it slowly, I see my pile of mail. I haven't gotten it in a few days.

Sure enough, there is a red envelope inside. I grab the pile and slam the mailbox door shut hard.

I run back up the hill to my house. I get up to the front porch and don't even bother to do a cool down. Now that I know there is another letter, the hair on my arms is standing up and I can feel a sweat coming on. That was not induced by my run.

I slam the front door shut, locking it behind me. I let the mail fall as I slump down to the floor on the inside of the door.

A few moments later Lexie walks up. "Liv, what the hell, are you okay? I heard the door slam." She stops when she sees the red envelope laying in the pile on the floor.

"I'm so sorry, I didn't mean to wake you up."

"Oh God, not another one. How many is this now?" She points to the red envelope.

"Number three, no, four," I say with an exasperated sigh. I pick it up off the floor and tear it open.

My dearest Olivia,

I always think of you – I do. Much more than once in a while. I think of how you smile, what you say, and the things you do to keep my heart beating. It's you baby, and always will be. You make me feel complete in a way nobody else can. I can't wait to make you mine completely.

See you soon,
X

"I can't wait to make you mine completely. What the hell?" I start to tear it up and Lexie stops me.

"Remember to keep them – what if there is something in there that helps you figure out who this is?" She is always one step ahead of me. If it was up to me none of these would still be in my house.

"You know what, today is not the day for this. Screw these letters, let's get beautiful for the wedding." I say, standing back up, slapping it down on the entry way table.

CHAPTER 16

LIV

WE BRIDESMAIDS ARE PRIMPING AND powdering ourselves to the max in the back room of the winery. My makeup is done, so I'm helping Lexie with hers. I love putting makeup on her. She doesn't need much, she has large features and long lashes, she looks glam very easily.

I'm bubbling with excitement to the point of almost getting a nervous stomachache. I'm so excited for Tim and Tina, and, not to mention I found out that Jay has been invited. I already asked Tina what his RSVP was, and she said he is coming.

I've been going over every detail of my hair, makeup, dress, and every other thing, just to ensure that I look as good as I can. If my dress doesn't do the trick of getting Jay's attention, then nothing will.

I picked out a red, long, and tight mermaid style dress with spaghetti straps. The back is open, and the front cuts into a V, showing off some cleavage. Lots of tape has already been attached to make sure this dress stays in the proper places; I don't need things slipping out when they shouldn't.

It really is stunning, I'm so glad each of us was able to choose our own dress. The only requirement was that they were the right shade of red. The other girls' dresses are a bit more conservative than mine. At first, I was a little uncomfortable with my decision, but after trying it on a few times I realized it's going to be amazing, and I let it go.

Tina's colors are red and gold, so all of us have matching gold heels. As a gift to us, Tina got us matching sets of beautiful gold dangle earrings. I decided to leave my hair down in curls, thinking it might help cover my overly exposed back.

The door of the adjoining room opens and Tina's mom steps out, a huge smile on her face and happy tears in her eyes. "Here comes the bride ladies!"

Tina steps out into the bright room, her beautiful white dress flowing around her, she is absolutely glowing and gorgeous. She chose an A-line dress with lace flowers embellished on it. It has a sweetheart neck, and the shoulders and back are covered with intricate lace, except for a cutout at the top of her back.

We are all in a frenzy with smiles, hugs, and tears of joy. Kleenex is being passed all over the room.

"Tina, you look absolutely amazing," I tell her as I give her a big hug. She's trying so hard not to cry and ruin her makeup, and we are all doing the same.

The next ten minutes seem to go by in a flash. A man steps in letting us know that it's time to start heading outside and to get lined up. I can tell Tina's nerves are kicking into high gear now.

As we cross the courtyard of the winery, I grab her free hand and give it a squeeze. I keep a hold of her, especially since we are going to be walking on cobblestones. We don't need the bride falling over. We have a small path to follow through the vineyard, leading to a beautiful large rectangular white gazebo with open sides. The sun is shining and there is a light breeze in the air. The greens of the vineyard are vibrant and set the perfect landscape for an outdoor wedding.

We come around the corner of the tan stucco winery, and the gazebo comes into full view. Guests have filled in the white chairs, and there are bouquets of assorted red flowers on pedestals spread around the perimeter.

Tina sucks in a deep breath. Her father is standing at the back of the gazebo, attempting to be slightly out of sight from guests as he hangs out behind a tree.

Sitting on a couple nearby benches are their grandparents, both mothers, and Tim's dad. They will be escorted in first by Tim, and then the wedding party procession will begin.

As we approach, Tina's dad gives a little wave, and Tim appears from around a tree at the back of the gazebo.

This is the first time Tim has seen Tina. Their eyes quickly meet, and a huge grin spreads across his face while he has tears in his eyes. Making quick steps he approaches, and I let go of Tina's hand.

"You are so beautiful," he tells her, giving her a long kiss.

"Thank you. You don't look so bad yourself," she tells him with a giggle. Now all of us girls are dribbling messes of tears.

Tim hesitantly pulls away as the music starts to play. He escorts the grandparents and mothers to their seats. After that he stays up front, taking his place at the altar.

We line up with our respective groomsmen in the back, the vineyard trees closing in around us.

I am greeted by a smiling face, my walking partner, James.

I don't know much about any of the groomsmen. Lexie and I talked about this last night too, trying to figure out who is single and who isn't. Apparently, James is single, and Tina put us together on purpose thinking we would hit it off.

He's a tall, very clean-cut guy. Dark black hair, and a dark complexion. He has broad shoulders and a decent smile.

"Hey there, Olivia," he says, giving me a smile.

"Hi. We can stay on good terms if you don't step on the bottom of my dress and trip me," I tell him with a quiet laugh.

"I won't trip you as long as you save me a dance later." It's a statement but it came out sort of like a question. I'm caught off guard. He was flirting with me last night too, but I'm just not into it.

"Um, yeah, sure, I think I can do that," I say with a small smile. I was really hoping to dance with Jay tonight instead.

Evelyn and her groomsman have already started walking. Lexie is about to start walking when she turns back and looks at me.

"Time to focus, put the flirting on pause," I roll my eyes at her comment. She and her groomsman start walking.

James and I take a couple steps forward, so we are ready to go. I quickly scan the crowd. There is only one person I'm looking for.

I'm trying to be discreet about it, and then I see him. He is sitting on the groom's side of the gazebo, toward the back, between an older couple and a younger couple. His head turns back, and he catches my eye. Oh God, he just caught me looking at him. A flush and a smile spread across his face. I'm mortified.

James nudges my side. "You ready, beautiful?"

I give him a quick nod, and we start walking down the aisle. I can feel Jay's eyes on me all the way from here.

As we approach the altar, I go to part ways with James, but he grabs my right wrist and pulls it back to him, giving me a kiss on my hand. I can hear the crowd make "aww" sounds. He's really turning on the charm now, this should make for an interesting evening.

CHAPTER 17

JAY

OLIVIA LOOKS STUNNING. I HAVEN'T been able to take my eyes off her.

All through the ceremony I can see the groomsmen looking at her, and I want to rip their eyes right out of their heads.

I want to cover her up, so other men can't look at her the way they are. But, at the same time, I'd love to rip that dress off her too. It would look great in a heap on the floor.

After the ceremony the wedding party exits, and the guests follow behind.

We have now moved into a large hall at the winery with white walls, high ceilings, and massive wood beams. There is brass accent lighting on the walls, and string lights flow from side to side above us in the large room. Greenery and flowers are on each table, and in large vases around the perimeter. The lighting is dim, and candlelight flows throughout the room.

We take our places at the round tables, each one seating six people. We are on the left side, only a couple tables off the dance floor and DJ area. I find my place card. "Jay Jones" it says in gold script. To my left is Brandon and Amanda. To my right is my dad Warren and mom Lisa.

"Who has the last spot at our table?" Brandon asks, and Amanda peeks over to steal a look at the place card.

"Randy Brennan," she says, and shrugs.

A few minutes go by allowing the guests to filter in and get settled. The DJ gets on the microphone, letting us know the wedding party will be entering in a couple minutes and that we need to take our seats.

A middle-aged balding man walks up to our table, inspecting the open spots place card and sits down. My dad strikes up a conversation with him. Apparently, he is Tim's unmarried, Uncle Randy, who claims he won't bug us long, as he plans on spending most of his time up by the open bar.

"Alright ladies and gentlemen let's welcome our wedding party," the young DJ's voice echoes through the large hall.

The lights dim even more, and a spotlight goes on, spiraling up the white wall across the hall from us. There are seven open archways overlooking the hall on the second level, with black wrought iron railings. There is a bridesmaid and groomsman couple in every other archway.

The DJ introduces each of the pairs and they each do their own unique thing together as they are announced. Olivia is the second from the last with the guy that keeps flirting with her. I can feel the tension rolling in me. I want her away from him, and she's not even mine.

When it gets to their turn, he gives her a twirl and leans her down backward, and it looks like he's going to kiss her. I can see her jerk a little and start to straighten back up, his ego deflating. I couldn't be happier that it didn't work out for him.

The wedding party walks to the front of the hall, coming down a set of stairs in pairs. At the bottom is the head table. Olivia keeps walking past her groomsman, but he grabs her hand, pulling her to him, and whispers something in her ear. It doesn't look like she says anything back, and she turns and keeps walking to her spot. If I wasn't mistaken, I'd say she looks a little irritated with him.

"And now, ladies and gentlemen, let me introduce you to the newlyweds, Mr. and Mrs. Tim and Tina Brennan!" We all stand and cheer as Tim and Tina make it across the second-floor hallway past all the arches, waving to the crowd as they go, and start their way down the steps.

Dinner is fantastic, you can't go wrong with steak and salmon. Everyone is groaning with full bellies and contentment after the meal is done. Soft music has been playing throughout the dinner.

"Time to attack that open bar. Come on." Brandon slaps me on the back, and we head up to the bar, taking note of what mom, dad, and Amanda want too.

"I made sure I timed this just right for you," Brandon says with a mischievous smile as we walk up. "Look who just came up to get a drink," he says, pretending to seem surprised, nodding his head at Olivia as she walks up near us and leans against the bar.

I take a deep breath. "I need some whiskey before I can talk to her."

"Fair enough, let's get you some whiskey then." He says with a hand around the back of my neck, dragging me through the crowd and finding an open spot at the bar closer to her.

I'm close enough that I can hear Olivia order a glass of Riesling. Within a matter of seconds James walks up to her, eyeing her up and down the whole time. He's leaning over her saying something, and I can imagine the stupid pick-up lines he's throwing at her. She looks bored.

As she gets her glass of wine she says, "excuse me" to him. She turns, and I catch her eye.

From this close I feel like I could melt, like being too close to the sun. My mouth is dry, and my brain isn't working, I have nothing to say. She gives me a look up and down and sends a flirty smile my way before heading back to the head table.

"Holy shit, did you see her check you out?" My brother is whispering to me, I can hear the astonishment in his voice.

"I did," I say, finally letting out my breath. The image of her in that dress is forever burned into my mind.

"If you don't ask her to dance tonight, then you are a fool. Here, drink this," he says as he hands me a low-ball whiskey on the rocks.

We grab our families' drinks and head back to our table. As we sit, Brandon gives Amanda a peck on the cheek and whispers in her ear, "Liv was checking out Jay." But it wasn't enough of a whisper that I couldn't hear it.

Amanda squeals with delight and tries to high five me. I make a lame attempt at a high five back.

"What's going on?" My mom asks leaning over. Amanda scoots out of her chair and goes over to my mom, squatting down next to her so they can talk. My dad leans over and listens intently too. Jesus! Now the whole family will know I like her.

"Jay likes the bridesmaid, the one sitting next to the maid of honor." She says, pointing in Olivia's direction.

"Oh, wow, she is so pretty. Who is she?" Mom asks, her question directed to both Amanda and me, with a smile on her face. Her dark brown eyes are intense; I can tell she's enjoying this conversation. She props her elbow on the table and leans closer to Amanda.

"Her name is Liv, she's in a band called American Obsession. She sings and plays guitar. She kicks ass." Amanda tells them.

"Oh, I've heard of that band, the do rock and roll covers. I hear they are good," Dad says, happy to be participating in the gossip.

"We need to get Jay buzzed up, so he has the courage to ask her to dance," she says, giving me a mischievous smile. I just keep sipping on my whiskey.

As the night wears on, Tim and Tina have their first dance, speeches and toasts are made, and things start to pick up on the dance floor.

Olivia has been to the bar a couple times to get more wine and some water, and it blows me away that every time she's up there, guys just swarm around her. I'm sick of watching it.

"Okay, after the next song we're gonna slow it down," the DJ says over the microphone.

Here's my chance. I get up, buttoning up my dark turquoise suit coat and push in my chair. I walk away from the table quickly before anyone in my family can make fun of me for what I'm about to do.

As I walk up, I see an older man with brown and gray hair and a gray suit coat on talking to Olivia. He's standing too close to her, and she keeps moving backwards as he talks, but he just keeps edging forward after her. I'm not sure what he's saying to her, but she looks uncomfortable.

"Come on, you and I need a picture together. Don't make me ask again," he says, trying to sound funny and leans close to her. He grabs his phone out of his pocket.

"Okay, I guess," she says and sets her glass down on the bar. She turns back and sees me, giving me a smile.

The guy grabs her around her waist and pulls her to him. He's smiling, and she's not. He takes a selfie and then looks up, seeing me as I stand in front of them.

"Can I help you," he says, looking squarely at me.

"I'm just waiting to talk to Olivia."

"Here, help us out. Take a picture of us," and he shoves his cell phone toward me. I hesitantly take it and hold it up to take their picture. He still has his hand on her waist and looks all too pleased being that close to her.

I hand his phone back and he doesn't say thanks, he just turns his attention to Olivia. "Thanks, see you later," he leans in close to her as he says it, and she automatically backs away more. Finally, he leaves, and walks out the door of the hall.

"Hi. Who was that guy?" I wonder if she knows him, or if it was just some random dude.

"An old friend of my dad's. He's my pharmacist, I know him a little bit but not well. I'm not sure why he wanted a picture with me," she says, shrugging her shoulders.

The song changes, the music slowing to Niall Horan's "Slow Hands". I can feel a knot in my stomach and a lump in my throat.

"Do you want to dance with me," I ask her hesitantly.

I'm ruined forever if she says no.

CHAPTER 18

LIV

A SMILE SPREADS ACROSS MY face. "Yes, I'd love to," I tell Jay. He has the biggest grin, and I can feel the excitement bubbling up inside of me.

He motions with his left hand to the dance floor and puts his right arm ever so lightly on my back, leading me out.

Once on the dance floor, he turns towards me, and I can tell he's a little nervous.

I slide my arms up and around his broad shoulders and neck, feeling the ripples of his muscles under his dark turquoise suit coat. He follows suit and puts his large hands on the bare skin of my lower back. It's giving me chills everywhere, and the butterflies are moving with unbridled joy in my stomach.

His deep hazel eyes are fixated on mine. I can feel the heat radiating off his body when he's this close. I hope it's not awkward that I'm staring back but I just can't look away.

"Are you having fun tonight?" I ask, trying to break the ice.

"Yeah, this is beautiful. Tim and Tina look happy together."

I nod my head in agreement with a smile. "Who are the people you are sitting with?"

"My older brother Brandon and his wife Amanda, and my parents, Warren and Lisa."

Both couples are out on the dance floor now, and I look over at them, and the one who is Amanda gives me a wink.

Immediately Brandon widens his eyes at her, and I can see he's appalled at what she just did.

Jay looks over at them and they both smile back at him, Amanda's cheeks reddening. Brandon shakes his head.

"So, I see the groomsman you had to walk with is working pretty hard for your attention," he says, and I can hear a twinge of jealousy in his voice.

"Yeah, he sure is. He's not really my cup of tea though," and I watch his reaction as he tries to suppress a smile.

"You know, you could really use a bodyguard with all these guys that hang around you. It's like watching monkeys fight over a banana."

I immediately laugh, and he drops his head and shakes it. "Oh my God I can't believe I said that out loud. I just called you a banana." I'm still laughing.

We keep dancing through the song, and I can feel his fingertips and hands slowly moving on my back and hips. Not moving around a lot, just finding the place they want to be.

I realize the end of the song is coming up, so I tighten my arms around his neck and lean in closer.

"So do I get to dance with you again?" I ask with my best flirty smile.

"There's nothing I want more than that," he says, smiling back at me. The butterflies are in a full frenzy now.

The song ends and I remove my arms from his neck hesitantly. I'm already missing the feeling of touching him.

He removes one hand from my back but keeps the other one there. The dance floor crowd is still mingling, and before we head back to the bar, he pulls me closer, grabs my right hand, and kisses it. Apparently, I do like it when guys do that, it just needed to be the right guy.

"Thanks for the dance," he says with a wicked smile.

We walk back to the bar together, his arm pulling me in just enough to keep me close.

"I'm going to use the restroom, I'll be back. Don't dance with anyone else," he winks at me and walks away.

After he leaves, Lexie comes up to the bar beside me. She's had enough wine now that she's good and loose.

"Hey! Oh my God, I seen you dancing with the hottie, way to go!" She gives me a hug and squeals.

"Jay is so charming and sweet. He said he'd dance with me again," I say as I do a little happy dance.

"Good for you. Wait! So, with that being the case, can I go after James if you aren't interested in him? He's kind of cute, and I need to get laid, bad."

"Hell yeah, go for it. Let me know if you need a wing woman." We talk for a minute, and I turn to notice Jay is on his way back towards us.

As he walks up, Lexie turns and introduces herself, a drunken happy smile plastered on her face the whole time. I'm not sure if she remembers me introducing them at Tina's bachelorette party. Hopefully, I don't have to carry her to the car at the end of the night.

"Well, I'm gonna go hit on your groomsman," she says.

As she starts walking away, Jay calls out to her, "please and thank you!" It's impossible not to laugh.

I'm about to tell him how nice he looks when Tara comes up behind me, tapping me on the shoulder. I can see her eyes go up and down Jay in appreciation and her cheeks redden. She snaps back and looks at me.

"Tina is going to throw the bouquet; you have to get up there – gather up anyone else you can find too."

"Okay, I'll be right there." I say and she turns and heads back to the dance floor.

"I guess I'm moving on to my bridesmaid duties now. Find me for the next slow song." I give him a sweet smile.

"Absolutely." He flashes me his charismatic smile again.

I turn and head to the dance floor, grabbing a few more girls along the way that are lingering by the bar.

The DJ announces that its time to throw the bouquet. There are about twenty girls gathered on the dance floor. Tina turns her back to us, launching the bouquet in the air. Sabrina's tattooed arm catches it, and she cheers out loud, holding it high.

I'm pulled around by Tina and the girls for a while, fulfilling my bridesmaid duties of the evening.

First, Tina had to pee, so I volunteered to help her out.

Then, Evelyn and I went and double checked that all the cards and gifts were picked up and brought out to Tina's parents' car.

After that, I had to pee, and decided to touch up my makeup a little since I was in there.

I collected money for the dollar dance, which ended up taking almost a half an hour. Talk about a way to kill the excitement of a dance, yikes. But Tim and Tina made some good money off it, so I was glad to help.

I keep glancing around during my bridesmaid duties to see where Jay is. If he ends up at the bar with another girl, I think I would have a meltdown. But he isn't. He's back at his table with his family. He looks happy and relaxed, sipping on his cocktail. Occasionally, I catch his eye, and it's impossible not to smile at him.

Finally, I catch a break as the DJ announces that another slow song is coming up. I'm finishing up collecting all the money from the dollar dance and handing it to Tina's dad.

The first notes of Gwen and Blake's "Nobody but You" begins to play. I look up at the table where Jay was sitting but I don't see him.

I jump when I feel two strong hands wrap around my waist and spin me around.

Once I've stopped, I see it's Jay. I can't help the enormous smile spreading across my face. He pulls me in close and I immediately wrap my arms tightly around his neck.

His hands are slightly lower this time than last time, and he's holding me a little closer too. I'm absolutely loving it.

I press myself into him and there is no awkwardness in looking into his eyes during the song, it just feels right.

We move through the song, finding our rhythm, inching closer as it plays on. We don't say a word the whole time, we don't need to. Our eyes say everything.

When the song ends, it takes us even longer to separate from each other. Just like before, he keeps one arm wrapped around my waist. He leads me back up to the bar, which is good, I could use a fresh glass of wine.

We order our drinks, and as we are waiting, I grab a hold of the lapel of his suit coat.

"If you would have told me before that a dark turquoise green suit coat would look this hot, I couldn't have pictured it. But this, this works." I give him a flirty smile, and I can feel myself blush. He smiles back at me.

At least I didn't make a superhero comment this time.

CHAPTER 19

LIV

AT THE END OF THE night, the wedding party is busy gathering up decorations and the remaining things that the happy new couple will be keeping. There is a van parked outside that we are helping load everything into.

I head back into the hall one last time to grab my purse. I look toward the table where Jay was and can't see him. A stab of disappointment runs through me, thinking that he left without saying goodbye.

There is a good size crowd of wedding guests still mingling in the entry way of the winery, on the edge of the hall. I scoot through the large crowd and decide waiting outside might be the best idea. Erik offered to give Lexie and I a ride home. So now, I need to find her too.

Outside in the cobblestone courtyard there is a fountain, and a breeze is making the water in the fountain spray across the ground around it.

I decide to step off to the side of the walkway near the fountain. From here I can see anyone coming out and can see the parking lot, so I will know when Erik pulls up.

I jump when a firm arm wraps around my waist. Startled, I look back to see it's Jay. A flush and a smile come across my face, and I immediately step toward him.

I have my arms crossed over me, the little bit of a breeze and the lack of back and sleeves to this dress making me cold.

Jay unbuttons his suit coat and starts to take it off.

"What are you doing?" I ask him.

"You're cold, I'm here to warm you up," he says with a sneaky grin. He wraps the warm jacket around my shoulders.

"Thank you. I was worried I wouldn't get to say goodbye to you. I'm glad you found me."

"Me too."

Erik's black car pulls up and a drunken Lexie starts walking towards it, giving me a wave. I hadn't even noticed she was out here; I was so distracted by Jay.

"Erik's here, I have to go." I start removing his jacket, but he stops me, sliding it gently back on to my shoulders.

He leans in closer to me, his large hands on my arms, holding me close.

"You keep it."

"I can't keep your jacket."

He leans in closer, his mint and whiskey tinted breath wrapping around me, his lips barely grazing my cheek.

"You can give it back to me on our first date," he says coolly in my ear, and doesn't pull away from my face.

"Okay," I say, and I can feel my heart pounding in my chest. I don't have enough air to get more words out.

"My phone number is in the pocket. Will you text me later?"

"Yes," I breathe out.

Moving one hand up to my neck and cheek, the other now wrapped around my waist, he plants the most perfect soft kiss on my cheek. My heart is hammering now in my chest. He backs away slowly, still holding my waist, and leads me to Erik's car. Every step is torture, I never want him to leave.

He opens Erik's passenger car door and raises my right hand up and plants a soft kiss on it.

"Good night. Text me later." He says with a flirty smile.

"I will. Good night." I turn to get in the car, and he closes the door behind me.

"Well, that was interesting," Erik says sarcastically as he starts to drive away.

"Oh my God that was the hottest thing EVER!" Lexie drunkenly calls out from the backseat.

I have nothing to add but a huge smile. I reach in the jacket pocket and find Jay's number on a piece of paper, signed "XOXO".

CHAPTER 20

JAY

IT'S AN AWKWARD RIDE HOME with my family. Brandon and Amanda are buzzing about how I was "so daring to ask her to dance," and at one point Amanda tells me she is "proud of me". In all honesty though, I'm proud of myself as well, I just don't want to tell anyone that.

We carpooled with mom and dad, and they drop me off at my loft first. They booked hotel rooms just a few blocks away, claiming they don't want to intrude on my small space.

I hear my phone beep as I'm getting out of the car, the anticipation of knowing it might be Olivia is killing me.

I quickly unlock the street level door going up to my place, lock it behind me and hurry up the steps. I slide the large door open and go into my loft. I don't even get the door shut behind me before I look at my phone screen.

An unfamiliar number has text me. I quickly swipe it open and pull up the text. It's from her. I save her number in my phone immediately.

> Olivia: Hi Jay - this is Olivia :)
> Jay: Hey! Glad you text me.
> Olivia: I had a great time with you tonight.
> Jay: Me too.

I stop and think. I don't want to be too forward, but I don't want her to slip away.

> Jay: So, when do I get my jacket back?
> Olivia: What nights are you free?
> Jay: I'm open any night, take your pick.
> Olivia: How about Thursday?
> Jay: Perfect. Pick you up at 6:00?
> Olivia: See you then ;)

I swear this huge grin on my face is never going away, and I'm not going to be able to sleep tonight. This girl is nothing I ever expected but ended up being everything I ever wanted.

CHAPTER 21

LIV

THE NEXT MORNING, I WAKE feeling lighter and bubbly. The early morning sun is shining in the windows, and I stretch out smiling at the previous night's events. I throw on some gym shorts and a blue spaghetti strap tank top and decide to start my day.

Lexie has taken over the guest bedroom, I see the door is still shut as I peek down the hallway. Erik is curled up on the living room couch. He's lying face down, his bare back peeking out through the mess of blankets, revealing the massive eagle wing tattoo that spans his back and shoulders.

I sneak across the living and dining room into the kitchen to make some coffee. I hit the button and my Keurig springs to life. I grab a French vanilla cappuccino pod and pop it into place. As the water begins to heat, I turn around and face the kitchen windows to the back yard.

My jaw drops, and I'm frozen in my tracks. This cannot be happening. There is a red envelope, I think the fifth one now, taped on the outside of one of my kitchen windows like a big ugly red scar.

Immediately I run in to the living room and shake Erik. "Erik, wake up! Wake up," I'm yelling at him.

His eyes fly open, and a second later his feet land on the floor. He grabs my arms. "What the hell? What's going on?"

"There's another letter...." I feel out of breath, panicked.

"Where is it?" He asks, rubbing his eyes, and I grab his hand and lead him to the kitchen.

I stand in the archway to the kitchen and point to the back window. Then I realize, there's more. In my back yard are at least a dozen small bouquets of red roses, scattered all over the back patio.

"What the fuck," Erik stammers out. "You stay right here." I'm not about to argue with him.

He unlocks and slides the back patio door open, and cautiously looks around, slowly walking over and takes the taped envelope off the kitchen window. He comes back in, locking the patio door behind him.

I grab it from him, tearing it open.

My dearest Olivia,

I have an insatiable desire for you. Always craving to kiss you, touch you, consume you, love you.

Your red dress took my breath away. I felt you deserved roses to match.

See you soon,
X

I can't stop shaking.

Inside is a picture of me from Tim and Tina's wedding, leaning against the bar in my red dress, holding a glass of wine. It looks like it was taken from a distance. I let it all fall to the floor. I feel like I could faint.

I wake Lexie up and tell her about the letter and flowers and send her home to her apartment. I don't need her getting wrapped up in all the chaos.

Erik and I pick up Darren and go around town looking for security camera systems for my house. Darren is the tech savvy member of our group; he has better insight on this than Erik or me.

While we shop, Waylon and Joe head over to the house and get rid of all the roses, making sure nothing else was left outside that we had missed earlier.

As we return, I see Waylon's truck and the Joe's Fiesta sitting in my driveway. Thank God they're still here. I need all the people I can get right now.

The front door opens as the three of us step on to the front porch, bags in hand. Waylon is filling up the doorway, big and built like a wall. I sling my arms around his muscular body, and I cry onto his chest.

"It's all right baby girl, we've got you," he says in his deep growl of a voice, leading me into my house.

"Thanks Way," I say, still burying my face in his chest.

Erik and Darren make quick work of setting up my new security cameras. There is one for both the front door and the back patio door that will double as video cameras and doorbells. They are both set up to capture video as far out as they possibly can, and I can shut them off any-time I need to. I was told I need to charge them once a month or so, hopefully I can remember to do that.

The guys are in the kitchen discussing this coming weeks' babysitting schedule. It makes me feel like a child.

I decide to remove myself from the conversation, so I sneak away into my bedroom. Flopping down on the bed I pull my phone out of my back pocket. I've heard it dinging multiple times today, this will be a good distraction.

I filter through and respond to the texts, nothing really catching my interest. Then one catches my eye. It's from Jay. The butterflies come to life just from seeing his name pop up on my phone.

How my heart swells more and more each time I see and think about him is wild. How does he have this effect on me so easily, and so quickly?

> Jay: I can't wait for Thursday. We will keep it
>   casual, I have something fun planned for us. :)
> Liv: What do you have in mind?
> Jay: I can't tell you.
> Liv: So, it's top secret? Hmmm….
> Jay: Yep. I'm counting down the days. :)

He is the perfect distraction from today's chaos. I'm counting down the days too, Jay.

CHAPTER 22

JAY

ITS TUESDAY NIGHT. I HAVEN'T seen Olivia in three days and haven't texted her since Sunday. I've wanted to, but figured I should lay off a little. I didn't want to seem overbearing after last weekend. If I came off too strong, I don't know, I wasn't there to witness how she felt about it all on Sunday. Maybe I was too overbearing, or maybe I wasn't. Flirting is not really my forte, I haven't dated much, so who knows, I'm probably going about this all wrong.

But tonight, this is a different story. Tim had told me awhile back that she and the band hang out at B&B's on Tuesday nights and shoot pool. So, I called Tim and asked if he wanted to go out and have a few drinks. He said he'd "checked with The Boss" and she gave him the green light.

I'm standing outside the main entrance of the bar waiting for him to arrive. People keep flowing in, this must be the place to be on a Tuesday night.

Tim finally rolls up, grabbing a parking space on the other side of Broadway.

"Hey man. Glad you called," he calls out to me as he crosses the street.

I give him a slap on the back as he approaches. "Hey. How's married life so far?"

A grin spreads across his face. "It's great. Thanks for coming out on Saturday, Tina and I had a blast. And, I'm guessing you had a good time too, being that you got to dance with Liv."

I can feel the flush in my cheeks. "Yeah, give a guy enough whiskey and he builds up a little courage I guess."

We both laugh and head inside, up the winding staircase to the busy bar.

"So, I'm going to venture a guess you picked this place because Liv and the boys come here on Tuesdays…" He gives me a sideways grin.

"Yeah, you got me. I knew you would figure out what I was up to."

"It's all good. Whatever I can do to help you land a date with her, you can count me in."

"Already took care of that, our first date is on Thursday." I can't hide the smile on my face.

"No freaking way. Holy shit, dude way to go! Where are you gonna take her?"

"Let me buy you a beer and I'll fill you in on my plan."

The bartender sets down our first round of drinks. Whiskey for me, and some kind of amber ale for Tim. I fill him in on my first date plans.

"Great idea, I think she will love that. She once told Tina she's sick of "cookie cutter guys", whatever that means, at least you are trying something different."

"Thanks. Glad I could run it by you. I have back up plans in case she thinks it's stupid," I say, shrugging my shoulders.

We are at a high top on the opposite side of the room of the pool table where the bands picture is on the wall.

There is a "Reserved" sign on that table, I'm guessing they know the bartender well enough that he saves it for them when they come in.

"Earth to Jay. Don't worry dude, she isn't here yet," and he starts laughing as he waves his hand in front of my face. I didn't realize it, but I was staring over there thinking about her. I decide to turn the conversation toward honeymoon plans.

"We can't afford much right now. Next weekend we are renting a cabin up north, and hopefully in six months or so we can go somewhere nice. Tina says it needs to be somewhere warm."

I look up and see a few guys sitting at the bar stools in front of us turn towards the door.

I turn my head to the side, and sure enough, the whole band walks in. I think half the bar is staring at them now, I wonder what they think when people do that.

Luckily, I've been studying up on them and have their names, faces, and instruments down.

First one in is Erik, the lead singer and the one all the girls go nuts over. He's wearing a black T-shirt and he looks like he owns the joint with a smirk on his face. He gives the bartender a wave as he goes by. He heads over to the pool table by their picture.

Behind him is Waylon, the bassist. Waylon steps around Erik and pulls the "Reserved" sign off the table and heads for the cues.

Right behind them is Olivia, Joe, Darren, and a girl I don't know with long black hair and tattoos. She's holding hands with Joe. Darren and Olivia are wrapped up in conversation, and the other two head up to the bar.

Olivia looks fantastic, not that I'm surprised. Her brunette hair is flowing in loose waves around her shoulders and down her back. She has smoky eyes and pink lips. She's wearing a crop top white T-shirt gathered up at the bottom in a little knot, and insanely short shorts. They are so short the pockets are sticking out the bottoms of them. Her top is just short enough I can see her belly button, and damn, she looks good.

"Helllooooo," I snap to and look over at Tim, who has a shit-eating-grin on his face. "You just zoned out looking at her for like two whole minutes dude. You need to bring better game than that on your date Thursday."

He's got a good point. I can't act like a lovesick puppy on our first date. I'm sure she likes guys that are in control of themselves and confident, not drooling all over her.

We order another round of drinks, and I make it a point to keep up with Tim in conversation. I don't want him to get bored and not want to come out with me again, just because I'm distracted by Olivia. I do keep checking on her though, it's hard to peel my eyes away.

As they play pool, multiple guys have gone over and talked to her. Most of the time the band keeps them at bay, with someone saying something cocky and scaring them off. I don't think she's noticed me yet. I kind of like it this way, just watching her interact with them.

As I take a sip of my drink, our table shifts and I'm caught off guard, my drink in one hand, the other hand attempting to grab the edge of the table. A lame and slurred, "sorry", is all we get from a tall dark-haired guy, finishing the last swigs of his pint and walking away without looking back at us.

He heads toward the far wall in the back. Looks like he's heading for the restroom. Before he gets there, he leans his forearm up on the wall by where the band is playing pool, and ogles Oliva. What a creep!

Waylon and Erik notice him right away, and stand in front of him, just to be jerks. Thank God.

The guy walks away and heads to the restroom. Waylon and Erik whisper something to each other. Olivia is laughing away with Joe and the dark-haired girl on the other side of the table, oblivious to the drooling idiot that was just staring at her.

A minute passes and Waylon, Darren, and Erik head up to the bar to get another round of drinks.

"So what time are you picking up Olivia on Thursday? Oh hey, if it goes well maybe you guys can double date with us," Tim is right, that would be fun.

"I'm picking her up at 6:00 Thursday. Fingers crossed, I can get to date number two and then we could absolutely do that."

I look back over and see the drunken idiot is out of the bathroom and hanging all over Olivia. Joe is doing his best to get in the middle of them, but the guy has a solid foot on him, and probably a good forty pounds too.

Before I know it, I'm out of my chair and crossing the bar. The guy's huge hands and fingers are wrapped around her, and he's swaying drunkenly, making her sway involuntarily.

"Knock it off, you don't get to touch me," I hear her telling him as I walk up. He's not budging.

"Not today, motherfucker," I spit at him. He turns and looks at me and doesn't seem the least bit affected.

He raises a fist toward me. Too bad for him I go to the gym every day. I beat him to the punch and clock him right in the face. He doubles over, grabbing his cheek.

"And who the fuck do you think you are," he asks me, with a hand over one eye.

"Nobody you will want to run into again. Get lost, asshole." He stands up straight, turns, and walks away, giving me the finger.

I glance behind me, and the entire bar is staring at us. All we need now is the music on the speakers to stop and it would be just like in the movies.

I look over at Olivia and she is looking at me in shock.

"I'm sorry, it just seemed like he was bothering you." I half choke it out in embarrassment.

"You don't need to apologize. Thank you so much. I went out with him once. He's a moron and has no boundaries. I've been waiting for someone to put him in his place." She looks over my shoulder as the bartender directs the bouncer to get the guy out of the bar.

"Who are you here with?"

"Tim. He's over there." I turn and point, and then realize he isn't at our table, he's standing in the small crowd that has formed behind me.

"Hi Liv. Good thing your personal bodyguard is here." He says laughing. Now I'm really embarrassed.

I look over around the pool table and I have four sets of eyes sizing me up. The AO boys. Shit, I really don't want to piss them off, they definitely outnumber me, and I'm pretty sure Waylon could take me in one punch.

Sensing my uneasiness, Olivia clears her throat and introduces me.

"Guys, this is Jay Jones. He's a friend of Tim's." They ease up a little, each reaching out and shaking my hand as they say 'hello'.

Erik keeps a hesitant eye on me as he shakes my hand.

"Next round is on me." Olivia gives a wave to the bartender and then points to Tim and me with a nod back at him.

"I got your next round too, and Tim's," Olivia says to me.

"You don't need to do that," I tell her.

"Yes, I do, you saved me from Mark. You must be paid back; your services cannot go unrewarded," she says eloquently with a chuckle at the end.

I sip my drink and decide to mingle with the band. I would like to get to know them, they seem cool, and if I'm going to try and hang out with Olivia, I need them to like me.

I decide to approach Darren first.

"Hey man, I'm Darren. So how is it that you know Liv?"

"Well, I've gotten to know her a little through our mutual friends, Tim, and Tina Brennan. And I'm taking her out on Thursday." His eyes widen and his jaw pops open and he looks over at Olivia.

"Seriously! And you haven't told me this yet? What the hell is wrong with you?" He's pointedly looking at Olivia in astonishment.

Olivia's face gets red, and she glances at me, embarrassed.

"I was planning on telling you."

"Girl, you need to tell me these things, otherwise I was totally planning on calling dibs on him." He says in a half whisper. Oliva rolls her eyes and smacks him in the arm before turning back to the pool table.

I glance around and realize all the guys in the band are staring at me again.

One by one, I walk around and casually reintroduce myself. But now that they know I'm taking her out, the conversation has turned in to whispers of "what to do" and "what not to do" with Olivia. This could not have worked out better.

Darren told me her favorite flowers are tiger lilies. And that if the date went south, I could always take him out instead. It made me laugh.

Waylon warned me she does not like smokers, pointing out that Joe is a smoker, and she gives him hell about it all the time. No worries there, never been one, and don't plan on starting any time soon.

Joe told me her favorite wines are Riesling and Moscato.

Erik shot me daggers and told me to be honest and, "don't fucking hurt her."

The night is winding down, and I finally catch Olivia for myself without being distracted by other people.

Done with her game, she lays her pool cue down and sits on the edge of the table. I've had enough whiskey at this point to be a little flirtatious. I walk up in front of her and place my palms down on the pool table on either side of her. I let my face get in close to hers and grin.

She smiles back at me, and I can see she's enjoying this. "So did the boys tell you all my dirty little secrets tonight?"

"Yep. You have nothing left to hide." I flash her a big smile and she laughs.

I lean in, placing my left hand gently on her hip, and whisper in her ear. "Two days left. I can't wait until Thursday; this is killing me."

I can feel her smiling next to me.

CHAPTER 23

LIV

THURSDAY HAS FINALLY ARRIVED. I'M beyond excited to go out with Jay. Ever since I woke up this morning it has been all I can think about, and now I'm making myself nervous.

I'm standing in front of my large full-length mirror in my bedroom. I have on an adorable short white sundress, with some ruffles at the bottom and a lace center that runs across my stomach. It has spaghetti straps that tie in the back, and it makes a "V" in the front. I've changed in to twelve different dresses and finally settled on this one. Some earrings are all I need with this; I don't want to look overdone. I grab my faded jean jacket in case I get cold, and my go-to tan wedges. Date night casual is what I'm going for.

I check my phone. I have a text from Lexie that reads, *good luck - knock his socks off tonight.* There's also an emoji with hearts in its eyes from her.

It's 5:51 PM. I can't stop looking at the clock. I hear the faint sounds of a vehicle and hurry out to look out my front living room window. I can see his truck pulling up. The butterflies in my stomach start freaking out. *Be cool Liv, just be cool.*

He pulls up in the driveway, and now I'm creeping around the window like a weirdo, I don't want him to see me watching him.

He's wearing jeans and a dark plaid button up. Perfect, he's not too dressed up, I don't have to change my outfit. I'm done watching, he's going to think I'm crazy if he sees me spying on him.

My fancy new doorbell rings on my phone, which is in my hand. I set the phone down on the entry way table and head to the door. I take in a deep breath and let it out before opening it. I do my usual mantra in my head: *he'll either be the one, or just another one.* I guess we're about to find out.

I open the door and there he is. A million-dollar smile plastered on his gorgeous, chiseled handsome face. His hair is a little longer on the top, and he has it slicked to the side in a neat, yet messy way. It's so freaking hot. It's the same way he had it styled at Tim and Tina's wedding. There is still the same little bit of stubble on his face. I start thinking about how I want to feel it on my skin.

"Hey," he says, and I can see a twinkle in his eyes, his grin not fading the least bit.

"Hi, come on in," I say in return. Now my nerves are really kicking into high gear.

I open the door wider and Jay steps in. He has a bouquet of flowers in his hand.

"These are for you," he says, and his cheeks redden a little.

"Thank you. They're beautiful. I'll make a trade with you," I say with a sly smile.

He cocks his head to the side in confusion as I turn to open the entry way closet behind me. I pull out his dark turquoise green suit coat from the wedding.

"I believe this belongs to you," I tell him smiling.

He takes the coat on its hanger and trades me the flowers. "From now on this is my lucky suit coat," he says with a grin.

I take a quick smell of the flowers. He did good, this spray has lots of tiger lilies in it.

"Tiger lilies are my favorite, you get extra points," I give him a wink. "I'm going to go put these in water, I'll be right back."

I step into the kitchen and grab a vase from one of the cabinets. I make quick work of it; I don't want to keep him waiting for me. I set them on my kitchen island.

As I come around the corner out of the kitchen, I watch him in the entry way. I catch his eye while crossing the dining and living room, and I can see he's giving me an appreciative look up and down. I must have done good on picking this dress.

"I'm ready when you are," I tell him. He goes to open the door and I grab my purse and phone, locking the front door behind us.

"So, what's the plan for tonight," I ask Jay as we approach his truck.

"That's top secret, you will see when we get there." He's looking over at me with a sneaky grin.

"Am I at least dressed appropriately? We aren't going to play paintball or something, right? Cuz I'm not doing that in a dress."

He's laughing at me. "You are good to go. You'll see when we get there," he says as he opens the truck door for me.

CHAPTER 24

JAY

IT'S ABOUT A FIFTEEN-MINUTE DRIVE out into the country. We are heading out to my uncle Mike's hunting land which is about halfway between Pine Lake and Greensboro. I had called him last Sunday to see if Olivia and I can have "date night" out there, and he happily agreed.

My idea for tonight was to load up the back of my Silverado with an air mattress, blankets, and pillows, and have a picnic while watching the sunset. I also brought a speaker to hook my phone up to so we can have music. I hope she's okay with this, I wanted to do something unique tonight.

I came out here on Monday night and picked out the perfect spot to park the truck. Way up on top of one of the hills, I found a spot that I can back up into, off the old dirt road that cuts through the field. There was an uneven spot in the CRP land that if I back up to it and open the tailgate, we can walk right into the back of the truck, which I'm sure she will appreciate, especially since she has a dress on.

I even went to the store and bought some lights. "Fairy lights" I think they are called. It was embarrassing buying them, I was so out of my element. I taped them up around the inside of the bed of my truck, so we have a little light for the evening. Luckily my tonneau cover is on, so she has no idea all the stuff is back there.

I picked up a variety of meats, cheeses, crackers, dips, and basically made a charceuterie board style meal, minus the fancy board.

I know she likes wine. I can't say I mind it, it's not my favorite, but I will drink it. I picked up a few bottles of Riesling and Moscato, and bought a couple wine glasses, since I didn't own any.

We make small talk in the truck on the way there. I tell her I'm from Greensboro, and that my family still lives there. My parents have a house there, and my dad is a judge. My mom is a homemaker, raised us kids, and spends a lot of her time working with charities and other groups around the area.

Brandon and Amanda live there as well, right in town. Amanda is a court reporter, and it was my dad who introduced them, given that he had known her through work. Brandon is the General Manager at a local vehicle dealership in Greensboro. He's been there since after high school.

I ask her if she grew up in Pine Lake and if she has any siblings. At first, she hesitates before answering, which is a little odd to me, but then she answers with, "yes, I grew up in Pine Lake. I don't have any siblings." It has a clipped feeling to it, not necessarily rude, almost like she doesn't want to talk about it.

We pull into the turn for my uncle's hunting land. I'm so nervous that she won't like this. I sneak a peek in her direction and see she has a confused look on her face.

"You aren't bringing me out here to murder me, are you?" She says it sarcastically, but I'm sure she is wondering what the hell we're doing here.

"Yep, all the murder stuff is in the back," I say, matching her sarcasm.

"Well, at least I have a hot murderer. Do me a favor and make it quick." Now we're both laughing.

We bounce slowly through the CRP grasses and past the cornfields that tower next to the truck like thick green walls. She has a smile on her face, thank God, it doesn't look like this bothers her.

I pull up to the top of the grassy hill and put the truck in reverse. I back into the spot I had picked out earlier this week. Good thing I practiced and know exactly where to go.

From this vantage my truck is facing the east, and the box of the truck is facing the west, perfect for watching the sunset.

"You wait here for one minute while I get things set up, and no peeking," I say as I lean over to her, closer than I need to, unbuckling her seat belt. I did it on purpose just to get close to her. Our eyes never leave each other. God, I wish I could kiss her right now. But I told myself I would find the perfect moment for that. I just need to wait a little longer.

I step out of the truck, giving her a wink as I close the door. I hope she doesn't think I'm crazy.

I hit the button so the side mirrors flip in, so she can't peek in them and watch what I'm doing. Rounding the back of the truck, I pull the tailgate open and flip up the tonneau cover.

Luckily, things haven't shifted too much during the drive. I get in and quick rearrange the blankets and pillows, so they look good.

I literally had to buy this stuff this week, I never owned throw pillows before. There's about a dozen of them in there, I might have gone a little overboard.

I flip the switch on for the fairy lights and they light up around the inside of the box. I dig out the cooler of food and wine, and the speaker.

I already had a playlist ready to go for tonight, so I fire up the speaker and hit "Play" on my phone.

I take in a deep breath and let it out. *You can do this Jay, just relax*, the voice in my head is telling me. I walk around to her side of the truck and open the door.

"I swear I didn't peek," she says, trying to make an innocent face.

"You ready gorgeous?" I ask as I hold out my hand to help her out of the truck. She takes my hand and gives me her perfect smile in return.

CHAPTER 25

LIV

I COME AROUND THE BACK side of the truck and I'm blown away.

Jay has the truck bed set up with blankets and pillows, lights, and music. This is literally the most thoughtful date I've ever been on in my life. I'm blown away, it's so romantic! Every girl deserves a date like this.

"If you feel like running away, I'd totally understand," he says to me quietly, seeing my shocked expression.

"Jay, this is absolutely perfect, I love it." I'm facing him, and I can see the tension and nerves melt away from him as I say it.

He grabs my hand and brings me to the tailgate. *Thank God I don't have to jump up into it, especially in a dress.* We walk into the back of the truck and now his hand has moved on to my lower back. It's giving me the most glorious goosebumps everywhere.

"Have a seat," he says as he motions toward the air mattress covered in blankets and pillows.

I turn and sit down, kicking my tan wedges off. He kneels in front of me, opens the cooler, and grabs two bottles of wine.

"I have Moscato or Riesling," he says with a charming smile.

"Riesling, thank you," and I'm wondering how he knows my favorite flowers, and my favorite wine. This guy is good. He pours it and passes the wine glass to me, then pours one for himself.

He takes out plates of cheeses, crackers, meats, fruits, and sets them on top of the cooler, using it as a table.

He crawls over and sits on the bouncy air mattress next to me. Just having him this close is giving me more goosebumps and it's impossible to hide the smile on my face.

We sit for a minute, sipping our wine, and look out over the beautiful landscape. A sea of grasses, trees, and fields are laid out in front of us, and we can see for miles. There are blues, pinks, oranges, and purples melting together in the sky, as the sun starts to move across it. The weather is perfect, still warm outside, the sky clear, with just a light breeze.

"This is beautiful Jay, thank you," I tell him, looking over at him through my thick lashes.

He's looking back, eyes on my face, searching my lips, and I want nothing more right now than for him to kiss me. He's so close I can smell his cologne, musky and sexy, it's just driving me crazy.

He breaks eye contact for a second, I can tell he's nervous. I take a sip of my wine and decide to dig in on some of this food, maybe that will help as an ice breaker.

We devour the spread, refilling our wine glasses another time.

"I thought you were a whiskey guy. That's what I've seen you drink before."

"I don't mind wine, but yeah, whiskey is my go-to drink of choice."

"How did you know Riesling and Moscato are my favorite wines? And that tiger lilies are my favorite flowers?"

A playful smile appears on his face. "The guys told me on Tuesday at B&B's. It was all helpful, apart from Erik who told me to *be honest and don't fucking hurt her.* I think he tried to murder me with his eyes."

"Oh God, I'm so sorry. They are like my brothers; but they can get weird and way overprotective sometimes. But I have to say, it seems like they like you. Normally they just tell guys to go away and leave me alone before they even get a chance."

He smiles at that. "Well, I hope they like me. They are intimidating. You all are."

I shoot him an incredulous look. "We are not intimidating, especially not me. We are just...*us*."

"Yeah, *us*, is a very loaded word there. You are all talented, you guys are basically out of everyone's league. Oh, and, you are gorgeous, which makes it terrifying to approach you."

I'm shocked. I really don't see it that way. I mean, I know we are popular as a band, otherwise we wouldn't have sold out shows all the time.

"Well, you are intimidating too, you know." I'm trying to bounce back from his comments, and I shoot him a sideways look. He casts a look back at me with shock.

"Just saying, you are very handsome, and not to mention charming. I'm not used to that with guys, usually it's just slobbering idiots drawn to me, like moths to a flame. Or what did you say at the wedding? Oh yeah, monkeys and a banana." I start laughing and his cheeks redden. He covers his face with his hands, trying to hide, removing them a couple seconds later.

"Wait. You think I'm handsome?" He sounds surprised, and he leans over and nudges my arm with his elbow. I can feel my cheeks burning.

"Um, yeah," I can feel the embarrassment radiating off me.

He takes my left hand with his right and holds it. "Well, for the record, I think you are gorgeous. Beautiful isn't a good enough word for you, you are beyond that, you are gorgeous."

I stare at him in pure astonishment. How does he always have the perfect things to say? My heart is beating out of my chest, and I don't know what to say, I smile and bite my lower lip.

He lets go of my hand, reaches up and pulls on my bottom lip with his thumb. He softly runs his hand over my cheek. I can't help but close my eyes and feel the tenderness of his touch.

The music over the speaker comes to a slow end, and I can hear the first few sounds of Ed Sheeran's "Perfect" start up. Jay removes his hand from my cheek, and I open my eyes and look at him. I already miss the feeling.

He stands up in front of me and extends his hand. "Will you dance with me?"

Hell, yes, I will. I take his hand as I stand up, then I slip my shoes back on. He keeps hold of my hand, leading me out to the tall grasses behind his truck.

He turns up the volume a couple notches on his phone, placing it in his back pocket, then places his hands on my hips, my arms automatically wrapping around his neck.

I can feel the warm sun on my skin as we slowly turn with the music, the tall grasses moving in sync with the soft breeze of the evening. By this point, the sunset is in full color. The bright displays of oranges, pinks, purples, and blues that surround us are all making the perfect backdrop.

Jay's grip on my hips tightens, his hands moving to exactly where they want to be. I pull myself in a little closer to him, pressing my body against his. Our eyes are locked on each other, as if we are afraid to look away for even a moment.

He removes his right hand from my hip, bringing it up slowly and wrapping it gently around the side of my neck, his thumb grazing my cheek. I close my eyes for a second, and when I open them, I see his eyes are full of desire. *Please kiss me,* I think to myself.

He tilts my head back slightly and brings his mouth to mine. It is the most tender moment I have ever experienced when our lips finally meet. Soft and gentle, as if he's asking for permission for that first second.

Cradling my head, he brings me closer, and kisses me harder. My hand moves from his shoulder to the back of his neck, and I hold him in place. This kiss is so good it should never end. I can feel the connections run between us like a current, and the entire world has gone silent around us.

We kiss through the rest of the song, and the one after that. It feels unbreakable, the spell our lips have put on each other.

Finally, Jay pulls barely away from me, his minty white wine breath still invading my nostrils. His hand is back on my cheek and neck and there is not an ounce of space left in between our bodies.

"I have always wished for you, without knowing your name, or when I would meet you. You are the one I've waited for."

I'm speechless, my breath hitches and my heart pounds in my chest.

"I've always wished for you too." And our mouths press together again in heated passion. His hands are moving around my back and hips, eager to explore.

He pulls barely away from my lips again. "Put your arms around my neck and hold on."

I do as he says. He grabs me with his strong arms and picks me up, holding me to him and walking us slowly back into the bed of the truck.

CHAPTER 26

LIV

JAY SETS ME DOWN IN front of the air mattress, and I kick off my shoes. I sit down and scoot back into the pile of pillows, never breaking eye contact with him. My breathing is ragged, desire pumping through me.

He kneels on the air mattress in front of me, his muscular arms planted on the truck on both sides of me, locking me in as if he's scared that I might run away.

He leans in, breathing heavy, and our lips crash together, as if those few seconds apart were pure agony.

I break the connection for a moment, still holding on to him, "I'm crazy about you," I say in a whisper. He smiles and brings his mouth back to mine.

Before I know it, Jay moves next to me on the air mattress, sitting down, his legs stretched out in front of him. In one swift motion he grabs my hips and swings my body on top of his, my legs straddling him, my short dress fanned out over us.

His hands immediately find their place on my hips, and his grip on me gets firmer. My right hand is planted on his shoulder, feeling down his muscular bicep and back up, the other is on the back of his head, keeping him right where I want him.

He grabs my hips harder and brings me down closer on top of him. I can feel his erection, and I move slowly against it, soft moans escaping his mouth as I move against him.

Our breathing gets heavier, and my movements on his lap a bit more driven. His hands are greedily running up and down my back, my hips, and my thighs, gripping me tight and keeping me close. I push against him harder and his head tips back, giving me access to his neck. I move down, kissing along his jawline, down his neck, not missing an inch, and back up, gently pulling on his ear lobe with my teeth. He groans in appreciation, and slides his right hand under my dress, resting on my hip. It sends chills all over me in appreciation of his touch. If he wanted to take me right here, I wouldn't bother to stop him, it just feels right.

His lips leave mine for a moment, and I can see the ecstasy in his eyes, they are on fire, looking deep into mine. "If date number one is this good, I can't wait until date number two," he says, and brings his lips back to mine.

— — —

We stay until dark, our bodies never leaving each other. No man has ever had such a sensual touch on me, igniting me like a fire from the inside out.

Its agony to pull away from each other, now realizing that its dark, and we probably should get things packed up. We work together quickly to put the cover back on the truck, and like a true gentleman he leads me hand in hand back to the passenger door, opening it, and then lifts me on to the seat. He kisses me and ends up half on my seat, our lips enjoying every second of the reconnection.

On the way home, my hand is in his and I feel a pang of sadness that the night is ending, but the butterflies in my stomach are having the time of their lives.

We pull up at my house. I'm battling internally if I should invite him to stay the night. I've never been that bold on a first date before. Everything feels right with him, but I don't want to do anything too soon, I want everything to be perfect and at the right time.

He shuts the truck off and walks around to my side, opening the door. He reaches out his hand and helps me out of the truck. We walk slowly up the sidewalk to the front door, both of us going as slow as possible, neither of us wanting our evening to end.

"I had a great time with you, thanks for going out with me," he says, one hand in mine, the other nervously at his side.

"Thank you. This was the best date I've ever been on. I can't wait until date number two," and I pull myself toward him, my lips finding his, my hand on his neck, holding him there and not wanting to let go.

He hungrily kisses me, as if he's getting his fix for the moments that we will be apart. Breathlessly, he pulls away a minute later, looking in my eyes.

"Goodnight gorgeous," he says with a smile.

A good night it sure has been.

CHAPTER 27

LIV

IT'S BEEN A WEEK SINCE my first date with Jay.

I've been an unfocused mess at work as I find myself daydreaming constantly of him. We've been texting back and forth, he keeps asking when date number two will be, but I've been so busy the last few days that I haven't been able to figure out when it will work.

On Friday we had an out-of-town show. I had texted Jay to see if he was coming, but he said he had a quinceanera job that he had to cover the photos for.

Saturday AO got together and practiced on a few of our original songs. After that we took a short break, each of us regrouping at home and met up again later to play at a wedding in town.

Sunday morning, I took the time and cleaned my house, I'd been neglecting it for far too long.

It was Joe's turn to "babysit" me that night, so he came over in the afternoon and he did the trimming in the yard while I mowed. It's impossible to be outside alone now with all the letters, I feel like someone is always watching me. Joe slept over that night, and I took some medicine to help me sleep, my mind too riddled over the red envelopes and Jay's hazel eyes.

Monday rolled around and I spent the day working, but feeling accomplished that I conquered a lot over the weekend.

Tuesday normally AO would end up at B&B's, but we were on a tear getting our music finalized, so we spent the evening in the shed, polishing things up. I kept getting distracted, my mind wandering to all things Jay.

Around 9:30 that night, Jay texted me, wondering if we were coming out. I had to send back a disappointed message, letting him know we were busy. I hoped he didn't think I was blowing him off.

Wednesday after work, I made a much-needed Target run, which included a stop at their in-store Starbucks. As usual, I left with way too much shit.

Thursday was another dull day at work, and I was once again distracted by all thoughts Jay. I wanted his hands back on my hips, his charismatic smile working its magic on me.

At noon that day, I walked down to the road where our neighborhood mailboxes are grouped.

I've learned to do this, along with my morning runs, with some pepper spray in my pocket, just in case. Waylon bought it for me, he was nice enough – and insistent enough – that I keep it on me as much as possible.

I opened my mailbox. I already had a sinking feeling that I was due for another letter. I popped the black metal box open and peeked in. Sure enough, I saw the red envelope inside. I decided to open it back at the house and removed my pepper spray from my pocket for the hasty walk back.

My dearest Olivia,

Have you been thinking about me? I have been feeling neglected by you lately, and I have a burning desire to be in your thoughts.

In case you ever forget - I am never not thinking of you, my love.

See you soon,
X

I had taken a picture of it and sent it to our AO group. They had advised me to keep them informed any time I received one. It made me feel bad that they get riled up over this, they each have their own lives to worry about instead of mine.

By Friday, I was so exhausted and sick of work that I could barely keep my eyes open. I had woken up that day in a fog from the previous night's dose of sleepy medicine. More thoughts of Jay clouded my attention. I really wanted to see him again.

AO had another private show that night, and by the time our show had ended, I had more texts from Jay, begging to see me. I also had a request to add him to my Snapchat friends list. I accepted that immediately, excited to see what snaps I would get from him.

He had insisted that if I didn't have plans for Saturday, he take me out for date number two. Luckily for me the band had a cancellation, so we ended up with a much-needed night off.

Date number two with Jay, here I come.

CHAPTER 28

LIV

IT'S 5:00 PM. JAY SAID he would be here at 5:30 to pick me up. I'm rereading his text from earlier where he suggested we go out for a nice dinner downtown. I'm standing in my walk-in closet, deciding what to wear.

In the racks of clothes, I spy a simple camel colored dress. All one piece, pencil skirt style bottom, with a rounded neck and cap sleeves, it's very slimming. I decide to pair it with my favorite gold dangly earrings and pull some of my loose waves around to the front of my shoulders. As I'm sticking my feet into some cream-colored pumps, the doorbell goes off on my phone.

Who the heck is that? I wonder to myself, double checking the time.

I walk to the front door. Looking out the peephole, I see Jay, nervously standing on the porch, hands shoved deep into his pockets.

I open the door quickly. "Hi. I thought we said 5:30." I say with a smile I just can't put away.

He looks up at me through his lashes. "I'm sorry, I just couldn't wait any longer."

Before I know it, he steps inside, closing the door behind him. He steps toward me, eyes intense, and grabs my face in his hands, bringing his lips to mine.

The rest of the week is instantly swept away from me, my lips entranced by his, my hands gripping on to his biceps, showing him how much I want him there.

His left hand leaves my face and moves to my hip, gently moving me backward to the wall. He steps with me, keeping his body locked into mine. He moves his leg in between mine, forcing me to spread my legs a little, letting him dip in closer.

His lips start to move to my neck, his heavy breathing sending waves of desire through my core. I can feel his erection pressing into me, and I grab his hips to pull him even closer.

"Well, I'm glad you got here early," I tell him breathlessly.

"Me too," he says with a grin. "I haven't stopped thinking about you since last Thursday."

"Same. My head was in a fog all week thanks to you." He just grins back at me, unapologetically.

He plants more soft kisses on my lips. I want a thousand more of them. "I'm sorry I'm early, if you need more time I can wait." He says, stepping back a little, but keeps his hands on my hips.

"It's alright, I'm ready now. What should we do tonight?"

"Well, you deserve a nice dinner, and some good wine. I was thinking we should check out VanBuren's, I haven't been there, but the reviews are great, and the menu looks good."

"That sounds great, I haven't been there in a long time. It's a really nice place."

I love VanBuren's. It's an old four-story brick hotel on the corner of Fourth Street and Broadway in downtown Pine Lake. The first floor has an upscale bar and restaurant, and the top three floors have some hotel rooms for rent.

I grab my purse, phone, and keys from the counter and lock the door behind us.

Jay holds my hand down the sidewalk and opens the truck door for me. *This guy is so charming, I am so lucky,* I think to myself.

— — —

We pull up to VanBuren's, the soft glow of lights pouring out of the windows, the red interior walls creating a romantic ambiance. I start to open the truck door and Jay touches my arm.

"You know the drill. Stay there," he says with a wink. I pull the door back shut and smile to myself.

He comes around, opening my door and holds out his hand. He leads me up the three steps to the main door of the restaurant.

We walk in, and I can't help but notice both the patrons and staff look up at us. Not everyone, but a lot of them. I'm used to it, but I wonder if Jay notices this or what he thinks of it.

We walk up to the hostess stand and the young girl eyes Jay up and down. He does look damn good tonight in his black long-sleeved button up shirt, which he has cuffed up a little, showing off his muscular forearms. It goes great with his dark wash jeans.

"We have a reservation, under Jay Jones," he tells the girl, and she flicks her eyes to the reservation list.

"Oh," she says, "you have *that* reservation."

I'm wondering what she means by that.

"Follow me," she tells us dutifully.

We follow her down a hallway with brick walls, a sign above the archway stating, "Employees Only".

What the heck is going on here? I glance back at the tables in the main room behind us in confusion. That's where we should be going.

She leads us to a service elevator at the end of the hallway.

She opens the door and motions us inside, following us, and hitting the button for "5". I glance over at Jay in confusion, and he gives me a sneaky smirk. He's up to something.

We arrive at the top, the elevator door opening, exposing the roof of the hotel.

"I didn't know there was anything up here," I look between the hostess and Jay in confusion.

Jay grabs my hand and smiles. We follow the hostess over to a small table set for two. There are twinkle lights surrounding the small space, the table covered in a white tablecloth, and a vase of red roses as the centerpiece.

"Have a seat, your server will be right with you," she tells us with a small smile.

Jay lets go of my hand and pulls out a chair, motioning for me to sit. He pulls out the other chair and sits across from me. I can't stop looking around, astonished, I had no idea this was up here.

Jay grabs my hand from across the table. "I called and made a special reservation with them. Originally, I had asked for the best table in the house, and they said they had another option we could try. This is it," he waves his hand around to the small rooftop.

"I'm so surprised, I had no idea you could do this," I'm delighted, my God he is thoughtful!

Our server appears a minute later off the elevator and introduces himself as Angelo.

We order off the menu. I have champagne chicken, and Jay has a New York Strip, medium rare. We share a side of rice pilaf, and fresh vegetables. We talk a little through dinner, but our food arrives so quickly, and is so good, it keeps us from saying too much to each other. We have a bottle of champagne chilled over ice. We finish off dinner with a slice of cheesecake with strawberries, it's to die for.

We sit at the table; our appetites satisfied. Soft music is playing over a speaker in the corner, and there is a light breeze floating around us. The sounds of the downtown crowd are muted from up here, barely floating over the walls and up to us. It's like we are in our own world. There are a few clouds in the sky, the lights of downtown casting reddish purple color on to them above our heads.

Our server comes back and checks on us again, and Jay tells him to bring a round of drinks since our champagne is gone. He has his whiskey, and I have Moscato. The sun is setting in the west, providing yet another great backdrop for date night.

"So, I want to know more about you. Tell me something I wouldn't already know from spying on you," he says with a sly smile.

"Hmm…where do I start? Let's see. I grew up here in Pine Lake, went to college here, and I now work from home as a mortgage underwriter for Mid-Central Bank. I have no siblings, but my extended family like aunts, uncles, and cousins live primarily around this area, which is nice." I pause, unsure if I want to tell him the next part. "I've lived in my house for six years now. I didn't buy it myself, I kind of inherited it from my parents…when they passed away." I can see the surprise sweep over his beautiful features. This was the look I was trying to avoid.

"Your parents passed away? Do you mind if I ask what happened? I get it if you don't want to talk about it."

"It's fine. I was in college. I was at home one night in my apartment, it was Friday, May 15. My cell phone rang, it was the Sheriff. It was around 11:00 PM, and he told me my parents were in a car accident. He didn't say they had passed, just that there was an accident. I just froze. I'm not even sure I said anything back to him, I can't really remember. He told me to come to the station immediately, so I did. I had pajama pants and a shitty T-shirt on, I didn't bother changing, just grabbed my phone and left. When I got there the Sheriff met me at the door and brought me to a small room. He told me he was so sorry, but that a drunk driver had blown through a stop sign and smashed into my parents car. They were pronounced dead on site, along with the drunk driver." I shivered at the memory but cleared my throat and kept pushing through it.

"I had talked to them just a few hours earlier, congratulating them. They had been out for dinner and were heading home, it was their anniversary."

Tears are pricking and burning in my eyes, and I'm doing the best I can to hold them back. It will be a lifetime before I can tell the story without breaking down.

"That was six years ago now. Like I mentioned, I have a lot of family around this area, and I'm so thankful for them. Everyone was so supportive during that time. My uncle Rick helped me with so much paperwork that I had no idea how to deal with, along with planning their funerals, and those types of things."

Jay is now kneeling next to my chair, holding my hands in his on my lap.

"I'm sorry. You had such a nice night planned, and I just killed the mood. I should have waited to tell you that."

"Absolutely not, I'm glad you told me." He's looking down at the ground, biting his lip like he's debating something.

"Since we're doing this, I have something to tell you too." He is deadpan, and the seriousness in his eyes has me worried.

"Okay," I manage out, and he gets up and grabs his chair and pulls it right next to mine, our legs touching. His hands are wrung together in a twisted mess in his lap.

"I'm glad you told me that. I know exactly the pain that you feel. When I was sixteen, living with my parents in Greensboro, we had an accident in our family. We were at my aunt Sarah's cabin, just outside of town. We spent a lot of weekends there growing up, my dad and his sister Sarah are close with each other. One Saturday, my parents were in the cabin with her and her husband, my older brother Brandon, whom you've met, and smaller cousin Chelsea inside playing board games."

He stopped, clearing the lump in his throat. It took him a minute to recover and keep going. I grab hold of his hands.

"My brother and I were outside, playing by the lake. There was a path through the trees from the house to the water. It was warm that day, and we wanted to jump in the lake."

"Wait, you said Brandon was in the house. There's another brother? Younger or older than you?" I feel bad interrupting, but I must know.

"Older. Two minutes older than me." He looks into my eyes, hard like granite, and I can see the sorrow running through him like a river.

"Oh, my God," I put my hand on my chest, I can feel where this is going and its already making me sick to my stomach.

"My brother's name was Casey. We were identical twins. We had been daring each other to jump off the rock ledge into the lake for a couple minutes, both of us wanting to do it, but neither of us wanting to go first. It was scary, it seemed so high." He inhales and exhales another deep breath, grabbing hold of both my hands again.

"Finally, I told him that since he was older, he should go first. He agreed that was fair, backed up, and ran for the ledge, jumping off. I watched him from up there, waiting for him to surface. I'm not sure how long it was before I realized it had been too long. I ran down the hill, down the path and got in the water. It ended up having some deep spots, and sadly some not so deep spots. I just kept diving down, every time coming up empty handed, not finding him. Finally, after what seemed like forever, I found him. He wasn't responding. He was gone. He had broken his spine. I pulled him up to the shore and left him there and went running to the house."

His hands are beginning to shake. I keep squeezing them reassuringly. My heart is breaking for this man.

"I ran in screaming, I'm not even sure what I said. They followed me to him, but there was nothing we could do." His hands are shaking harder now, big heavy tears rolling down his face.

"Jay, it's not your fault," I say, crawling over to sit on his lap. I take his head and bring it close and put my arms around him.

I can feel his tears slowing as we sit together for a minute just holding each other.

"It's been ten years since he passed. I feel like half of me died with him. We were inseparable, we were twins. After that I breezed through the rest of high school, doing fine enough, but not wanting much for social interaction. After high school I went to college, I did date a couple girls, but never really felt that I wanted a relationship with anyone, I never felt like I deserved to. After all, Casey will never get the opportunities to do those things in life."

He is so vulnerable right now, I feel so connected to him, but in such a sad way, its breaking my heart.

"I have been in therapy for ten years, dealing with the guilt, the loss, the constant void of him and the fact that he can't live a full life. I can honestly tell you now, that I have lived a shell of a life because of that day, until I met you."

Now I'm crying. I wrap my arms around him, and we sit for a few minutes holding each other.

"That's why I chose to be a photographer. I cherish every photo that Casey is in because I know there will never be more of them. I want people to photograph their families, friends, their *lives*. You never know when it will get taken away, and those photos will be what is left."

As if I wasn't already falling hard enough for this man, this just drove it home.

CHAPTER 29

JAY

WE SIT TOGETHER FOR A while on the rooftop of VanBuren's, just holding each other.

It's the most comforting moments I've had in my whole life. No therapist can deliver this kind of healing. This healing comes straight from the heart, something I've needed so badly for so long.

I'm nervous as we leave the restaurant, I don't have anything planned for us, and now the night has taken a turn I hadn't anticipated.

Olivia and I get back in my truck, and we sit in silence for a minute with the engine running, music playing softly over the speakers.

"I'm not sure what we should do now," I finally say to her. I'm being honest, I'm not sure. I don't want her to get bored and go home, I realize how much I need her next to me.

"I'm game for anything, I'm not ready for the night to be done," she says as she grabs my right hand and squeezes it, giving me a smile.

Then I have an idea. "Hey, my studio is a few blocks from here. Do you want to come and see it?"

Her eyes light up with excitement. This will be the perfect way to wrap-up our evening.

CHAPTER 30

LIV

JAY PARKS THE TRUCK IN front of a two-story old red brick building with big windows in the front on the street level. Small spotlights illuminate the canvases in the four windows, with enlarged photos on them. They are beautiful. A sign that says "JJ Photography" is lit up above the door.

The second floor has two large windows facing the street, like half-moons, with intricate designs in them.

Jay comes around to my door and opens it for me, taking my hand. I swear I will never get sick of this.

We walk across the sidewalk up to the front door. He takes out his key and inserts it into the keyhole, an alarm going off inside. He quickly goes in, punching in a code and the beeping stops.

"Sorry, it goes for fifteen seconds before anything happens. I'm finally getting used to this thing," he says, pointing to the alarm box on the wall.

He flips a few light switches on, and the large room becomes bright and beautiful. Hardwood floors, brick walls, very simple and understated, its perfect.

"Wow, Jay this is great." I start walking around, my heels clicking across the floor in the silent room. He lets me go in front of him to check out the space.

He has a simple desk and chair by the front door. I run my hand across the wood as I pass by it. Random pieces of furniture are scattered around the room with different varieties of backdrops and lighting equipment.

He grabs my hand and leads me to the back wall. "This is my office. Don't judge, it's a mess."

He opens the door to a small room with papers covering a desk, and a computer. There is a filing cabinet in the corner. "I'm still getting it set up."

He closes the door, and we go to the other door along the back wall.

"This was a storage room, and it was in pretty bad shape, but I cleaned it up to be my dark room," he says as he pops open the door. Everything he needs is laid out in front of us, I'm impressed by how organized it is.

We soon come out and stand in the middle of the large space. "So, what do you think?" He says as he places his hands on my waist, watching my eyes as they scan the room.

I put my arms on his biceps and give him a kiss. "I love this, it's amazing." And I continue kissing him.

Before I know it, he dips me backward, kissing me harder, his hand supporting my back. It's enough to leave me breathless.

He brings me back upright slowly. "Do you want to see upstairs?" He says, trailing a few kisses on my neck.

"What's upstairs?" I ask.

"My home," he says, and nervousness is creeping back into his face.

"Absolutely," I tell him with one more kiss.

Holding my hand, he pulls us out of the studio, resetting the alarm and locking the door. *Holy shit, I'm going to his place. Be cool Liv.*

He leads me toward a door on the side of the building. He grabs another key and opens the door, flicking on a light. Taking my hand, he brings me inside and locks the door behind us. A set of stairs leads up to a platform and a large metal door. He slides it open with ease, gesturing for me to go in first.

It's dimly lit so I don't go in far. He turns a light on, and it comes into full view. This guy lives in an awesome loft; this is like the ultimate bachelor pad.

"Living upstairs has its perks. Only one mortgage to pay. It's not much, basically one huge room, but I don't mind it. Make yourself at home," he says as he gives me a peck on the cheek.

He walks over to the kitchen and grabs a couple glasses out of the cupboard. I roam around the room slowly, scoping things out. Looks like he's still unpacking a little, a few boxes are sitting in the corner.

I go over to the half-moon window and look down at the street. "These windows are gorgeous," I tell him, tapping on the windowpane.

"Yeah, I keep thinking they could be fun photo settings." I can hear ice clinking into a glass.

I make my way around to the couch and sit down in the middle of its cool leather seat, crossing my long legs.

On the back side of the room is his bedroom area. His bed is made – he gets more bonus points for that. Then, immediately I think *I'd love to mess those sheets up.* I need to get my mind out of the gutter, but I also kind of like it being there.

He walks over to me, handing me a glass of white wine.

"Thank you," I say. He's got whiskey and gives my glass a clink. I think about where my mind just was, and it makes me flush a little.

"Are you okay?" He asks, sitting down next to me.

"I'm good. I love this place. This is like, the ultimate bachelor pad."

He glances around, smiling. "Yeah, I guess it kind of is. Too bad I don't want to be a bachelor anymore." He gives me a sideways smirk and takes a sip of his drink.

He sets his glass down on the coffee table and grabs my wine glass, setting it next to his.

He turns and faces me, bringing my face toward his with both of his hands. Our lips crash together, and it feels like an eternity since I last kissed him.

Slowly he eases me back on to the smooth leather of the couch, leaning over top of me, propped up on his elbow. I can feel his excitement growing and pressing into me, and I'm not sure how much longer I can hold out before I rip his clothes off.

I hear my phone buzz in my purse on the coffee table. Shit, Way is supposed to stay with me tonight. Now is the time to decide – do I stay here and let Way know he should not bother to come over, or do I go home, and be miserable without Jay all night?

Jay senses something and stops kissing me. "Do you need to get that?" he says as he nods his head in my phone's direction.

"I don't know, but it has me wondering where this is going. Tonight, I mean." Hopefully I didn't word that weird, or make it sound like I want to leave.

"Where do you want it to go?" He is breathless and I can see the want in his eyes.

"Well," I say, raising myself up, with him sitting up in front of me on the couch. I bite my lower lip, I'm nervous and not sure how I want to go about this.

He pulls my lip out with his thumb and gives me another passionate kiss. My eyes close and in that moment, I know, this is right. There is no leaving tonight.

I give him a polite little push back so I can get up off the couch. I turn and look at him, and he looks anxious, thinking I might leave.

I grab my phone quick, texting Way not to come over, that I won't be home. I toss my phone back down on the table.

"Come here," I say, wiggling my finger at him. He stands up and I turn my back to him.

"Unzip my dress." I look back at him and his mouth is open, excitement flashing in his eyes.

He's hesitating. "I mean, unless you don't want to," I say teasingly.

He moves my thick hair out of the way and finds the zipper at the back of my neck. He slowly starts to slide it down with one hand, holding my hip with the other. His hands feel like butter, caressing smoothly across my skin.

He stops at the bottom and pauses; both his hands are on my hips now. I grab the short sleeves of the dress and start to slowly pull them down off my arms, exposing my back to him. I can hear his breathing get shallow.

I get the dress down enough where he can see the back of my bra, and I teasingly slide it the rest of the way down over my hips, and let it drop to the floor. His hands instantly move back to my hips, pulling me close to him. His breath is hot and heavy on my neck, and I can't wait for him to devour me.

All I have left on is my black Chantilly lace bra and panties, and my heels.

His hands run over me, over my thong, gently pulling on it, running his fingers beneath it across my skin. Before his hands get too greedy, I turn around slowly, watching his gaze as his eyes move down my body, focusing on every detail.

"Jesus Olivia, you are gorgeous," and I can see his chest moving with his heavy breathing.

He runs his hands up to my bra, the black lace just barely covering my nipples. Before I let him touch me, I give him a light push backwards. His eyes light up and he looks at me with curiosity.

I gently move him back toward the couch, pushing him down to a sitting position. I spread his legs and kneel between them, unbuttoning his shirt. He hasn't taken his eyes off me yet.

Once I have all the buttons undone, I slide it down his arms, exposing the half sleeve he has on his right bicep. I'll have to check that out later, I'm too distracted by the rest of him right now.

I run my hands deliciously over his pectoral muscles and arms, taking in all of him. He's looking at me with such a hunger, I shouldn't keep him waiting any longer.

I move my knees so I'm straddling him on the couch, kissing him, showing him how much I want him.

Deep down I'm a hopeless romantic but with a filthy mind. I want Jay to treat me like a lady in public and absolutely ravage me in private. Tonight, I'll show him that's exactly what I want.

CHAPTER 31

JAY

MY MIND IS REELING. I can't believe this gorgeous, perfect woman wants me. I have a weakness for her, for her touch. A longing for her kiss seconds after kissing her, I can't resist this woman.

I've got my hands gripped tightly to her ass. I would move them around but I'm loving this new place I'm allowed to touch on her way too much. She keeps grinding into me, letting me snake my fingers through her black lace thong.

Her breathing is heavy, and I can feel the desire coursing through her, through me. Her hands have been exploring my chest and arms, her kisses on my lips and neck making me want more.

I bring my hand up to her back, I want this bra off her, even though it is beyond sexy. I fumble for a minute and can't find the hook. Not that I have much experience with this.

She pulls away from me, smiling, laughing a little.

"Looking for this?" She says it with a seductive grin as she grabs a tiny clasp I hadn't seen on the front. I can hear a little click, and slowly she undoes it, sliding it off her, exposing her perfect breasts.

I can't move. I'm pretty sure my jaw is on the floor; I think I'm in shock. She is more perfect than I ever could have imagined.

She grabs my hands and brings them up to her, wrapping my hands around her. It's perfect. She's perfect. The way she fits into my hand is seamless, and I can feel her excitement through her nipples.

I can't take it anymore. I remove my hands and wrap them around her back, pulling her up to me. I suck and tease her, and it's exquisite. She's grabbing the back of my head and my hair, pulling me harder into her, showing me how much she likes it. Her soft moans are like music to my ears. And I want more.

Looking up at her, I finally catch my breath. She looks down at me, confused why I stopped. "Stay with me tonight baby," I say, looking into her eyes. She nods in return with a smile.

In one swift movement, I wrap my arms around her, standing and picking her up. She makes the cutest squeal, her thighs wrapping around me. I notice she still has her heels on, and damn, there's another turn on that I'm finding I can't resist.

I carry her in my arms to the other side of the loft where my king size bed is.

Setting her down slowly, I let her sink into the soft mattress. She is looking at me with so much want and desire, I can't wait any longer.

I slowly push her back, flat on the bed. I lift her arms up and take her wrists, holding them above her head.

Leaning over I kiss her, hard. Pulling away I look in her eyes, wanting to make sure it's very clear, and whisper, "I want you to be mine."

She moans and I feel her squirm under me, wanting me to take her, right then, right there, heels and all.

CHAPTER 32

LIV

I'M PINNED TO JAY'S BED, breathless and full of lust. There is nothing holding either of us back now, his full lips on mine, hips grinding into me, evidence to his eagerness.

He lets up on my lips for a second, and I take the opportunity to lift off the mattress, and he releases my hands from his grip.

I slide away from him off the bed, he has one knee on the edge of it, arms at his sides, looking at me like a hungry animal fixated on its prey.

I stand next to the bed, taking my time to slide my black lace panties down my legs, dropping them to the floor. *The heels can stay on*, I think to myself. I feel his gaze like a burning heat on my skin. I move toward him, hooking my fingers through the belt loops of his jeans.

I don't say a word as I unbutton and unzip his jeans, sliding everything down his legs to the floor. Without losing his gaze, I move back on to the bed, licking my lips, silently willing him to come to me.

He pauses for a second, giving me one long sensuous stare, then leans forward slowly on his forearms, his large frame towering over me.

He leans in and kisses me with intensity, letting his lower half rest against me. I voluntarily spread my legs for him, willing him to do as he pleases.

His mouth moves from my lips to my neck, my collarbone, to my breasts where they linger, teasing me into a frenzy.

He looks back up at me through his lashes as he pushes back up, grabbing me by my hips, and in a slow and steady motion, feels his way lusciously into me.

I gasp and throw my head back, moaning with pleasure. He never releases my hips and starts moving inside me, ever so slowly. I can feel every inch of him, and I can't help but grind against him in appreciation. It's slow and exquisite, and we take our time taking pleasure in each other.

His motions get faster as we keep moving in sync. His right-hand stays on my hip as he leans down and continues to suck and play with my breasts. The combination is incredible.

"Jay, I'm close," I say, my breaths ragged.

"Me too baby," and his motions are faster, harder, and more driven.

He sits up straighter and I wrap my legs tightly around his body, tightening myself around his erection. He loses control in that moment, saying my name as he comes undone inside of me. I let go with him, my hands and nails gripping the smooth sheets of the bed in exquisite desire.

He collapses on top of me, his face in my chest, breathing hard, my arms wrapped around him. I have never felt this amount of ecstasy before, and there is no better feeling. This is pure blissful magic like no other.

He sits up quickly, unexpectedly. "Oh my God, Olivia…" he trails off. The look of concern on his face is appalling.

"What? What is it?"

"I came inside you; I didn't wear a condom. Oh my God." He starts to raise up off me farther, but I pull him back down.

"Jay, it's okay. I wouldn't have let you do that if I wasn't on birth control." He relaxes against me again.

"Thank God." He leans up and kisses my lips, holding my neck and cheek in his large hand.

Even if this could only be for one night, if this was all I could have from him, I lived it with a burning passion I never knew I could feel, with a man I never expected to meet.

"I want you to be mine," is the last thing I hear him whisper to me before I drift off to sleep, completely sated in the comfort I find lying next to him.

CHAPTER 33

JAY

I OPEN MY EYES AS I feel the morning sun pouring through the windows, warming my skin.

I'm on my back, tangled up in the black sheets, and the most beautiful sight appears in front of me: Olivia, in pure sleepy bliss, curled around my left side, her leg draped over me, her face on my chest, brunette hair spilling out around her.

She looks so peaceful that I don't want to wake her. But I also do.

Last night was perfect. I had thought date night number one was the best night ever, until last night. It was mind blowing, and I loved every second of it.

I place my hand on the back of her head and stroke her hair gently. She stirs at my touch, and I'm already at full attention, ready to relive some of last night's moments.

Her sleepy eyes open and she looks up at me, her hand slowly caressing my chest.

"Good morning gorgeous," I say with a smile.

"Good morning," and she gives me a kiss on the cheek.

We lay there for a few minutes, savoring the comfort and warmth of being curled up with each other. I could stay like this all day.

She's rubbing my right bicep where my half sleeve is, her fingers sliding smoothly across the part that reads, "Casey, gone but never forgotten". Its surrounded by roses from my elbow up to my shoulder.

"This is beautiful," she says quietly. We go back to laying with each other in complete comfort.

She starts to sit up, "I'll be right back," as she sashays herself off to the bathroom.

As she gets to the doorway, she turns, "do you have any mouthwash I can use?"

"Yep, I think it's in the second drawer down in the cabinet, help yourself."

"Thanks," she says with a smile and closes the door behind her. She better hurry, I want her back in bed with me.

She returns, looking refreshed, crawling slowly across the bed to me, with not a stitch of clothing on. She leans partially over me, grabs my hair, and holds on, kissing me. I can't help but moan, I'm so ready for her again.

She sits up, and slowly pulls away the covers, exposing my huge erection. She pivots and slowly crawls on top of me, sliding ever so enticingly over me. I groan in response.

Her palms resting on my chest, she lowers herself on to me. She's just as ready and full of desire as I am. Once I'm fully inside her, she rolls her hips and enjoys the fullness, letting out moans of pleasure.

Her hips are working, slowly, and I've grabbed on to her, ready to kick things up a notch.

I pull her close to me, whispering in her ear, "baby, I'm all yours." She sits back up and grinds up and down on my full length, enjoying every inch.

Watching her move on top of me is spectacular. I grab her perfect breasts and she calls out my name.

This is how I want to wake up every morning, forever.

We are moving in unison, and I'm not going to last much longer.

"Come with me babe," I say breathlessly, as she moves quicker, clenching herself around me.

"Jay, oh God, Jay," she calls out, and it's my undoing. I grab her hips hard and pull her down on me, giving her everything I have. Her head is thrown back in pleasure as she grips my hands, which are firmly planted on her hips.

She collapses on top of me, in the same position we woke up in.

We spend the next two hours tangled together in bed. I want to beg her to stay all day, but I don't want to seem too needy, so I gladly take all the time that she is willing to give me.

I have no clue how things are going to work out with us, or what's going to happen, all I know is that she makes me so ridiculously happy, and that she is everything I need.

CHAPTER 34

LIV

IT'S SUNDAY EVENING, AND IT'S Darren's turn to "babysit" me. I'm so glad its him, I can't wait to dish about Jay. My new fancy doorbell goes off, letting me know that he's here. He opens the door and steps in. "Dude, you are supposed to keep your doors locked," he says with a stern stare.

"Sorry, I forgot. I'm too distracted." And I can't help the mischievous smile on my face.

"Oh my God – date number two. How did it go? Tell me everything and leave out no details." He kicks off his shoes and flops down on the couch and pats the seat next to him, motioning for me to sit.

I tell him about last night. I didn't tell him all the juicy details, but I mentioned spending the night and he easily figured out what that led to, most likely by the smile on my face. By the end of it, he was looking at me like my life was a dirty soap opera, and he couldn't wait to hear more.

"So, I have to know..." he trails off.

"Have to know what?"

"I think you know the one, well, *big* or *small* detail I want to know," he says with a dirty grin on his face.

"Oh God." I bury my face in my hands. He peels them away, waiting for his answer.

"Let's just say, *that* detail is big enough to make you *very* jealous of me. I'm a lucky girl," I say with a shy smile.

"Olivia!" His hand covers his mouth for a second then he jumps off the couch, grabbing me, pulling me into a hug.

"I'm so happy for you, I like him, I hope you keep seeing him." And this is why he's my best friend when it comes to dishing about guys.

"When are you seeing him again?" He asks, and I shrug my shoulders, unsure.

"Well damn, if you keep this going, he will be the one "babysitting" you at night, not us. And I guarantee you'll enjoy that way more." He's laughing now, and I can't help but do the same.

"He planned the first two dates; I feel like I need to plan the next one. Especially since he's not from here, I need to find something unique to do." I've been thinking about this already today and haven't come up with anything.

"Honestly, just take him out to dinner, and as long as you rip your clothes off for him after that, he's not going to care," he says laughing. I roll my eyes.

"Hey, what if I took him to the quarry? We could do some late-night swimming."

There are multiple granite quarries in the area, and there is one that is nice that has been turned into a park. Growing up here it was a rite of passage to sneak out there at night to swim after the gates closed.

"There you go, I bet he wouldn't mind that at all," he says with a smile.

CHAPTER 35

JAY

MY MIND IS STILL IN overdrive since Saturday night with Olivia. It's Monday and I know I should focus on the studio, but she is taking over all my thoughts.

We've been texting and calling back and forth asking questions about each other. And I may have asked too many times when I can see her next. *Stalker Jay in full force.*

I've learned that her favorite guilty pleasure foods are crab legs and good Chinese. I like her taste; those are a couple of my favorites too, along with a medium rare steak.

She also told me that the band is working on some original songs, and that they plan to roll them out soon at a local show, where their most die-hard fans have the chance to hear them for the first time. She said she's excited and nervous at the same time about it, excited because their dream is to land a record deal as a rock band but scared that she will have to move to a big city that she might not like, leaving everyone behind.

She asked me what my favorite music is. Rock is my favorite, but I am a sucker for a good old school country song.

When I asked her, she said she loves rock most of all, but she finds that she likes different genres of music depending on her mood, and that all music has its place in her life. I had never thought about it that way before.

Her favorite movies are both Zombieland's, Super Troopers, and Practical Magic. I'd never heard of Practical Magic, so I'll have to watch it. She says she watches it every Halloween.

I made a joke that Magic Mike was my favorite, and she was dying laughing over the phone. She argued they were good movies, and I said that would be the one thing I would never do with her was watch them. I finally told her you can't go wrong with a comedy like Ferris Bueller's Day off, or something that is classic like the Godfather. She agreed.

One of her texts was, "what crime would you commit if you knew you would get away with it". I responded (probably too quickly) and said, "steal your heart." She sent me a blushing face emoji. I had meant every word and forgot to ask her the question back.

She asked me, "if I could have one superpower, what would it be?" I said X-ray vision. What guy wouldn't want that? She said reading people's minds.

Her favorite song is Dorothy's "Black Sheep." I wasn't familiar with it, so I downloaded it. Turns out its awesome, and I downloaded all the rest of their songs. I told her mine is anything by Godsmack, I couldn't pick just one, it's my favorite music while I'm at the gym. She said at the next show I'm at, she will have Waylon do a Godsmack song just for me, and that he has a great voice for their music.

I asked if she would be at B&B's Tuesday night. She said she wouldn't because they had an outdoor concert to do in a town about two hours away. Luckily, they start at 7:00 so it wouldn't be too late for a weeknight show. It disappointed me. I need to find another way to see her.

— — —

It's Wednesday and I can't wait to see her anymore. In a last-ditch effort, I decide to get her flowers and stop by her house unannounced.

It's about 8:00 and I drive through her neighborhood slowly, suddenly getting nervous that I am making a stupid decision.

As I pull up in her yard, I see an old black Chevy Impala sitting in front of her two-stall garage. My heart sinks, instantly I begin to wonder if she has a date tonight.

I pull up in the driveway and shut off my truck and grab the flowers from the passenger seat.

I approach the front door, and I can see a red-light flick on the new doorbell. I press the button and wait a few seconds. The door opens abruptly, and I see its Erik. He doesn't say anything right away and he's giving me an odd look, like he's judging me or wondering what my intentions are.

"Hey Erik, is Olivia home?"

"Yeah, she is. Liv!" He bellows back behind him as he chews on some popcorn he has in his hand. He looks back at me and eyes the flowers in my hands, giving me a shake of his head with an eye roll. We wait a few more seconds and Olivia doesn't appear.

"Obsession Olivia! Where are you?" He calls out again, a little more forcefully.

Olivia comes from around the corner. "What? I was changing, cut me a break." She says as she finishes pulling down a sweatshirt around her waist.

She stops dead in her tracks when she sees me. Holy shit, I hope they aren't on a date. I hope they never have dated, and I hope they never do. What if he's spending the night?

Her eyes light up and she smiles, "Jay." She bites her bottom lip, never taking her eyes off mine.

Erik moves out of the doorway and heads toward the kitchen, shaking his head again. "I'm getting more popcorn."

"I'm not interrupting anything, am I?" I say nervously.

"Absolutely not. They boys don't like it when I'm alone. They come over to babysit. This is normal." And she waves her hand around behind her in the direction where Erik just disappeared.

"Ok good. Um, I was thinking about you…I decided to bring you flowers." Now I'm embarrassed. I feel like such a juvenile.

"Thank you. Get in here," she grabs my free hand and pulls me in the door.

I step inside, hopeful that she doesn't think I'm being too clingy. She's smiling, so that's a good sign. I set her flowers on the entry table. Tiger lilies, of course.

She has on a sweatshirt, and the shortest tight spandex shorts I've ever seen. Her hair is in a messy high bun, and she looks like she would be the perfect cuddle buddy on the couch right now.

"I'm glad you're here. I was going to text you. I was wondering if you have plans tomorrow night." She bites her lower lip again.

"I don't have plans. What do you have in mind?" I'm trying hard not to smile.

"How about you stop over here around 7:00, and I'll cook for you. Then I have a fun idea for after that. Bring your swim shorts," she goes right back to biting her lip.

I lean in close to her, putting my hands around her waist, pulling her to me. "I'd love that," I say, and run my hand up and pull on her bottom lip. "You know, you shouldn't do that."

"Do what?"

"Bite your lip like that."

"Why?"

"Because that's my job." I grasp the back of her head, pulling her in for a deep, slow kiss, and take her bottom lip in between my teeth teasingly. It's greedy and hungry with lust, I've been dying for this since Sunday morning.

After a minute I finally let go of her, reluctantly.

"See you tomorrow gorgeous," I say with a wink. I'm so glad I stopped over.

CHAPTER 36

LIV

JAY AND I HAVE BEEN texting on and off since he stopped over last night. Every time I pass by my dining room table I stop and smell the tiger lilies he got me.

I guess after kissing a lot of frogs, I finally found a prince. Charming guys are hard to come by. I hope he sticks around; I'm liking how this is going.

It's Thursday, and we're meeting up for our third, much anticipated date. I told him to get to my place around 7:00. I'm finishing up in the kitchen, trying to make it look like I didn't just make a huge mess.

I check the time – its 6:47. I dig out the bottle of whiskey I picked up and set it on the island with a low-ball glass. Our first two dates were perfect, I want him to enjoy this night that I planned.

I hear the close of a car door and before I know it my phones doorbell alarm is going off. I hope he didn't dress up because I sure didn't. I went with a nice tight pair of jeans with a white tank top and a black bralette under it.

I walk over and open the door to a smiling Jay.

"Come on in," I say with a return smile. I'm relieved, he didn't dress up either, he looks perfect in an army green fitted T-shirt and jeans. His shirt is tight, and I can see his muscles beneath it. It's ridiculously distracting.

He steps in and holds up his swim shorts in front of him. "Look what I remembered. So, where will this swimming take place and why do we need to be dressed?" He says in amusement, and I can see a twinkle in his eye.

"Well, that's top secret. You'll see later." I say as I turn and head slowly back toward the kitchen.

"See the secret swimming place later or *see you* later? And you know that I mean see *all of you* later," he says with a teasing raise of his eyebrow as he kicks his shoes off.

"If you play your cards right it will be both," and I turn into the kitchen, with him not far behind me.

"What are we having tonight? It smells good."

"Don't laugh, but it's a casserole called *Marry Me Chicken.*" He breaks out in a laugh instantly.

I turn and pull the pan out of the oven and set it on the hot pad on the island. "It's chicken, baked in a cream sauce with garlic, spices, parmesan, sundried tomatoes, and I add a little white wine."

I've only made it twice, but I know this is a fool proof recipe. I just feel dumb that I picked *Marry Me Chicken* as the first meal I make for him. He probably thinks I'm some desperate clingy girl.

"It smells amazing, thank you. And I'm thinking you might not be Minnesotan because you just called it a casserole, not hotdish." He leans over and kisses me.

I'm laughing as I pick up the whiskey and pour him a glass. I pour myself some wine. We sit at the island and eat, talking about our week and how we're so glad it's almost over.

The chicken must be alright, his is going down quick and he's not saying much between mouthfuls.

"Marry me," he blurts out with his last mouthful of food. I start laughing and almost spit out my wine.

"So, let me get this straight. You are hot, you are a badass guitar player, and now I find out you can cook like this. I'm sold." He leans over and gives me a kiss.

After dinner we change into our swimsuits. I throw on the same white tank top and some distressed jean shorts over my bikini.

It's about a twenty-minute car ride to the quarry where I want to take him to swim. Timing should be just about right, it's 8:30, perfect for a night swim.

We talk a little on our car ride over, and he is either holding my hand or rubbing my leg as I drive us in my Tahoe.

Finally, we arrive, turning into the dark parking lot. There are no other cars here, the swimming area is technically closed, but the gate to the park never really gets locked, so it's easy to sneak in any time you want.

There is one large quarry pit that filled with water years ago. I drive around it to the west side, where there is a smaller off shoot of a pond. It's shallow and more private for us in case someone else should show up. Since they've turned this into a park, they brought in some nice soft sand for around the edge so you can sit with your feet in the water and be comfortable. It's a great place to spend a nice hot day. We could have stayed home and used my pool, but I thought this would be a fun and different experience for him.

I put the SUV in park and shut it off. I grabbed a battery powered lantern to set in the sand, so we have a little light.

"You ready," I say, turning to him in the car, wiggling my eyebrows at him.

"Hell yeah," he says with an excited smile.

We jump out, peeling off our clothes, leaving just our swimsuits on. He has charcoal gray board shorts on, and I have a white bikini, with small pink sequins embellished on a little bit of the top half. It's my favorite bikini from Victoria's Secret. It's nice and tight and small, I thought he might appreciate that.

He turns around and faces me, his eyes lighting up. "Damn, that looks good enough to peel off of you." He walks over and scoops me up in his muscular arms, swinging me around and kissing me.

He walks us toward the water, never putting me down. He slowly steps through the soft sand, and wades into the clear water. It's just deep enough that you can stand up in it and still touch. He still has me in his arms, and I can feel him getting hard beneath me. I wiggle a little against him to show him I notice.

"Sorry," he says, blushing.

"Oh, I definitely don't mind," I say, wrapping my legs around him, kissing him.

We make out in the cool calmness of the water for quite some time, the moonlight casting just enough light for us to see each other. We pause for a moment, and he picks me up and starts to walk us back toward the edge. He lays me in the soft sand, where the shallow water meets it.

He leans down over me on his elbows, caressing my cheek, kissing me. I know where this is going, and my body is on fire in anticipation.

His kisses trail down my neck, to my collarbone, then he stops before getting to my breasts. Slowly reaching up, he slides one of my bikini tops to the side, exposing me. Gently he takes my nipple in his mouth, sucking gently. His other hand reaches up and removes the other side, his hand finding it.

I arch my back in response to his touch, and he begins to suck harder. He reaches around and undoes the strings in the back, tossing my top to the side in the sand. He buries his face into my breasts, taking his time savoring them.

I can feel his erection, and I open my hips wider, suggesting him to take me. He pulls up, and quickly removes his shorts, tossing them to the side, and makes quick work to remove my bikini bottom. He lays back on top of me, kissing me again, his eyes burning with lust.

He slides his length into me slowly, relishing in me. I arch my back again and call out his name between soft moans.

He pulses inside me with a steady rhythm, running his hands up and down my body, his mouth continuing to give attention to my aroused nipples. The water laps around us as we find our rhythm in the soft sand.

"I'm close baby," he says breathlessly, his movements quickening, getting more forceful.

"Me too," I say breathlessly back.

He pulses inside me a few more times, grabbing my hips with his strong hands. I squeeze myself around his firmness, and we release together. I call out his name multiple times, extasy coursing through me in waves.

He collapses on top of me, breathing hard. "Fuck, that was good," he says in a tired voice.

All I can do is nod, my body still buzzing.

We lay in the sand a few more minutes, then retreat to the coolness of the water, holding each other under the soft glow of the moonlight, the crickets chirping a continuous song in the background.

CHAPTER 37

JAY

THIS NIGHT HAS BEEN AMAZING beyond belief. Every minute with Olivia is like being in Heaven.

I've been so closed off for the last ten years, I never imagined myself doing these things, or feeling this way. All I had ever wanted was to hide behind my camera lens and fast forward through my days.

We dry off with our towels and get back into her Tahoe, our wet suits clinging to us. They are cold, I can see Olivia shivering.

I lean over to her, "You okay there, babe?"

"I'm freezing," she says, shaking.

"I could help you take this off again," and I'm already reaching over, undoing the delicate strings in the back of her bikini. She laughs. I eagerly slide her bikini top off.

"I've never had sex in a car before." Shit. Maybe I shouldn't have told her that. I'm instantly embarrassed.

"Really?" I can hear the surprise in her voice. She opens her car door and gets out. "I'll meet you in the back seat," she winks at me.

Holy shit. The old Jay would never have done anything like this. I jump out, opening the door to the back seat of the SUV, and she's getting in the other side.

"Sit in the middle, no clothing required back here." She smiles at me. I slide my swim trunks off and toss them on the floor. She does the same with her bikini bottoms.

She crawls on top of my lap but doesn't let me inside her yet. She's kissing me, on my lips, down my neck, sucking on my ear lobe gently with her teeth. I try and maneuver her hips so I can get inside her, but she doesn't let me.

She stops kissing me. Her eyes dancing wildly.

"I have a better idea…" she trails off. *A better idea? What is a better idea than having sex?*

She turns around and sits backwards on my lap. She is sitting on me, facing the front of the vehicle, holding on to the front seats. She lifts and lowers herself on to my erection.

From this angle I have the perfect view of her tight ass. Holy shit, this is uncharted territory for me.

She begins to raise and lower herself on top of me, moving slowly. She throws her head back, calling my name, as her grip on the seats gets firmer.

I can feel the blood pumping through me with excitement, and I move my hands from her breasts down to grasp her ass.

She started off the first few minutes moving slowly, but now she's moving faster; I don't think I'll last very long like this. I give her ass a squeeze and slap it. She groans out in pleasure and throws her head back again. It's enough to put me over the edge.

"I'm coming," I choke out between ragged breaths.

"Yes…yes…yes," and we release together. She lets go of the seats and leans back on to my chest. I wrap my arms around her.

We're both breathing hard, resting for a minute. I've never felt this comfortable doing something so new and raw with someone before.

"Well, that was a perfect way to say goodbye to this vehicle," she says.

"You're getting rid of it?"

"Yeah, I have an appointment Monday after work to go get a new one at Pine Lake Motors. This one is getting traded. The transmission is slipping, and it's getting up there in miles. Time for an upgrade before she blows up."

"Well, we'll have to break in the new one then too," I say, sucking on her neck.

We finally get enough energy to get dressed and head back to her place.

It's almost midnight as we walk up the sidewalk. We haven't discussed yet if I'm spending the night or leaving. I hope I can spend the night. Nights alone are torturous now.

She gets her house key out, unlocking the door. She opens it and stands inside the door frame. "Um, I'm not sure if you want to spend the night but, I'd love it if you would." She says, her eyes drifting down to the floor nervously.

I close the space between us, wrapping my arms around her.

"There is nowhere else I'd rather be than wrapped up with you in bed." I plant a soft kiss on her lips.

We kick off our shoes, and she grabs my hand, leading me to her bedroom. She strips off her clothes, throwing them on the hardwood floor.

"There's a bathroom there if you need it, and there is another one just off the kitchen. I'm going to brush my teeth. I have an extra toothbrush you can use. Don't worry its brand new. I'll set it on the sink. I'm a stickler about always brushing teeth, it's one of my pet peeves."

"Thank you," I say, looking around taking in her bedroom. I haven't been in here before.

The walls are painted a dark emerald color, the trim and hardwood floors are a rich brown, which run through the rest of the house. In the center of the room is a king size bed with cream-colored sheets, elaborately stacked with throw pillows and blankets. There is a lamp on a nightstand on either side of the bed, and a vintage chandelier hangs in the middle of the room, giving off a soft glow.

She comes back from the bathroom, wearing a set of pink lingerie. I can feel my pulse quicken. I didn't realize she had gone and gotten them; I was so distracted looking around. I walk over to her and plant a soft kiss on her lips and tell her I'll be right back. Just like she promised, she left me a toothbrush, new in the package. I brush my teeth, give myself a once-over, and exit the bathroom.

The only light left on is the lamp on my side of the bed. Hers is off and she's laying under the cream-colored comforter, her brunette hair flowing around her. She gives me a smile. The image is going to be burned into my mind as one of my favorites. This is exactly how I want to go to bed every night.

CHAPTER 38

LIV

MONDAY HAS COME TOO QUICKLY. I could have used about three more days of weekend.

Jay and I have been texting and snapping a lot since our date Thursday. I can't get that boy off my mind. I was once again distracted by thoughts of him while working today.

I pick up Erik on my way to Pine Lake Motors. Not that I couldn't have done this myself, I just feel better bringing someone with me, just in case I have questions, or the salesperson is sleazy.

We pull up to the lot, the white building with large glass windows sitting in the middle of the large, paved parking lot. There is a sea of cars around us. Luckily, I was here before doing test drives and know which one I want. I can see the black Tahoe that I previously looked at. It's not brand new, I wouldn't be able to afford that, but just a couple years old. It is a much-needed upgrade for me, not to mention it's the extended one, so it will help the band get more stuff to and from shows in it.

As we are doing a final walk-around on my new vehicle, I get the feeling someone is watching me. I give a quick glance around but am quickly pulled back into the conversation with the salesperson.

We sit and do our paperwork, and everything checks out. Erik and I leave the lot and decide to do a cruise around town to test it out, just like the good old days when we would cruise Broadway, thinking we were so cool because we were teenagers, and we could drive.

I drop Erik off at his apartment and thank him for his help.

Heading home, I realize I haven't gotten the mail since the end of last week. I've been putting off getting mail more and more lately, due to the stalker letters.

I pull my new ride up to the grouping of mailboxes. I pop open the door and immediately slam it back shut. I could be losing it but I'm pretty sure I just seen a dead bird in there.

I pull my vehicle ahead to the side and put it in park, get out, and walk back to the box. I grab a couple sticks, so I don't have to touch it.

I slowly open the box again; sadly, the bird isn't moving. Who puts a dead bird in someone's mailbox? My first thought is, *probably some kids being dumb*, and then I see the red envelope, lying next to the bird.

I reach in slowly and grab it. This one is different, it doesn't have a postmark or stamp on it, and the bird's blood is smeared on the outside. I put it back, and use the sticks and maneuver the bird out, leaving him to lay in the grass. I grab the pile of mail and head up to my house.

My dearest Olivia,

This bird is a representation of how I feel when I can't be near you. Dead. And if you refuse to start noticing me more then I'm afraid I need to take more drastic measures.

See you soon,
X

I drop the letter to the floor. They seem to be taking a more sinister turn. I instantly call Waylon and tell him to get here immediately. He was supposed to be coming over tonight anyway, but I need him here now.

I text the AO group a picture of the letter and tell them about the bird. Waylon texts back and makes the rest of the group aware that he is on the way. Great, now they are going to be even more worked up over this than they already were.

— — —

Waylon pulls up about twenty minutes later, his brow furrowed and a worried look on his face.

"I told everyone else to come over too. We need to talk about this. They'll be here in a few minutes."

"Yeah, I suppose we do. Thanks Way." I give him a hug, and he wraps me up in his large arms.

"No one fucks around with our girl. We'll figure this out," he says seriously in his deep voice.

The guys each roll up shortly after. They are on edge, which is not normal for them. I don't like seeing our group like this.

We sit uncomfortably at my dining room table for a minute before anyone talks. The light from the chandelier is casting shadows on each of our faces.

"You need to go to the police." Joe says with a firmness I don't usually hear out of him. Everyone nods their heads in agreement.

"Fine." I say, staring down at my hands. I will go in tomorrow after work and talk to the police.

"We are going to keep staying with you at night, and if you need us here more, we can do that too," Darren adds.

"Do you think it should be more than one of us at a time?" Erik asks, looking around at the rest of the guys.

"No, you guys, what we have been doing is good enough. I don't need you all worn out and exhausted all the time from babysitting me."

"The good news is that Jay can be here now sometimes too. You just need to let us know when he's here, so we don't double up," Darren says.

"Yeah, what's going on with you and that guy? Is it getting serious? You let me know if he gets out of line at all." Waylon says with a playful look on his face. I think deep down he has a thing for confrontation.

"Thanks Way, but I don't think he'll get out of line. We've been out a few times, I really like him," I can feel myself blushing, and all four sets of eyes are on me like overprotective brothers.

Thank God for these guys. I don't know what I would do without them.

One more thing lingers in the back of my mind...should I tell Jay about this?

— — —

The next day I stop into the police station after work. I decide to bring Lexie with me for moral support.

Luckily, I end up talking to Sheriff Hayden, the same man who notified me when my parents had been killed. He's very sincere and I trust him explicitly. Although being in here with him again is stirring up bad memories and feelings that I would rather leave trapped in a deep, dark place.

Throughout the years he has stayed in touch with me, probably feeling sympathy for what I went through at such a young age. He's an older man, with jet-black hair, a little bit of a belly, a big warm smile, and an even bigger heart.

He gives me his personal cell phone number and tells me to call or text him any time. He claims until there is something threatening, there isn't much they can do. He also advises me that it was good that I saved the letters. Lexie gives me a little nudge, acknowledging she was right all along to keep them.

When I mention the flowers and the bird, he gets more concerned. He tells me to keep letting the guys stay with me at night. He also says to not to apprise the situation, as there could be other people that might jump in on it as a joke, and it would just complicate things.

He pulls a pocketknife out of his pocket and tells me to always keep it on me.

I have to say I feel a hell of a lot better after meeting with him. After I get home, I make sure to update the guys on how it went. Joe is scheduled to babysit me, but I call him off. Jay had texted me earlier asking if he could come over. I feel awful that I have gotten so wrapped up in all this that I haven't invited him over. I want to feel more secure and have things figured out before I bother him with it all.

My doorbell goes off and my phone is buzzing. That should be Jay at the door.

I look out the peephole and see Jay leaning against the porch post in front of the door. He looks a little uneasy. I open the door wide and invite him in. This time he has a small backpack, I'm guessing it's his overnight bag.

He seems a little unsure of himself and doesn't kiss me right away. His hands are shoved in his pockets, and he's looking at the floor.

"Is everything okay? You seemed off the last couple days. Is it something I did?" He looks up at me and he looks like he could cry. I feel awful.

"Absolutely not. I have been going through some stuff, but it's nothing to do with you. Just some stressful bullshit, that's all. I got some of it figured out tonight after work. It will be okay." I let a deep breath out and close the space between us, wrapping my arms around his neck, kissing him.

"Good, I was getting worried. I can't lose you Olivia," he breathes into my hair, kissing the side of my head.

"Oh, one more thing before I forget. This Saturday.....is my birthday. The guys are organizing a night out on the town for me.

I want you to be there. That is, if you want to go." I'm holding his hands now, looking at him nervously. *What if he doesn't want to go?* "I'd love to babe, you just let me know the plan and I'm all in." He kisses me again.

"Come on, I'm tired and I need some Jay cuddles." I grab his hand and lead him to my bedroom.

I can't wait to be wrapped up in the sheets with this man.

CHAPTER 39

LIV

LEXIE SLIDES THE ZIPPER OF my dress up my back and secures it at the top.

"This dress is amazing," she tells me. I got lucky and found it at an online boutique. It is a short, tight black dress, the neckline rounded, with long sleek sleeves. The entire thing is glittery. It would be a perfect New Year's Eve dress too. It's form fitting, and I paired it with some black heels. I'm hoping Jay loves it and wants to rip it off me with his teeth.

Lexie has on a sleek black maxi dress that looks great on her curves. She borrowed a chunky silver necklace and bracelet to go with it. For my birthday we told people they could dress up if they wanted to but didn't have to.

Tonight, the AO boys decided to rent a party bus for my birthday party. This will be the first night Jay really hangs out with the guys, I hope they all get along. The AO boys can be a little overprotective.

My phone rings, it's Darren. "I'm almost there, picking up your mail on the way, hope that's okay."

"Yep, go for it. If there's a red envelope in there just light it on fire."

A minute later he steps into the front door. "The party has arrived, bitches!" He announces with a flare in his step. Lexie and I give him hugs.

"Dang dude, you look good," I tell him. I make him spin for me, showing off his black jeans and white button up shirt. He loves short sleeve button up shirts, especially ones with prints on them. They look good on his lean figure.

"I'm hoping to not go home alone tonight, so I had to bring my A-game. And speaking of A-game, look at you two," he eyes us up. "It looks like Jay might need to cut that dress off you Liv," he says eyeing me up and down and spins me around.

"He won't need to, I'll gladly rip it off for him," and I do a little shimmy.

"Speaking of Jay, look who just pulled up," Lexie says, pointing out the window.

I can feel the butterflies come to life in my stomach. I peek out the window as he gets out of his truck.

He has dark wash jeans on, and a cream-colored button up shirt. His hair is that neat and messy slicked to the side look that I love. I'm staring like I'm never going to see him again.

"Hot damn," Darren says, peeking through the window next to me.

Jay comes in, and immediately I can smell his musky cologne.

"Hey," he says with a smile.

"Hey, you," I say as I walk up to him, wrapping my arms around his neck. He kisses me, then dips me down backward.

"Happy birthday gorgeous," he quietly says, his eyes burning into mine, and kisses me again.

He leans me back up, and I feel flushed.

"Aww," I can hear Lexie and Darren catcalling us. Jay's cheeks redden and he steps back a little.

"This is for you," he says, holding a gold bag with white tissue paper in it.

I set the bag on the entry table beside me and pull the tissue paper out. I hold it up, it's a T-shirt. It's white with black bold lettering that says, "SORRY BOYS, I'M TAKEN." Instantly I'm laughing, this is amazing. I would love to wear this at a show.

"Thank you so much, I love it." I wrap my arms around Jay and kiss him.

"More people are showing up," Lexie points out the window. Multiple cars have driven up, including Erik, Waylon, and Joe. Tim and Tina pull in too.

Everyone gathers inside, bringing coolers and overnight bags. Tim and Tina, and Joe and Molly aren't staying, they will drive home. Jenna and Bo should be here any minute too, they said they won't spend the night either, Bo will drive them home. Everyone else that was invited is spending the night. Lexie and I already have air mattresses blown up in the basement for people to crash on.

Finally, our last two people show up. Two of my girlfriends, Bridget, and Cassie.

Bridget and Cassie are best friends, and I met them one night at a party. Our friend Ben was throwing a post-AO show house party, and they were there. We hit it off immediately. Bridget is a bartender at Loco's here in Pine Lake, and Cassie is a Realtor.

From what they've mentioned to me, Bridget has a thing for Waylon, and Cassie thinks Erik is the sexiest guy alive. Maybe I can play matchmaker tonight for them.

We are all gathered in the kitchen, raising cheap disposable champagne glasses in a toast.

"Here's to Obsession Olivia, I hope your birthday is as amazing as you are," Darren says, raising his glass up. Everyone clinks their glasses together. I shake my head and laugh at his toast.

I take a sip of my champagne, and my doorbell app goes off on my phone.

"Are we expecting anyone else?" Lexie asks in confusion; I shake my head "no".

I walk to the front door, opening it slowly. I'm surprised to see a familiar face. John, my pharmacist, my dad's old friend.

"Hi John. What are you doing here?" I ask, and there is a pretty evident confusion in my voice.

"Hello Olivia. I remembered it's your birthday, and I wanted to stop and drop these off for you." He hands me a bouquet of assorted flowers. I take them hesitantly, feeling a bit odd about this.

"Thank you. They're beautiful," I tell him. I'm wondering how long this encounter will last. I don't feel comfortable inviting him in.

"You are welcome. I hope you have a very happy birthday." He turns and leaves, looking back at me once. I'm just awkwardly frozen in the doorway.

I close the door as he walks back to his car. That was weird. I turn around, and see Jay standing in the living room, leaning against the light gray wall, watching me with a stone face.

"You okay babe?" I'm sure he notices my weird expression.

"That was strange. John just brought me flowers for my birthday."

"Who's John?"

"He is my pharmacist. He was kind of friends with my dad. He's the one who asked you to take a picture of us at Tim and Tina's wedding. I'm not a big fan of him, he creeps me out a little."

Jay grabs the flowers from me and sets them on to the coffee table in the living room.

"If he bothers you too much you let me know," and he grabs my face and kisses me.

"I will," I tell him.

"Let's get back to your friends, they are waiting for you. And by the way, you look smoking hot tonight," he says, slapping my ass.

I re-enter the kitchen, and there are multiple conversations happening. I'm not even sure where to jump in. Erik looks up from his phone, "the driver of the party bus just called me, he'll be pulling into your yard in a couple minutes."

In a fluster, we all grab our coolers, purses, phones, and everything else we think we need. The boys get the coolers and gear loaded on to the bus.

Lexie is busy handing out necklaces with shot cups on them as each person gets on the bus. I take mine, giving her a hug and a kiss on the cheek. I couldn't ask for a better best friend.

The bus is painted black on the inside, all the seats removed and modified to run along the edges, so we can all face each other.

Halfway back is a speaker with a phone hookup for music. Darren is all over it. There is a stripper pole in the back, and color changing lights run around the top of the bus.

I feel a hand on my lower back. I turn to see its Jay. "Where you wanna sit babe?"

"Next to you," I smile.

He grabs my hips, pulling me down to a seat right next to us, and I lean into him. He wraps his left arm around my shoulders.

Cassie and Bridget are sitting across from us. Bridget leans across the bus toward me, "you guys are adorable together," she says with a smile. "How long have you been together now?"

"We've been on three dates, I guess we aren't even *official* yet." I tell her, shrugging my shoulders.

I glance at Jay, and his brow is furrowed. "What do you mean we aren't *official?*"

"I mean, I guess we haven't really decided if we are a couple or not, it's only been three dates." He looks a little surprised. I can see he hadn't even thought of this yet.

Darren gets the music going, Jonas Brothers "Cool" flows through the speakers, and everyone is piled onto the bus, reaching into coolers of beers and seltzers to find what they are looking for.

Erik is up front giving instructions to the driver. He told me he already picked out the best bars, and to not worry about logistics, to just have fun.

As we pull out of my yard I turn toward Jay, giving him a kiss on the cheek. He squeezes me tighter into him. I can see the wheels turning in his head.

CHAPTER 40

JAY

I FEEL LIKE AN IDIOT, I hadn't even considered the fact that Olivia and I aren't officially a couple. Until she said it, I hadn't even thought of it. I'm on a mission tonight to change that, I just need to find the right way to do it.

We cruise through Pine Lake, heading to the south side, into an older part of town, the bus coming to a stop in front of a bar called "O'Malley's". Looks like an Irish pub.

Everyone starts piling out, Olivia and I are in the middle of the crowd heading across the parking lot.

"This is one of Liv's favorite bars," Joe leans over and tells me as we walk toward the door.

We get inside and it's exactly how you would picture an Irish pub to be. Green walls and dark wood trim, dark hardwood floors, with neon bar signs and flat screens surrounding us.

We all gather at the long bar, the two bartenders scrambling to make our drinks. Waylon orders shots for everyone that wants them – Irish Car Bombs he calls them. We all take one and cheers the birthday girl.

After a couple drinks I head toward the back to use the restroom. I pass by an arcade room, filled with games like Ms. Pacman, pinball, and lots of those canisters where you put in a quarter and get a cheap prize.

I use the restroom and start heading back. Suddenly, I have an idea. I go in the arcade room, looking at the canisters of cheap prizes. Sure enough, I find what I'm looking for.

I head back to the bar, where I find Olivia talking with Bridget and Waylon. It looks to me like she's trying to set them up. I wait for a pause in the conversation.

"Olivia, do you have a minute?"

"Yeah, what's up?"

I don't say anything, I just grab her hand and lead her back to the arcade room. I bring her over to the red and clear canisters of prizes, where I've already stuck my quarter in one of the machines and turned the metal dial.

"What are we doing in here?" She looks confused.

"Oliva, I should have done this already. I'm sorry I haven't." I pause and take a breath. "You make me so unbelievably happy, there is nobody else I would rather be with..." I trail off, grabbing my prize out of the metal door, popping the plastic container open. Inside is a simple silver band, probably not even worth a penny.

"Will you be my girlfriend?" I hold up the ring in my fingers, trying my hardest to keep a straight face.

She starts giggling, a huge smile spreading across her face. "Yes, hell yes."

I close the space between us, kissing her passionately, my hand holding the back of her head, pulling her close to me.

I pull away for a second, slipping it on to her ring finger. She examines it for a second with a smile, then wraps her arms around my neck, kissing me hard, pressing herself into me.

It might be *her* birthday, but this is one of the best days of *my* life.

CHAPTER 41

LIV

I FEEL LIKE I'M WALKING on cloud nine since Jay and I talked in the arcade room. It was unexpected, but perfect. All this time I was hoping he felt the same way I did.

We have been bouncing from bar to bar for a few hours now.

First was O'Malley's, then a karaoke bar not far from there, where a few of us got songs in, one of them being "Happy Birthday" and the whole bar got in on it. I got it on video, it was awesome.

We stopped at B&B's and had a couple drinks. While we were there, I reintroduced Bridget and Waylon. I had started to do it at O'Malley's but was interrupted when Jay brought me to the arcade room.

They ended up carrying on a long conversation at B&B's, maybe my matchmaking skills aren't so bad. They are both bartenders, so I thought they might have something in common to talk about. I made sure to bring that up when I introduced them. Bridget has had a thing for him for a while, so this was the perfect opportunity to get them talking.

Across the room at B&B's, I spotted a familiar face. Kevin. I hadn't talked to him since our date. He was a nice guy, just not the guy for me. My brain was in matchmaker mode, and it hit me: I should introduce Kevin and Lexie. They are both single, friendly, and I think they would get along well.

I had grabbed Lexie and walked her over to him. He was sitting with another guy about his age. It was a little challenging with

Kevin being so quiet, and Lexie being so nervous around guys. Still, I think it was a good start, and they both seem interested.

— — —

Erik decides that we end the night at the Whiskey Whistle. It has a livelier crowd and is a good place to be at for bar close.

I find the first bartender where I can and order a round of shots. The Irish Car Bombs went over well last time, so I decide to repeat those.

As we take them, I see Cassie is having a hard time getting hers down. I think she's about had her limit. I walk over to her; I need to make sure she's okay.

"Liv. Liv," she says, slurring her words, reaching her hand out to me. I lean in closer, giving her a small smile.

"I tried hitting on Erik, he isn't interested. So, I'm drinking my sorrows away," now she's teetering on her feet and Lexie wraps an arm around her to steady her.

"Don't worry, we will find someone for you Cassie," I tell her with a reassuring smile.

Lexie carts her off to the ladies room. I look over and see Bridget, Tina, and Molly chatting. I walk up to them, placing my elbows on the high-top table.

"Hey guys! Having fun?"

"We are. But that doesn't matter. What matters is that *you* are having fun, it's your birthday," Tina says, leaning over and giving me a hug from the side.

"I'm having a great time. Hey Bridget, I see you and Way talked for a while. You guys hit it off?"

"Yes, I'm crazy about him, thank you so much for introducing us. We got each other's phone numbers; I hope he asks me out!"

"That's awesome, good for you," I say as I give her a high five.

I look around the busy room. Darren, Joe, Waylon, and Erik are talking with Steve, the bar owner. We do shows here on a regular basis, Steve is a great guy to work with.

Tim, Bo, and Jay are in a quiet conversation about something a couple tables over, so I decide to belly up to the bar and grab a drink for myself. Hardy's "Truck Bed" is playing over the speakers and the bar patrons are singing along.

I slide on to a bar stool, making sure my dress doesn't ride up too high, and just a few seconds later, I feel a hand on my back. I look back, smiling and expecting to see Jay, but disappointed when I see a drunken Mark. He botched the one date we had, and now feels the need to bother me every time we run into each other.

"You can remove your hand," I tell him, giving him my signature "piss off dude" look. He does slowly, but not without an appalled look on his face.

"You still playing hard to get?" I can hear a drunken slur in his words. It's my birthday and I've been drinking and even I can pick it out.

"No, I'm playing not interested."

"You know Olivia, you should give me an actual chance, instead of just shutting me out." The beer in his pint glass sloshes a little.

"No thank you," I tell him. I decide to turn my focus to ordering a drink and maybe he will go away. It's crazy to me that every time I see him, he's absolutely hammered.

He's still hovering around me, just staring. It's very uncomfortable and the bartenders are busy way on the other end of the bar. Screw the drink, I need to get away from this guy.

"Excuse me," I say, which was probably too polite for him.

"What the hell? Running away again?" His voice trails off.

I get up and decide to use the ladies room. Weaving through the thick crowd of people, I move my way toward the back of the bar. The restrooms are around a corner and down a hallway in the back.

As I round the corner and start to head down the hallway, I feel a hand wrap around my waist and pull me backwards. It startles me and I jerk away and end up hitting my head on the corner of the wall. Mark has his arm firmly around me, holding me in place.

"Why won't you listen to me. You don't always need to be so shut down," he whispers in my ear as he spins me to face him, and I can smell the beer on his stale breath.

"Leave me alone Mark. I'm not going to tell you again." I try to push away from him, but his large frame overpowers me.

He spins me around, facing him. "Come on, let's just have a little fun tonight," his beer-stained breath is in my face. He's trying to sway me back and forth as if I'm dancing with him.

The next thing I know, Waylon's tattooed arm wraps around his neck, pulling him back into his chest. Erik comes around the side of him and stands between us, pushing me up against the wall. I sneak a look over to see Waylon dragging Mark down the hall and in one swift kick opens the door marked "Exit" to the back alley.

"I'm sorry, he just wouldn't leave me alone, thank God you guys noticed," I say to Erik.

"Are you okay? Did he hurt you?" He's looking me up and down, assessing me to make sure I'm alright.

"I'm fine. It's all okay, I think maybe we should just go."

"Waylon's taking care of him for you. Joe and Steve noticed too, and I'm guessing Steve is already out back with them. Let's get you back to Jay." He slings his arm around my shoulders, leading me back to the front of the bar.

As we approach Jay's table, he looks up at us, a look of apprehension on his face when he sees Erik's arm around me. Erik removes his arm.

"I believe this belongs to you. Some guy had her in the back hallway against her will," he tells Jay.

"What the hell? Olivia, are you okay?" Jay stands up and his arms wrap around me, rubbing up and down my arms and caressing my neck and cheek.

"It's fine. He's gone now," I tell him, trying to blow the whole incident off. I should have just brought my pepper spray and gave him hell. Then these guys wouldn't have to worry like this.

"It's not fine. I think we should leave."

Waylon and Steve walk back up to us. "I'm so sorry about that Liv, he won't bother you anymore. He's kicked out."

"Thank you, Steve." I say with a small and grateful smile.

Waylon has scratch marks on his arms. I touch one, giving Waylon a hug.

"Way, are you okay?"

"Don't worry girl, you should see the other guy." It makes me smile. I look over at Bridget and she is watching Waylon intently, impressed.

We gather the group up and head back to the party bus. I find a spot near the back of the dark bus, sitting down. Jay is hot on my trail; he is sitting down close to me, with our bodies touching. He wraps his arm around me, pulling me into him. He kisses the top of my head.

"I'm sorry I wasn't there to help you, I should have been there," he says into my ear. He sounds hurt about it.

"It's okay. There's a lot of jerks out there. It's not the first time, won't be the last."

"Well, that's what I'm for. I need to protect what's mine," he says as he tilts my chin up and kisses me.

CHAPTER 42

LIV

THE NEXT MORNING, MY PARTY guests clear out, and I'm getting some much-needed time alone, just hanging out on my couch in leggings and a sweatshirt. Jay left early to go to the gym.

Sipping on my coffee, I notice Darren left yesterday's pile of mail sitting on the coffee table. I reach over and spread the pile out, noticing a red envelope tucked in the middle.

I set my coffee down and tear it open, nervous about what this one might say.

My dearest Olivia,

Happy Birthday my beautiful girl. You are so vibrant and full of life, 27 will be our year.

See you soon,
X

Twenty-seven will be our year, that's unnerving. How does this guy know how old I just turned?

I take a picture and text it to the guys as well as Sheriff Hayden. I bring it to my room and toss it in the box in the walk-in closet dresser with the others.

I will not allow myself to get wrapped up in this. Some random guy is probably having a hay day knowing that he is driving me insane. I'm not going to let it get to me.

I decide to focus my time and energy on more important things. My friends. The band. Jay.

CHAPTER 43

LIV

THE NEXT TWO WEEKS GO by in a blur.

I have gotten two more letters from the red envelope stalker, but there have not been any details or clues as to who is sending them.

We finally finished our original songs, there are three. We are super proud of them and are waiting for the right show to share them with the world. We have been practicing almost daily on them, it has taken up so much time, hopefully in the end it will pay off.

But most importantly, Jay and I have been getting closer.

We have been out on numerous dates, and we are spending a lot of nights together. The nights I don't spend with him feel lonely. His place in my world is becoming so big.

We both keep trying to think of unique dates we can go on.

One night, I decided we would try paintball; it was a blast. It had been a while since I had laughed that hard; we were able to get in with a random group of people and had the best time. He totally kicked my ass. At first, Jay didn't want to shoot me, so I took a couple shots at him to get things rolling, and then it was on. We ended up getting back to my place that night and taking a shower together, which was the highlight of the evening.

One hot September day, we went back to the quarry and swam. It wasn't as exciting as the first time, because it was daytime and there were other people there, but it was still fun. We invited

Tim and Tina to go with us and decided that double dates with them should happen again.

I invited him over one night to the shed where AO practices. We played one of our original songs for Jay, so that he can officially be the first in the world to hear it. He said he loved it. He looked so touched when we told him we wanted him to be the first person to hear it. "If You Leave Me", is a rock song that both Erik and I sing lead on, interchangeably through the verses. We feel it is the strongest of our three originals.

– – –

Now it's the beginning of October, and it is Jay's turn to pick what to do tonight. I see him pull into the driveway, so I open the door and lean in the frame.

I have on distressed jeans, a black bralette with a gray tank over it, and a knit sweater, open in the front.

Jay gets out of his truck, smiling at me. He is in a cream and gray sweater and dark jeans. I think he gets sexier every time I see him.

"Hey handsome," I call out to him.

"Hey gorgeous," he says, kissing me, wrapping his arms around my waist.

"What's the plan for tonight?"

"Well, I was thinking we could relive date number one," he looks down at me, hopefulness in his eyes.

"Really? That sounds amazing." I'm instantly grabbing my keys, phone, purse, and jacket and heading out the door, bubbling with excitement.

On the way there, we listen to old country songs, and Jay runs his hand up and down my thigh. I could happily do this every day with this man.

We pull up to the same spot we parked last time. This time I know what's coming, so I hop out right away and help him get things unpacked and ready.

We unroll the tonneau cover, and the same barrage of pillows and blankets are in the back, along with the speaker and cooler of food and wine.

We climb into the back and waste no time getting snuggled into each other. The sunset cascades above the grasses in front of us, and it's beautiful. The sky is streaked with oranges and blues, highlighting the tan grasses around the truck.

Jay is sitting on the air mattress with his back against the truck, and I'm sitting in front of him between his legs, his muscular arms wrapped tightly around me. We don't have to say much to be comfortable with each other, the feeling of each other's touch is enough for us.

Finally, after minutes of watching the sunset, Jay clears his throat. "Olivia, I have something to ask you," he says, anxiously.

"What is it?" I turn slowly so I can see him better.

"Um, I was wondering…." he trails off, looking down, sucking in a deep breath.

I grab his chin and tilt it up, so he's looking at me. "What is it?"

"Next Sunday, would you want to come to Greensboro with me and meet my parents?" His cheeks are flushed, and I can tell he's nervous. "My parents are having Brandon and Amanda over for lunch, and I was hoping you would want to come with me."

I'm speechless. He wants me to meet his parents. This is a huge step.

"I'd love to," I say as I take his face in my hands and kiss him passionately.

CHAPTER 44

LIV

IT'S SUNDAY MORNING. I HAVE been nervous for days about meeting Jay's parents.

Things keep rolling through my head like, *what do I wear? What questions do I ask? Are they going to like me? What are they like?* It has my stomach in knots.

Jay is here, he spent the night last night, and he keeps reassuring me that no matter what they are going to love me. I'm not feeling as confident.

I chose to wear a ruched T-shirt dress, it's a light green blue color, and I thought it was the perfect mix of casual and dressy.

My hair is down, and I paired my dress with a gold multi-chain necklace and a matching bracelet. I grabbed my jean jacket too in case it gets cold, the weather this time of the year can be unpredictable.

Jay looks classy as usual with dark wash jeans, and navy-blue pullover sweater.

The whole thirty-minute drive there, I'm fidgeting with nerves. I haven't met a guy's parents in a while, and I want so badly to impress them. Jay keeps grabbing my hand over the center console and giving me reassuring squeezes, although when I look over at him, I can see he's nervous too, maybe those squeezes aren't just for me.

I've spent a little time in Greensboro, doing a show here or there, but I'm not very familiar with it. It's not quite as big as Pine

Lake, maybe about half the size. We drive through town, turning into a nice development called "Richmond Hills". My stomach is really doing flips now because I know we're getting close.

The houses are huge, and each has a manicured yard and nice cars in the driveways. It makes me feel a little out of my element. These aren't the kind of places I'm used to spending time at.

"Here we are," he tells me, as we turn into a paved driveway, a large brick house with white trim looming in front of us. It reminds me of Kevin's house in "Home Alone". It's at the end of the cul-de-sac, in a nice lot with mature trees and perfect grass. It puts my place to shame.

I take a deep breath as he puts the truck in park. "I'm so glad you came with me. Just relax. They are so excited to meet you," he says and gives me a kiss.

He steps out of the truck, and I do the same. "Hey, you know the rule, I always open the door for you," he says with a smile, coming to my side of the truck and takes a hold of my hand.

Before I can answer, I hear the front door open. We both look up from the driveway. A long dark-haired woman with a sleek face and deep brown eyes steps out.

"Oh my gosh, you're here!" She turns back to the house, "Warren, they're here!"

She comes a couple steps closer, waving for us to come in.

I approach the front door, my left hand in Jay's. "Hello, I'm Liv," I reach my hand out to shake hers.

She comes at me and gives me a hug, and I pull my hand out of Jay's, hugging her back.

"I'm so happy to meet you. I'm Lisa, Jay's mom. Come on in, please make yourself at home."

I turn to look at Jay and he laughs quietly, shaking his head. I follow her in, looking up at the two-story grand entry way, mesmerized.

"Wow, you have a beautiful home Mrs. Jones."

"Thank you, and please, call me Lisa. Do you want to be called Liv or Olivia?"

"Either is fine, most people just call me Liv though."

A tall man with salt and pepper hair walks into the entry way. He is built just like Jay. Same square jaw, same nose, and remarkably similar hazel eyes.

"Hello, I'm Warren, Jay's dad. And please don't call me Mr. Jones, I get that enough at work," he smiles at me. I reach out and shake his hand. They both are so warm and inviting.

I look back at Jay, he's leaning against the front door. He looks uncomfortable, like he doesn't know what to do with his hands or something.

"Come on you two. Brandon and Amanda are already here, and they are so excited to meet you," Lisa exclaims, grabbing my hand.

I follow her through the house, the entry way leading into a huge two-story living room, with a dining room off to the left, and an open kitchen next to it.

A hallway goes down past the kitchen, to what looks to be the mud room area. On the other side of the house is a massive open staircase and a hallway.

On the backside of the living room are two sets of patio doors, facing the backyard. The lawn is perfect, and there is an in-ground swimming pool with a cabana next to it.

"Look who I found," Lisa calls out cheerfully. Brandon and Amanda are sitting at bar stools at the large kitchen island and turn toward us.

They both get up, smiling. I nervously look back at Jay, who is walking behind me, hands in his pockets.

"Hi Liv, I'm Amanda, Jay's sister-in-law," she says with a genuine smile. I'm sure she knows exactly how I'm feeling right now.

"And I'm Brandon, Jay's brother, Manda's better half," he says, and Amanda slugs him in the arm with an eye roll.

"Dinner will be ready shortly. Jay, why don't you show Liv around the house while I finish things up." Warren joins Lisa and they start working on last minute things in the kitchen, and Brandon and Amanda get to work on setting the huge dining room table.

"Come on gorgeous," Jay whispers to me and grabs my hand. He points down past the kitchen. "Bathroom, laundry room, and door to the garage."

We cross the large living room, and he points out the patio doors, "maybe next summer I can get you in that pool," and raises his eyebrows at me. The butterflies in my stomach are jumping into a frenzy.

In the main floor hallway, we pass by open double doors, looking into a huge and beautifully decorated master bedroom with decadent gold and black colors and a beautiful chandelier.

"This is my parent's room," he says, and then we cross to the other side of the hall. "Guest bedroom here, and this one is my dad's office." I look in and see rich green walls and a large mahogany desk in the office. The colors remind me of my bedroom.

We come back down the hall and head to the staircase, making our way down first.

"Down here is the rec room, utility room, another extra bedroom, and Brandon's old room. Him and Amanda sleep in there when they spend the night here."

I nod, noting that my whole house probably fits in their basement. The rec room is amazing. There is a bar with beautiful granite countertops, leather couches facing a flat screen TV, a pool table, and another table that looks like it's made specifically for playing games. This is the place to be.

We head back up, then climb the staircase to the second floor. There are four doors. Jay tells me one is a linen closet, and one is a bathroom. He points to a door on the left.

"This one is Casey's old room. We really don't use it; we try to leave it the way he left it." I can see he's having a hard time saying it out loud. I squeeze his hand and bring him to me, giving him a gentle kiss.

Wrapping his arm around my waist, we open the door next to Casey's at the end of the hall. "And lastly, this is my room."

He opens the door, with his hand on the small of my back, guiding me to go in front of him.

It's a light blue room with white linens on the bed. There is a walk-in closet, a dresser, and a desk. There isn't much on the walls, which surprises me. "So, this is where you bring all your girlfriends then huh," and I give him a wink and a mischievous smile. I sit on the end of the queen-size bed and bounce a couple times, looking around the room.

He runs his hand through his hair nervously. "You are the first girl I've had in here. You are the first girl I've brought home to meet my parents."

I look up at him, surprised. I knew he hadn't dated much, but I wouldn't have guessed that I'm the first one to meet his parents. So, this is why he has been so nervous, he has no idea of what to expect.

I stand up from the bed and cross the room to him, where he is leaning back against the dresser.

I pull on the collar of his sweater, so his face is almost touching mine. "Well, I hope I'm the first and last," and I give him a passionate kiss, his hands finding their way around me, grabbing on to my back and my ass, squeezing like he will never let me go.

We kiss for a couple minutes, and I've nearly forgotten we are at his parents' house. I pull away, holding his biceps.

"We should probably stop, before we get busted." As I say it, I see a playful twinkle in his eye.

"Dinner's ready," I hear Amanda call from the bottom of the steps a few seconds later.

I check myself in the mirror before heading downstairs with him. I can already smell the food in the dining room, and it smells amazing.

Warren and Lisa are taking their places at the ends of the table. Brandon and Amanda are finding their spots on one side, leaving Jay and me to the other side.

Like a true gentleman he pulls out my chair for me. I can see Warren give him a proud smile as he does it. Clearly this guy trained him well.

"Everything is family-style, so dig into whatever looks good. We did roast chicken, fresh garden green beans, mashed potatoes, and buns. Help yourself." Lisa smiles, undoubtedly enjoying that her dining room table is full of family.

Everyone digs in, passing dishes around the table to one another. I'm thankful it isn't a stuffy setting. Everyone is relaxed and at ease, not like some families where there is an uptight feeling at the dinner table.

I've had a bite of each thing when I look over at Lisa. "Everything is amazing. Thank you so much. It's been a long time since I've sat around a dinner table with family." I can feel old tears welling up in me, from memories past, and memories I never got to have with my parents.

Lisa gets up, placing her cloth napkin by her plate. She comes around the table, leans down over me, and gives me a hug. It's completely unexpected, but a hundred percent appreciated.

"You are welcome here any time, we are happy to have you," she says, and I smile at her. This is probably the most heartfelt gesture I've had from a parental figure in years.

She starts to go back to her spot, then stops and skirts around her chair, heading over to Amanda.

"And we love you too Amanda, we have since day one." Amanda gives her a big hug back. I already love this family.

Partway through the dinner, Jay slides his hand high up my thigh under my dress. I look over and he's not giving anything away about the gesture. I quickly slide my thigh a little to the side so his hand slips to the inside. He drops his fork loudly on his almost empty plate, clearing his throat.

"You okay Jay," his dad asks. Jay nods in embarrassment and tries to brush it off as nothing. It takes everything in me to keep a straight face.

After dinner Amanda and I help Lisa in the kitchen to get things cleaned up and put away. Lisa insists that we go relax, but I love feeling like a part of the group, like I did my part for the day.

Warren, Brandon, and Jay are watching football in the living room. Random chants keep coming from them, but I don't pay much attention, I'm not really into football, I honestly just don't understand most of what's going on. I would probably like it more if I understood it.

The dinner cleanup is done, so we gather in the rec room in the basement, playing a game of Scrabble at the game table. The football game plays on the big TV on the wall.

It has been years since I played a board game like this. I hadn't realized how much I missed the comradery of a family, and how the simplest things are so much better with the right people around.

The game is done, Warren absolutely wiped the table with all of us.

"Well, next time I'll be sure to bring my A-game, now that I know you play at expert level," I say, chiding Jay's dad.

Warren smiles and laughs. "You are welcome to come over any time and try." Now everyone is laughing.

"Well, we better get going," Jay says, and he stands slowly. I stand up too, smoothing my dress down my legs.

"We'll walk you out," Lisa tells us. Everyone gets up from around the table and goes upstairs.

As we get to the front entry way, Warren leans in and gives us both hugs.

"Thank you for coming over today," he tells me with a smile.

Brandon sneaks in behind him, awkwardly approaching me, and kind of motions that he's not sure if he should hug me or not. I stick out my right hand to shake his, laughing. He takes my hand and comes in for a half hug, patting me on the back awkwardly.

Amanda shakes her head at his gracelessness and gives me a hug.

"Get my number from Jay, let's get together some time. I'm so glad there is another girl to hang out with." Her enthusiasm is awesome, I have a feeling we are going to get along great.

And finally, Lisa gives me a million-dollar hug. It's warm, exactly how a mom should give hugs.

"Thank you so much for coming today. And thank you so much for making my son so happy," she whispers in my ear. I pull away and see tears welling up in her eyes.

I quickly look away, otherwise I will start crying too.

"Alright, now that I know you guys like her more than me, it's time for us to go," Jay says with a quiet laugh. All of them surround him in one big hug and laugh together.

We turn and head out to the truck, turning to wave goodbye before we get in.

"I love your family so much," I say before Jay closes the passenger door behind me.

"I told you they would love you. Thank you for coming, it means a lot to me." He leans in, grabs my face, and kisses me.

CHAPTER 45

JAY

I TAKE A SEAT ON the uncomfortable brown leather couch in Dr. Stangel's office. It smells like vanilla and pinecones in here.

"So, Jay, how have you been? It's been a while since you've been here, last time we spoke was early August. What's on your mind?"

"Well, Dr. Stangel, do you remember I told you about Olivia last time?"

"Yes Jay, I have it in my notes that you had brought her up. Are there any updates there?" He's giving me a skeptical look, and it's kind of bothering me.

"Yes, we've been going out since August. A couple days ago I brought her home to meet my parents, and Brandon and Amanda. Things are going great." I blow out a breath after saying it, already feeling better, wanting to wipe away any doubt he has about us.

"That's great to hear Jay. One question. Have you told her about your brother?"

"Yeah, we talked about it. She lost her parents in a car accident when she was in college. So it feels like every day we are helping each other heal. Because of her, I feel like I've found a way to clear my anxiety, frustration, and anger."

"Interesting. Well, I'm sorry to hear about her parents. I'm just going to say one thing about this, please don't take it in any negative context. You've gone through a lot and have spent years keeping people and relationships at an arm's length. Just be mindful that you should take things slow. I don't want to see you go backwards in all your progress if things don't work out with you and Ms. Dunne."

I sit there for a minute, stunned that he would have the audacity to say that. I feel unnerved and I want to leave.

"I'll keep that in mind Dr. Stangel." And that's all I can manage to get out.

I never want to come back to this office again.

CHAPTER 46

LIV

IT'S WEDNESDAY. ONLY MID-WEEK AND I feel like it's never going to end.

I'm in the AO practice shed with the guys. We just got done recording our three original songs. We've been in here for hours.

We are all sprawled out on couches and chairs, reeling in the fact that we just recorded our first demo. I feel a multitude of emotions right now. Excitement, anxiety, self-doubt, and more excitement. It's all morphing together in an uneasy, anxious feeling in the pit of my stomach.

Darren is finishing things up on the computer. None of us had a clue how to do this, thankfully we have Darren who can figure it out. He's working on getting the recordings on to CD's. We are going to mail them out to different recording studios to see if there would be any of them interested in us.

I stand up and cross the room to the table he's sitting at. I sit down on his knee and lay my head on his shoulder. All this waiting and anxiousness is exhausting.

"I have some done, got about half to go yet," he says, handing me a clear case with our CD inside.

"How do we do this? Do you think we should dress these up somehow? I feel like we need a cover on here and on the back list the names of the songs, even if there are only three," I say, looking around the room to see if anyone agrees with me.

"Good idea. We should do a band picture on the front, something edgy and cool," Erik says, standing up from the couch. He comes over and grabs the clear case from me, turning it over in his hands.

"Liv, maybe you should talk to your boyfriend and see if he will do a picture for us," Joe chimes in from a rolling chair across the room. He exhales and smoke billows out around him. He's sitting by an open window, with a joint in his hand.

"That's a good idea. I'm sure he wouldn't mind. He's been getting more and more business at the studio, but I'm sure he could handle doing that for us quick in between jobs. I'll text him." I stand up and move about the room, texting Jay.

> Liv: Hey! So, we are recording our demos tonight on CD's. We need a photo for a cover for the cases. Do you think you would have time this week to take a band picture for us?
> Jay: Absolutely babe. How about we do a bunch of them, then you can pick your favorite for the CD, and post the rest on your website and FB page. I noticed there weren't many on there.
> Liv: That sounds awesome. Thank you. When are you free?
> Jay: Tomorrow night work for you? Just come to the studio, I'll be here.

"Guys, how about tomorrow night?" I look around and they all nod in agreement. Waylon works but he says he will get someone to take his shift.

> Liv: Do we need to bring anything?
> Jay: Multiple outfits for each of you. Make sure you each have an all-black outfit too. And guitars. And Joe's drumsticks.

Liv: Thanks babe. XOXO.

"Alright. It's on for tomorrow night. We need guitars and drumsticks, and multiple outfits, including one all-black one." There is a new buzz about the group now.

"I'm going to finish working on these, you guys can head home, go get your beauty sleep for pictures tomorrow," Darren says with a smile.

We all head out the door, hugging and high fiving one another. This was a big day for AO, hopefully it will all pay off.

‒ ‒ ‒

I get home and Lexie's car is in my driveway. I had texted her earlier and asked if she wanted to spend the night. I wanted someone here but needed a little distraction from the band. We have been working tirelessly together lately and I'm scared they will get burnt out between work, AO, and babysitting me.

I pull my car in the garage, leaving the door open for her to come in. She has her usual overnight bag.

"Hey lady. How was your day," I ask as she walks up and into the garage.

"It was alright. Long though, I'm shot," she has a tired look on her face.

"Ditto. We got our songs recorded tonight. And Jay is doing pictures for us tomorrow for our CD covers. Things are coming along well," I say as I grab her bag, slinging it over my shoulder and bring it in for her, dropping it on the kitchen island.

"Glass of wine before bed?" Lexie asks me, and I nod by head. I'm always game for a glass of wine.

"Thanks for coming over. Sometimes I just need a girly hang out instead of having the guys over. Guest bedroom is all clean and made up for you when you are ready," I say as I set our glasses on the counter.

We talk for a little bit as we sip on our wine. Lexie has been dying to know how it went on Sunday meeting Jay's parents, and honestly, I'm excited to tell her about them. I can't wait to see them again.

The wine is gone, and the conversation has slowed. It feels like it's time for bed.

"Since it's nice and cool out, can I open the bedroom window tonight? It cooled down a little the last couple days and it would be good sleeping weather."

"Absolutely. Goodnight." I tell her as I give her a hug and then start towards my room. I leave the bedroom door open; it will be nice to have a cool breeze in the house tonight while we sleep.

I brush my teeth and slip out of my clothes, putting on a light pink silk nightie.

Laying down I fall asleep in a matter of a couple minutes, the days stress melting away from me, the cool breeze cascading into my room.

CHAPTER 47

JAY

I'M CLEANING UP THE LAST of the day's mess in the studio. Olivia and the guys should be here any time.

I have so many ideas of what we can do for the band pictures, I hope we end up on the same page and they like how they turn out.

Cars begin to pull up outside the window, and I see them stepping out of their vehicles. I don't know what it is, but I still get nervous around them, they are intimidating, especially when it's the whole group.

Opening the front door, I give them a smile. They've each got a bag of extra clothes, along with some guitars and drumsticks. Perfect.

"Hey guys, come on in," I say as they cross the sidewalk to the door. Olivia stops next to me.

"Thank you so much," she says, and she kisses me. I'm doing this for her. Everything is for her.

They set their things down by the desk near the front door. They are already dressed in the perfect outfits. A lot of black, leather, and ripped denim. It's exactly what I would expect them to wear.

"First shot I have in mind we are going outside for. No instruments needed. We are going to use what is left of today's sunlight, so let's get right to it," I say as I grab my camera and put it around my neck.

There is a set of old worn-out cement steps in front of the building next to mine, the grass peeks through in the small cracks, and if I can get the coloring right in this during editing, it will look great. I position them on the steps, staggered around each other, with Olivia and Erik in the front.

I kneel on the sidewalk, getting a shot up at them, my shutter taking multiple pictures. Most of our shots will be more serious or stoic, with a couple funny ones in there just for kicks.

I motion for them to get up, and we go in the alley way on the other side of my building.

"This is going to feel weird, but I'm going to lay on the ground, and you guys all stand above me, forming a circle of sorts, looking down at me. If your hair is long let it fall around you, however it happens naturally."

I lay down like I said, and they file in above me. A couple smiles peek out, the rest serious stares. I take multiple pictures. As I stand back up, I show them the preview screen. I'm getting all smiles from the group now.

The third group of shots, we go around the back of my building. There is a cement ledge about waist high where a large old window used to be. I instruct them to sit on the ledge in a row.

At the back is Joe, and as they get closer to me it's Darren, Waylon in the middle, Olivia, and Erik closest to me. No smiles again, and I do one shot with Erik looking at me and the rest of them looking down and in other directions, then decide to do another where they all look down and away from the camera, at random angles. The last one I tell them to smile and act goofy, and it felt haphazard, but when I checked the screen, it all worked out well.

"Let's head in now guys," I tell them, and they start walking down the alley to the front of the building. I snap pictures of them walking ahead. One of them Olivia is turning back to look at me, that sultry look on her face that I love, and I snap the picture. That one will be a gem.

I have rolls of different colors of backdrop in the studio. I have a very bold red one down already, I knew I would want to use this one for at least one shot.

"Okay, I want everyone in all black for this one. If you need to go change you can use the back two rooms there and the bathroom," I point to the doors, and they scatter and grab their bags.

While they are gone, I roll through the shots I've already taken. We've got some good ones to work with already.

They all return, as expected, in all black. I position them in front of the red back drop, Waylon and Darren standing in the back, Erik on a black chair, Joe sitting on the floor next to the chair, and Olivia laying on her side, arm draped over her hip, laying in front of all of them. I take lots of shots, then I grab a couple of their guitars, passing them out, along with Joe's drumsticks, and snap a few more.

For the next hour we change backdrops and props. They get a little more daring as the evening goes on.

"Okay, one last group of shots. We are going to go upstairs to my loft to get these." I get a couple funny looks from Waylon and Erik.

We head up the stairs to my loft and I slide the heavy door open, letting them in. Thank God I picked up before they got here. I haven't been home as much lately, and it was turning into a disaster.

"We are going to do one set by that half-moon window over there, that faces the street," they all turn and look, and it starts to make sense to them.

"Babe did you bring what I told you to for an outfit?" I ask Olivia quietly, hoping she had what I was looking for. I text her late last night and made an outfit request.

"Sure did, I'll go change in the bathroom."

"Guys, you can stay in what you have on, the all-black will work great. She's gonna slip something else on quick," I say, motioning behind me.

A couple minutes later, she steps out of the bathroom, and I'm blown away. She's wearing a low cut tight black short mini dress, tall black heels, and sexy lace black stockings, with intricate patterns sewn into them.

I feel like I can't breathe, I'm frozen in my spot. She walks over to me, running her hand down my arm, giving me a wink. My gaze follows her across the room to where the rest of the guys are.

They are starting at her in awe like they've just seen her for the first time. Waylon's jaw is on the ground, Darren is giggling like an idiot, and Joe and Erik look like they are in shock. I bring my camera up and snap a random shot of them.

Olivia turns her head back to me, a wicked grin on her face. I get that shot too. She looks amazing, I'm going to have to go to her place tonight. Hopefully she'll keep that dress on for me.

I get them in to position in the arch of the window, trying multiple different angles and configurations. All these shots are going to look great.

"Alright guys, I have everything I need, good job," I tell them as I slip the camera off from around my neck.

I walk to the kitchen and grab some beer out of the fridge. I set them on the counter and pop the tops. They each come and grab one, holding the brown bottles high.

"Cheers to AO, you guys' truly *rock*," I say with a smile, and we clink our bottles together.

They talk amongst themselves, and I take the opportunity to be one on one with Olivia.

"Hey babe," I say, wrapping my arm around her small waist.

"Hey. Thank you so much," she says, kissing me.

"So, I was thinking about payment for this little photo shoot."
She cocks her head to the side in interest at my comment.

"I'll come over later, you leave that outfit on, and I can rip
those clothes off you with my teeth," I quietly say, leaning in
close to her ear.

I hear her take a quick breath; I can tell she's turned on.

"Deal," she says with her sexy smile.

CHAPTER 48

LIV

I'M DOING JUST AS JAY asked and leave my sultry outfit on. I just got in my house, he said he would be over once he locked up his place and the studio.

A few minutes later I hear his truck pull up. I'm sitting on the kitchen island when he walks in. He comes around the corner, and a wicked grin forms on his face when he sees me.

Neither of us say a word as he closes the space between us. He grabs my face in his hands, holding me there, kissing me firmly. His right-hand slides down the front of me, caressing my breast, sliding one of the tiny dress straps down my arm. His hand rests firmly on my hip. He grabs me and pulls us closer together and I spread my legs open to him.

He runs his hand down my leg, over my stockings. I have my arms around his neck, and he reaches down, grabs my ass, and picks me up off the island. He carries me to the bedroom.

He sets me down on the bed, reaches around and unzips the back of my dress. I lay back on the bed and he slides it off me, along with my black lace panties. He wastes no time, his mouth working on my nipples, my back arching in pleasure.

He leans back up and pulls my heels off but leaves my stockings. He pulls his white T-shirt off, never breaking eye contact with me. The rest of his clothes end up in a pile on the floor.

He crawls back on to the bed, laying on his back, his head on the pillow.

I crawl over to him slowly, stopping perpendicular to him while on my knees, and take the length of his erection into my mouth, moving up and down him slowly. He grabs my hair and moans my name, I repeat it a few more times before I slide over and straddle him.

I look down at him before I let him enter me. I can see the passion in his eyes. He grabs on to my hips and I lower myself down on to his erection, moaning with pleasure as he fills me up.

I leisurely grind myself on top of him, slowly, enjoying every second.

I begin to get faster and faster, and a little harder. He moves one hand up and cups my breast, the other firmly on my ass, pulling me into him.

It feels so good on top, my rhythm quickening.

"Jay I'm close," I say breathlessly after a few minutes.

"Me too baby," as he grabs my ass with both his hands, squeezing me hard.

I say his name between moans, and tighten myself around him, finally letting go, and he is right behind me with his release.

I lean down and lay on his chest, both of us panting wildly. After a few minutes I drag the stockings down my legs, and curl back into him.

We drift off to a blissful sleep, never letting go of each other.

CHAPTER 49

LIV

FRIDAY IS FINALLY HERE. I'M taking a much-needed day off from my day job. I have errands to run, and just need some personal time.

Jay left this morning, like usual, and went to the gym. I'm planning on stopping by his studio in a little bit to peek at the pictures he took last night.

First thing first though, I need my daily run. I slip on my running clothes, stretch out on the front porch, and head down the driveway. I roll my eyes as I run by the mailbox. I'm not ruining a perfectly good day off with the possibility of a red envelope.

It's a great run, excitement bubbling through me, with thoughts of the band and Jay occupying my mind.

After I'm done, I decide to take a bubble bath instead of a shower since I have time. All I can think about is Jay, and I wish he was in the tub with me. *Next time*, I tell myself as the dirty fantasy plays out in my head.

Getting out, I slip on some distressed jeans and a fitted long sleeve black T-shirt. I go in the bathroom and open my medicine cabinet. I grab the bottle with the Methotrexate in it. Playing guitar has led to arthritis, which typically my medication can keep in check. I've been on it for years.

I pop the little orange bottle open, counting how many I have left. It doesn't take long, there is only one in there. I knew it was getting low, I had gotten a text from John at the pharmacy that it was time to come in for a refill. I check my birth control pills and see I have plenty of those yet.

I grab a glass of water in the kitchen and take my birth control pill and the last arthritis pill, tossing the empty bottle in the garbage. I grab a banana for breakfast and head out the door.

I make it into Jay's studio about fifteen minutes later. He's sitting at his desk, focusing on his computer. As I open the door, he looks up and smiles.

"Hey babe, I'm working on your stuff right now."

I come around the side of his desk, kissing him and then sit on his knee. He scrolls through all the pictures, there are way more than I expected. I point out some of my favorites as he scrolls past. Damn, this guy is talented, they look amazing.

"Erik says he is going to stop by this afternoon and pick one for the cover. Is that okay with you?"

"Yeah, we already discussed that," I say, nodding. The group already decided one person should just pick the cover photo, so we don't bicker over the decision. Erik happily announced he would do it, so we let him.

"I need to go; I need to pick up a prescription and have other errands to run this afternoon. Should we stay here at your place tonight?"

"Sure, just text me when you are on your way, and I'll make sure I have it cleaned up for you," he says, smiling at me.

— — —

I run around town, accomplishing all the things I need to. I love having a random weekday off to get things done. Last stop is to get my prescription refilled.

I walk in the door of the pharmacy. I've been coming here for years. Luckily, the only things I need to take are my arthritis pills and birth control.

I walk up to the counter, and John is standing there. "Olivia, hello. Nice to see you. I'm guessing you need your Methotrexate for arthritis refilled," he says with a smile.

"Yes, I do. I took the last one this morning. And again, thank you for those flowers on my birthday, you really didn't need to do that."

"It was my pleasure."

I give him a small smile. I still think it was weird.

John motions for me to move over to the consultation window. He opens a white paper bag, with the same orange bottle of pills in it that I usually get.

"Now, I know you obviously know how to take these, but I do want to tell you, they changed the look of the Methotrexate, so they are different looking but the same prescription," he says as he pops open the childproof cap and turns the open bottle to me so I can see inside.

"Oh yeah, I can tell. Thanks for warning me." I pay my copay, sign off on the insurance, and put the pills in my purse. "Thanks, John."

"No problem, Olivia, see you soon." He gives me a wave and a smile, and as I turn away, I have an uneasy feeling in the pit of my stomach.

As I pull on to my road to go home, I decide I'm ready to get the mail. I open the door slowly. I must have this idea that the red envelopes in the mailbox are like a Jack-In-The-Box toy or something, that they are going to jump out and attack me.

Sure enough, there is a red envelope. I shake my head in disbelief.

I get up to the house, bringing the mail in, and lock the door behind me.

I rip open the red envelope, and much to my disgust, it's not just a letter. I open the letter first, afraid of what else this will lead to.

My dearest Olivia,

Your beauty knows no bounds. You have ruined me to the core so that nobody else will ever compare. I can't wait to set your world on fire.

See you soon,
X

I let the letter fall to the table. I pull out what is left in the envelope. Pictures. I flip them over. They are pictures of me. Sleeping. I have on the light pink silk nightie, I just had this on the other day when Lexie spent the night. Oh. My. God. The realization hits me. This person must have snuck in Lexie's open window that night. The cameras would not have caught it, as that window is on the side of the house, not the front or back.

I go into the spare bedroom, peeking around the partially open door. The window has already been shut, but I look around anyway, making sure it's locked.

I bend down, and can see a little dirt on the floor, smushed into the carpet. I look out and can see a large boot print in the dirt right outside the window.

I'm frozen with shock. I can't be here, I need out. I need Jay. It's probably time to tell him what's going on. I put the disturbing contents back into the envelope and file it away with the rest of them in my closet then grab my phone.

> Liv: Hey. Chinese takeout sound good tonight? I
>   want to come over now.
> Jay: Mmmm yes.
> Liv: I'll pick it up and will be there shortly.

I swing into the Chinese buffet and get two to go boxes. I load up with a variety of things for each of us, there is enough food here to put us in substantial food comas.

I can't get my mind off the pictures, it's the most violated feeling I've ever had. Tears are pricking the back of my eyes, and I feel like the entire world is staring at me, its unnerving. The short drive to Jay's loft is torturous. I can't focus on anything; I'm just so rattled.

As I pull up, I see him waiting by the first-floor door to the loft. "Hey gorgeous," he says, kissing me, and takes the takeout bags out of my hands.

"Hey," I say in reply. I already feel better and safer that I'm here and not alone at my house, like a weight has been lifted off me.

It has started raining and the clouds are darkening in the sky. Its making it feel later in the day than just 6:00. We don't waste any time standing outside getting wet, we make our way up the steps to the loft.

"Erik picked out a great shot for your cover. It was one of them we took in the half-moon window upstairs."

"I'm so nervous about all of this. I think Darren was going to try and get those mailed out yet today."

"It will all work out, don't worry about it," he says as he slides open his loft door. There is soft music playing in the background, and it smells good in here, like his musky cologne.

He notices me smelling it, he waves his arm around and says, "yeah, I finally cleaned," he lets out a little laugh.

We flop down on the couch, spreading out the Chinese take out in front of us. We stuff ourselves to the point of stomach pain.

"It's always too much, but it's so good," he says, licking the last of some sweet and sour sauce off his finger, leaning back in exhaustion.

We relax into the couch, just laying together listening to music.

My mind is still reeling. *Do I tell him about the red envelope stalker? Would he think I'm seeing someone else? I haven't mentioned the letters, pictures, flowers, or the bird yet. Would he be mad I haven't told him already?* I wonder what my parents would tell me to do. I wish more than anything they were here to help me with all of this.

"This might sound stupid because I know it's early on a Friday night, but I could totally go to bed now, I'm so full," he says, slowly, rubbing his stomach.

"I vote yes to that idea." I'm more than ready to be done with the stress of today, I need to shut my mind off.

He sits up, giving me a peck on the cheek.

"A lazy night in bed it shall be then." He grabs my hand and leads me across the room to his bed. "I'm going to lock the doors, shut the music and lights off and get us some water," he says, turning away.

I stand on my side of his bed and take out my earrings. I set the first one on the nightstand. The second one falls out of my hand and rolls under the bed.

"Shit," I say out loud. I get on my hands and knees and start feeling around in the shadows under the bed.

My hand runs across something, it's not an earring, but I pull on it anyway. It feels like a box. I slide it out and look, sure enough it's a shoebox.

I glance up and see that Jay isn't back yet, so I open the lid out of curiosity.

At first, I'm confused at what I'm looking at.

I pick up a picture of me. It's from the day I bought my new Tahoe. *But Jay wasn't with me.* It looks like he was down the street, it's a picture of me, with Erik and the salesperson behind me. I look past it and find a few more from that day. I find another one of me shopping at Target. Then I find about twenty of me on stage during shows. Then there is one of me walking into my house, the night of Tina's bachelorette party. The next one is of me at the grocery store, pushing my shopping cart of groceries.

I'm confused. Why would he have these? Does he follow me? Then it hits me like a ton of bricks. He calls me Olivia. The red envelope stalker calls me Olivia. They started arriving around the same time he moved to Pine Lake. My stalker sends me photos, and he's a photographer.

I'm shaking now, still holding one of the pictures. I hear footsteps behind me.

"Olivia, what are you doing?"

I'm frozen with fear. This can't be happening. He can't be my red envelope stalker. It could make sense though; he did know I was going to be at the car dealership that day, he was at Tim and Tina's wedding to take that picture of me in the red dress, he knows the ins and outs of my house. Holy shit, did he sneak in and take pictures of me sleeping the other night? Maybe he's not the person I thought he was.

I slowly turn my head and look at him. He swallows, I can see the uneasiness in his face as he sees the shoebox. Now he knows that I know. I'm scared to know what happens now.

"What the hell! You've been stalking me?" I'm in shock. I let the picture fall back into the box and I stand up, wrapping my arms around myself.

"Olivia, let me explain." He trails off, but I hold up my hand to make him stop.

"No, Jay. This is unacceptable. What you've been doing is unacceptable." I turn and walk through the loft, grabbing my purse.

"Stop Olivia, let me talk to you!" He sounds more forceful this time.

"No, Jay. You need to stay away from me," I say as I flip the lock on the sliding door and slam it behind me.

I run down the staircase, trying to put space between us, but he's following me.

As I run, I grab my key fob out of my purse. I quickly unlock the door to the street and run faster. I get out to the sidewalk and hit the unlock button on the Tahoe.

"Damnit, Olivia stop!"

I jump in the SUV and lock the door behind me as fast as I can.

Jay stops at my door and tries to pull on the handle. I refuse to look at him, I'm just staring at my steering wheel, my chest rising and falling as I take heavy breaths.

"Olivia, unlock the door, let me talk to you." He pounds his fist on my window, and it makes me jump.

I turn the ignition. I look over at Jay in the window and heavy tears are streaming down his face.

"Olivia, please, babe, talk to me. Please," he's begging.

I can't. I put it in gear and drive away.

CHAPTER 50

JAY

I'M SITTING ON THE CURB of the sidewalk in front of my place where her vehicle was just parked. I can't move. Tears are running down my face and I feel like I can't breathe. I'm crying so hard. My hands are shaking.

What the hell was I thinking? I should have known to not do any of this. Although in my head, I never expected her to find any of that. I realize now how ridiculous it all was.

I sit there for quite a while, watching the sky darken around me as a heavy rain starts to fall. I let it pelt off my skin as I sit.

Finally, I make my way inside to my loft, not even bothering to lock the door. If she decides to come back, she will be able to get in. Even though deep down I know she's not coming back.

I stand next to the bed and look down at the pile of pictures in the shoebox. It's now the only thing I have left of her. Just like Casey. Pictures and memories. I pick up the earring that's left on the nightstand. I'm guessing the other one is under the bed, and that's how she found this. Fuck!

I give the box a kick across the floor. I flop down on to the bed, it feels so cold now, knowing she won't be laying in it next to me.

I lay in bed, fully clothed, all night without falling asleep. I bounce between being depressed and angry at myself. I'll be lucky if I ever sleep again. Life seems meaningless now.

Dr. Stangel was right. Now I'm right back to the pit of hell where I started.

CHAPTER 51

LIV

I SPENT LAST NIGHT IN the AO shed. I laid alone in the dark and the desire to go back to him was a burden on my soul, it felt like a weight on my chest and gave me restlessness. I didn't want to call any of the guys. I didn't want to relive the pain of what happened yesterday just to get them caught up on the situation.

I also didn't want to stay at my house, knowing Jay would expect me to be there. Although, I didn't hear my doorbell alarm go off either, I guess he didn't bother to stop by.

I laid awake on the tattered old couch last night wondering when the last time was that I heard the doorbell alarm go off. I haven't charged it like I was supposed to. It's probably dead. I'm sure they both are.

— — —

The next morning, I wake up, having gotten barely any sleep.

My eyes are red and puffy. I need to get out of here before Joe gets up and asks questions on why I'm sleeping in the shed on the couch.

He was out last night when I arrived. Sometimes one of us will end up staying out here, I'm sure he didn't find it unusual when he got home and saw my vehicle outside.

I exit the shed and head to my Tahoe, willing it to be quiet so I don't wake him up. As I drive home, I think about what happens next with Jay.

I do know a few things after thinking all last night – I am not ready to speak to or see Jay, I need to charge that damn doorbell, and I need to fill in the guys on what's going on. Do I tell the cops? I probably should but I'm not sure I want to.

I pull into my garage, shut the Tahoe off and close the door behind me. I sit in the quietness of the car for a minute. I could fall asleep right here as I'm so exhausted.

I finally get out, putting one slow foot in front of the other.

I unlock the door from the two-stall attached garage into the mud room of my house. I set my purse down on the ledge and meander into the kitchen.

I grab a bottle of water out of the fridge and a banana out of the basket on the counter. I need to take my pills. I go back to my purse, finding one of each and pop them into my mouth with a swig of water.

I lean against the kitchen counter and slowly eat my banana. I toss the peel in the garbage. I stand for a minute, trying to think of how I want to go about my Saturday and what I need to do. I should probably tell the guys what's going on before our show tonight. My brain feels like mud.

I walk over to the front door, unlocking it. I pull the black cover off my doorbell camera and notice that the inside of it is gone. I'm pretty sure the thing on the inside was what I'm supposed to plug in and charge.

I put the cover back on, confusion clouding my mind. I close the front door behind me and walk to the back patio door doorbell camera. I open that one, and again, there is nothing inside.

My eyelids feel heavy, and my legs are so tired. I lean back and start to slide down the outside wall of my house next to my patio door, heavy fatigue washing over me, dropping the doorbell cover on to the cement patio. My head feels so heavy. Am I really *this* tired? My arms are starting to go numb, and I can barely keep my eyes open. This doesn't feel right.

I finally give in, slumping to the ground, letting the blackness take over me.

CHAPTER 52

JAY

I HAVEN'T SEEN OR HEARD from Olivia since she stormed out Friday night.

It's Sunday night now. I haven't slept, and my thoughts seem to be taking drastic turns. I'm sitting on the floor, my back propped up against my living room couch. A low-ball of whiskey is in front of me, but I don't have the ambition to drink it.

I get my phone out and decide to call Darren. He answers on the third ring. I'm so glad Liv gave me all the AO boys' numbers.

"Hey Jay, what's up?"

"Hey Darren. I'm wondering if you've talked to Olivia."

"You know, we've been worried about her. We were supposed to have a show last night, but she messaged the group yesterday morning and said she can't do it because she's sick. She said you were coming over last night to stay with her and that she would be fine. We've been texting her but haven't heard back. How is she doing?"

"Her and I had a fight on Friday night, and she stormed out of here, that's the last I've heard or seen of her. She wasn't sick at that point, and I didn't go over there last night. I don't want to bother her, but I just need to make sure she's okay. I figured maybe she would reach out to you."

"Oh shit," I can hear the concern in his voice. "Something's not right."

"Should we head over to her house and check on her?" I'm already getting up off the floor.

"Yeah, I'll text Erik, maybe he can meet us there too. I'm going to head over there right now."

I run downstairs to my truck. I get in, start it up, and peel out of my parking spot.

As I pull onto the road for her development, I see Darren's car pulling in right in front of me past the mailboxes. The sun is starting to set, twilight setting in around the trees that line the road.

We drive up in her yard, and Erik is just getting out of his car. He peeks in the glass of the garage as we get out and walk up to him. "The Tahoe is here, so she must be home."

"Weird there's not hardly any lights on though," Darren says.

We walk up the sidewalk and Erik tries the door. It opens right up. "Damnit Liv, lock the fucking door," he mutters. The light on the doorbell camera system doesn't light up.

Darren flips open the doorbell camera lid. "Um, the battery isn't in here. Maybe she's charging it?"

We both stare at him with questioning looks.

Opening the door, we step inside. The lights are off, except for a light in the kitchen. The back patio door is wide open.

"Liv, where are you?" Erik is calling for her, but we aren't hearing any sounds or movement.

We walk to the patio door, and Darren slides it shut and back open, confused. He calls her name out into the backyard. No response. He looks down at the doorbell camera cover laying on the ground on the patio. There is no battery in this camera either.

"Do you see the camera batteries in the house anywhere?" He asks us, looking around. We split up to look but don't find anything.

"Her purse is back here," I call out to them from the garage entry way.

I open the tiny purse and find her keys, phone, two pill bottles, and her wallet. "Her phone is here," and there is fear rising within me. Why is her car and phone here but she's not?

We search the rest of the house and find nothing. She is nowhere to be found, it's as if she vanished right into thin air.

"We need to call the police," Erik says, panic building on his face.

— — —

About twenty minutes later the Sheriff pulls up into Olivia's driveway in his black squad car. I can see him looking over at us as he shuts the vehicle off.

After calling the police, we called Waylon and Joe. The five of us are standing on Olivia's front porch, anxiously waiting.

"Looks like the whole posse is here huh," he says, getting out and adjusting the belt on his black pants. None of say anything, just give him small smiles or nods, a surreal and uneasy feeling has settled upon us.

"I know four of you, but I don't know who you are," he reaches his hand out to me, and I shake it.

"I'm Jay Jones, Olivia's boyfriend."

"Alright. Nice to meet you. I'm Sheriff Hayden. I've known Liv for a long time. I'll have the three of you that were here when you called follow me through the house and we will replay what you found. I don't want you to touch or disturb anything. If she is missing, anything and everything is evidence. I also want you to tell me what you have already touched and moved when you were in there."

We nod in agreement and turn towards the house. Darren is the first to speak up.

"We helped her install a doorbell camera system for the front door and back patio door awhile back. When we got here, I checked them and noticed that the battery is missing in both, so nothing is recording. I thought maybe they would be in the house charging, but we can't find them anywhere."

The Sheriff writes some notes in his notepad and snaps a picture of the front doorbell camera. We walk him through the main part of the house, noting that nothing looks disturbed to us anywhere.

We cross the house and reach the back patio door.

Darren speaks up again. "When we got here, the patio door was open, just like it is now. I closed and reopened it; in case you dust for prints."

"Our prints will be all over this house, all five of us. And probably a bunch more people that are friends with Liv." Erik adds, a little shortness to his voice.

The Sheriff takes another picture and writes a note.

"The backyard doorbell camera is missing the battery too, and the cover is laying there, on the ground. I think someone messed with them that didn't want to be seen."

The Sheriff inspects the cover and takes a couple pictures. He stays there for a minute, searching for more details. He gets his phone out again and takes a picture of the edge of the patio door, right on the trim.

"Look here, there is a clump of long hair that's stuck. It's not at Liv's normal height for her head, it looks like she was sitting or bending over here, and some got caught." He points at the clump of hairs with his pen and takes a closer picture.

He walks around the back patio, watching where he steps so as not to disturb anything. "You boys stay where you are, we don't want to step on anything that might be important." We obey and watch him scour the backyard.

"Sheriff. There is something you should know," Erik clears his throat.

"What is it, Erik?" He stops and looks at him.

"Well, she has been getting those stalker letters. I know she mentioned it to you. She was still getting them up until, well, this. She had gotten some pictures and there was a dead bird in her mailbox. Did you know about those or just the letters?" I don't give the Sheriff time to respond. "What stalker letters are you talking about? Why didn't she tell me about this?" I'm shocked and a little appalled. There is nothing I want more than to be the one to take care of her and be there for her. Why wouldn't she tell me about this? My pulse quickens and I'm pacing the cement patio.

"Yeah, she told us probably about a few weeks ago. It's why the nights you weren't here we were staying with her; we didn't want her to be alone. It really freaked her out." Darren says, he looks at me and I can tell he's a little uncomfortable.

"Yes, I knew about the pictures and bird too. Once we're done looking around, I'm going to have to confiscate all those letters, hopefully she saved them." Sheriff Hayden says.

I'm still stunned. I watch him continue to walk around the yard. He bends over, eyeing something on the edge of the cement patio.

"I have a large men's boot print here, it looks a little smeared in the dirt, its heading for the direction of the patio door and the hair. Might be nothing but might be something." He takes a picture of it and notes it in his notepad. I can see him glance over sideways and look at all our shoes.

I want to walk forward and look at it but hold myself back.

"Did Liv tell you about the guy watching her in the trees? That was back in like July or August." Erik adds, looking at me with uneasiness.

"I knew about that. That was the night of Tina's bachelorette party. Why didn't she tell me about any of the rest though?"

"She kept saying *she didn't want to bother you with it.* She figured it was just some weirdo and eventually it would end." Darren sounds dejected, like he's filled with regret.

I'm pacing with anxiety. This is horrible and there is nothing I can do about any of it. I head back inside the house and pull up a chair at the dining room table, resting my head in my hands.

The Sheriff, Erik and Darren come back inside.

"Jay found her purse back there," Erik points to the mud room area. They walk over and I can hear a couple snaps of pictures being taken.

"Did she keep those letters? It will be very helpful if we can find them all."

"I think she had them in her room," Darren says, and he turns to head to her bedroom. I follow the group in there.

Darren is opening the nightstand drawers and looks under the bed but finds nothing. He goes into the closet and pulls open a few drawers, finally pulling out a cardboard box. I look over his shoulder and see it's full of letters and ripped open red envelopes. The one in front is cockeyed.

"Oh, by the way, I've touched most of these too, sometimes I would get the mail." The Sheriff has his eyes squared at him, listening intently.

"Holy shit, I hadn't seen this one." He checks the postmark on the first one in the pile. "I bet she opened it on Friday."

He unfolds the piece of printer paper, and we all look over his shoulder and read it.

My dearest Olivia,

Your beauty knows no bounds. You have ruined me to the core so that nobody else will ever compare. I can't wait to set your world on fire.

See you soon,
X

A sob escapes him when he turns over the picture of her sleeping in the light pink nightie.

"Did he fucking come in here and take her picture while she was sleeping?" His voice has changed, a different pitch, fury taking over.

I feel the blood drain from my face. This guy was in her house. My mind starts reeling and I feel sick to my stomach. This can't be happening.

If she got this Friday, then came over to my place and found my box of pictures.... oh my God, she thinks I'm her stalker. It's coming together in a terrible, twisted way.

"Okay boys let's put that back in the box. I'm calling in back up on this. I need all three of you to step outside." We step outside and join Waylon and Joe on the front porch. The Sheriff gets his cell phone out and starts making phone calls from inside the house.

"Well, what's going on," Waylon nervously asks us.

"I think he has enough pieces to put together that she is missing. He's calling for back up right now," Darren choaks out, tears falling from his eyes.

And before I know it, the four of them are hugging and crying. I bury my face in my hands and turn away. I can't handle this.

The Sheriff steps out of the house. He hands each of us his card, pointing out his cell phone number. We are instructed to call him immediately if we hear from her, or if we think of any other details that might help.

He gets out his pen and pad of paper and writes down each of our names and numbers. He said his office will be calling each of us for statements, so that they have everything on file.

I feel a numbness taking over, I collapse to my knees on the patio and sob uncontrollably. This can't be happening.

CHAPTER 53

LIV

I SLOWLY OPEN MY EYES. They are so hazy, it's almost like a cotton ball has been spread across them. It takes me a solid minute to get them to focus and fully open. They feel heavy, like I could go right back to sleep. I try to rub them, but when I move my arms, they won't budge.

I look to the right and see that my wrist is handcuffed. I come to a little more, shaking my arm, it not budging at all. I look to the left and see my other arm is in another handcuff. I'm hooked on to metal bars that are built into the wall behind me.

I'm on a bed, on top of a beige comforter. I look around, panicking, trying to get my bearings. The last thing I remember was standing in my backyard, looking at my doorbell camera. How long have I been sleeping? Where the fuck am I? There is a piece of cardboard duck taped to the bedroom window to my right, and there is a dim lamp on across the room from me.

I try to call out, but my voice is hoarse and dry. I clear it a couple times and try again. I keep repeating this for a minute until finally, my voice makes a sound.

"Hello? Is anyone there? Where the fuck am I? Let me go!" It's not loud or clear, but it was something.

A small red light catches my attention, high in the corner of the room, on a surveillance camera. I stare right at it and say as best I can, "get me the fuck out of here!" I want to scream but can't.

I shake my arms in the handcuffs, but all they do is cut my wrists, stinging.

The bedroom door opens, slowly. This will be the person who decided to shackle me to this fucking bed. My jaw drops in shock.

"John? What the hell? Did you do this to me? Where am I? Let me out of here." I shake my arms again, and I can feel blood running down where the metal has been cutting me.

"Olivia, honey, don't struggle. You're hurting yourself." He sits down on the bed next to me and I attempt to scoot away from him, the cuffs digging even more.

"See, you shouldn't do this. You are too perfect to be scarred like this," he says as he grabs a tissue and wipes the blood off my arms.

"Why the hell do you have me handcuffed? What day is it? Is it only you here?" I have so many questions I don't even know which one I want answered first.

"Today is Monday. We've been together since I got you at your house on Saturday morning." He is talking so calm, as if this is something so normal, like he does it often. "I have been watching you honey. I could tell your door cameras were dead, they weren't lighting up. But I took them apart anyway just in case."

"It's Monday? Have I been asleep since Saturday? Why would you do this to me? Why were you watching me?" I feel hysterical.

"I gave you a little something to help you sleep, so you wouldn't panic. I can see we might need a bit more, as you aren't comfortable here yet."

"No, shit!" I try and scream it at him. If looks could kill, he would be dead.

"Now sweetie. That is no way to talk to me. I am here to take care of you and give you a good life. If you just stay calm, we will both get what we want and be happy together."

"Fuck that. All I want is to get away from you." I try to kick my legs at him, but they are weak. He grabs a hold of my ankles and holds them to the bed.

"Well, have it your way. I need to go to work today, so looks like you will be napping again. And if you try and kick me, I'll shackle your legs too, so don't push it." He grabs my arm, finding a vein. He grabs a syringe from his pocket and stabs me with it.

"What is that?" I try to move away, but I can't. I can feel the strain of metal against my wrists.

"Just a little something to help you relax. I will be home from work later and we can work things out then. I can't wait to spend time with you, my beautiful girl." He leans over and kisses my cheek.

I feel my head getting heavy, my eyelids heavy. I try to move my mouth and form words, but nothing comes out.

The blackness takes over again.

CHAPTER 54

JAY

IT'S TUESDAY. IT'S BEEN FOUR days since Olivia was last seen or heard from.

The police combed through her house, looking for any pieces of evidence they could find. Sheriff Hayden told me that the hair on the patio door was "interesting". It had bothered me that he used that word. That hair came off my girlfriend's head, it's not "interesting".

He said he found men's boot prints in the backyard, coming from the trees behind the house.

When they investigated in the trees, he said they found lots of prints, as if someone had been there many times. It looked as if someone also came in and tried to cover up as many of them as possible.

They have taken the letters and are examining them. The Sheriff said in the first review there wasn't any obvious clues about who sent them.

AO had to put out a statement that they are canceling their shows for the foreseeable future, until they find Olivia.

Of course, the media has taken this and put two and two together, and Olivia's missing person story is plastered all over the news. At first it irritated me but after talking with the Sheriff, he said that the publicity is good, the more people that know she's missing, the more people will be on the lookout for her.

The police have blocked off the development where she lives. People had been driving in her yard and putting flowers and things everywhere. Now they can't get that far and have resorted to leaving things by her mailbox.

This morning the police organized a couple walks around wooded and grass covered areas near her house. It was a huge turnout. They had dogs with them too, but nothing turned up. The only scent any dogs have caught of her were in her yard, and in the backyard by the trees where the Sheriff found all the footprints.

— — —

I decide I'm going to go to the pharmacy to get some medication to help me sleep. I don't think I've had more than a few hours since Friday night.

I walk into the pharmacy, the bell on the door dinging behind me. It's cold and has a sterile smell and the fluorescent lights hurt my eyes. I walk toward the back to the tall counter, and I see an older woman on the phone, and the top of a man's head as he is working on something I can't see.

"Can you help me?" I ask the man.

His head pops up and I recognize him. It's the guy that brought flowers to Olivia on her birthday. John. I think she said his name is John.

He clears his throat and eyes me up for a second, not smiling at me.

"How can I help you?" He clears his throat and asks in a professional tone.

"I have insomnia, I'm wondering if you have something to help me sleep that is non-addicting."

"Yes, go into aisle number three behind you, you will see a bottle of Z-Quil. That's what I would do if I were you. You can take a little more than recommended."

"Thank you." I start to turn away. "You are John, correct? You know Olivia."

"Yes, Olivia and I know each other."

There is something about the way he said that. Almost possessive. I can't quite put my finger on it, but it seems a little off. He's still not smiling at me, like I'm bothering him.

"Thank you," I turn and grab two bottles of what he recommended. I walk to the front of the store to the check out. I don't want to talk to him more than I need to.

As I'm walking back to my truck, my phone rings. It's my mom.

"Hey mom," I say, there is a clear lack of emotion in my voice.

"Hey sweetie. How are you doing today? Any news on Liv? I am so worried about both of you."

"Not doing great. Just left the pharmacy, I bought some medicine to help me sleep. No new news on Olivia, the search parties came up empty handed." I can feel tears pricking in the back of my eyes.

"How can I help? What do you need us to do?" That's mom, always willing to help others.

"Nothing really. I have no idea. I don't even know what to do with myself."

"I'll tell you what. I'll come there tomorrow and just stay with you. You need someone to watch over you too. I'll bring food and help you with whatever you need. Sound good?"

"Sounds good mom. Thank you. Just text me when you are on your way."

"Love you sweetie. And don't worry, they will find her."

"Love you too mom."

I sure hope so. I won't survive without her.

CHAPTER 55

LIV

JOHN TELLS ME IT'S WEDNESDAY.
My brain is fuzzy, but I think this is five days with him now.
During the days he leaves for work. He keeps giving me shots
of something, and it makes my entire day fill with blackness.

My head always feels heavy when I'm awake. I've been
shackled in this bed for days and every part of my body is aching.
I feel like if I would try and stand up, my legs wouldn't remember
how to walk. Every second I'm awake all I want is to see Jay. I
keep imagining him busting through the door with the police to
rescue me from this hell.

The bedroom door opens, and John steps in. My heart sinks.
He changed into a plain white T-shirt and some gray sweatpants
after he got back from work.

"Time for a bath honey," he says it in an endearing way with
a smile, but it just makes my skin crawl.

He leans in over me, kissing me on the lips, and I impulsively
try to wiggle away from him, turning my head, the restraints
pulling at my wrists again. Blood has run down my arms and
crusted on to me. It's on the bed and in my hair. He grabs my
jaw hard and turns my head back toward him, kissing me again,
harder. Tears are rolling down my cheeks.

The first day I was here, he left me in bed in the clothes I had
on. I don't remember it, but he must have given me a bath, and
he put pink lingerie on me.

Each evening he gives me a bath and changes the lingerie, and leaves me here with no blankets, no food, no water, strapped in like an animal. My gut tells me to try and fight him off or outsmart him, but I can't move and I'm so dehydrated, I'm unable to put up any kind of a fight.

"You really need to stop fighting these cuffs, they are hurting your wrists."

"Maybe you shouldn't have put them on me then," I try and spit it out as mean as I can, but my throat is so dry it gets choked out. My lips are so dry they have been bleeding.

"If you are a good girl in the bath tonight, I will give you some water." He's talking to me like I'm a fucking three-year-old. But the second I hear the word water I start salivating, craving it.

"Remember, if you fight me at all I will put the cuffs back on, and I can always add more." He's giving me a stern look and taps on my ankle.

He pulls a key out of his sweatpants pocket and unhooks the cuffs. I try and move my arms down by my sides, but they hurt so bad I can't move them. John pulls them down, and tears break out of my eyes, my arms are searing with pain.

"A hot bath will take care of that." He says, bringing me into his arms.

He brings me into the master bathroom and lays me down in the clawfoot tub. It is cold on my skin and makes me shiver. He removes my bra and panties and puts them on the floor. He grabs a jug of bubble bath from the cabinet and pours some into the tub, plugs the drain and starts running the hot water.

I try to move my arms to cover myself, but they just won't work right. He doesn't take his eyes off me the entire time the water is filling up, looking me up and down like he owns me.

"You know, I think I will take a bath with you tonight."

My eyes widen in horror. No. No. No. It's bad enough that he washes me every night. The last thing I want is him in here with me. He turns the lights down low and lights a candle that is sitting on the vanity countertop.

He stands next to the tub, still watching me. He removes his T-shirt and tosses it on the floor. He takes the handcuff keys out of his pocket and sets them on the vanity. He removes the rest of his clothing, leaving it in a pile. I refuse to look anywhere but his eyes. He shuts the water off after a couple grueling minutes. I'm so scared that I'm shaking and can't stop. The blood on my wrists has tinted the tub water pink.

"I've waited a long time for this Olivia. I've known you all your life, I've been waiting so long for you to grow up and be mine." He steps into the large tub, lifting me forward so he can slide in behind me. The feel of his skin against mine is repulsive. I wish so bad that I had any amount of energy to run away from him or try to fight him.

He grabs a rag and starts running it over my skin. He starts with my arms and neck and moves to my breasts. I can feel him harden behind me, and I squirm with all my might to move away from him. I move my arms as much as possible, and I'm able to scratch his legs hard with my nails.

He stops washing me and grabs the side of my head, turning my right ear toward him. "Olivia, remember honey, if you scratch, bite, or do anything to hurt me, you will regret it."

He leans close, his mouth touching my ear, and whispers slowly. "I'll make you crawl, and fucking beg in return. You will only be hurting yourself."

My eyes widen in alarm.

He releases his hand from the side of my head and moves it to my shoulder. I can feel him drop the rag next to my arm. He puts his right hand on my other shoulder, and before I know it, he pushes me down, submerging me under the hot bath water. He pulls me back up by my hair, twisting my head so he can see my face. My breaths are quick and staggered. He pushes me down one more time, holding me under, finally dragging me back up. I'm coughing, hot soapy water filling my mouth and lungs, and I feel like I can't catch my breath no matter how hard I try.

"There are consequences of you breaking my rules. You will pay. Don't forget that." He releases his hand from my wet hair and my head flops back forward.

He picks the washcloth back up and begins to wash me, running it over me, and there is nothing I can do to stop him. I continue to look forward to the front of the tub, trying to regain my breathing. He's still hard behind me, it terrifies me that he is finding enjoyment in this.

After the long and antagonizing bath, he pulls me out of the tub like a rag doll and carries me back into the bedroom, laying me on the bed. He opens the nightstand drawer, and it's full of lingerie.

"I think this looks good," and he holds up a black lace nightie.

He slips it over me, pulling it down, and adjusts me on to the bed and fastens the handcuffs tightly around my wrists. I start crying so hard I can't breathe.

"I did promise you water, but you weren't a good girl, so you don't get much," he says, and takes a cup and spills the tiniest splash of water into my mouth. It isn't nearly enough, but I'm going to savor anything I can get.

He has his gray sweatpants on again, and he grabs a blanket and pillow from the closet.

"Time for bed honey," he looks at me lovingly. It makes me want to throw up.

This is the worst. He lays in bed next to me at night cuddled up and holding on to me like I'm his favorite toy, rubbing his disgusting hands all over me. He covers himself with a blanket but not me, and before he falls asleep, he just stares at me, looking me up and down like he's studying me.

"But first, time for your bedtime meal." My ears perk up at the thought of food. Am I going to be lucky enough to have food today? I haven't had any since I've been here.

He grabs a saltine cracker off the tray on the nightstand, and a small glass of water. I barely manage to choke down the cracker, my throat is so dry it feels like I'm trying to swallow razor blades. He gives me only one small sip of water, and I close my eyes for a second, the relief of a little water making me feel slightly better. It doesn't last long though, before I know it; another syringe is being shoved into my arm, and the blackness takes over for the night.

At least tonight I won't have to be conscious while he lays next to me. I'd rather be dead than give him what he wants.

CHAPTER 56

JAY

OLIVIA HAS BEEN GONE SEVEN days now if you go by the last day that I talked to her. It's Friday.

Mom has been staying with me since Wednesday, helping me take care of myself, and helping me keep organized and on top of different search missions and things I can help with.

She contacted Sheriff Hayden Wednesday after she got here and asked if there was anything she could do. They formulated a plan to have a vigil tonight in Central Park in Pine Lake. She told me not to worry about any details, and that she would get me there.

I've turned into a shell of a person. I can barely keep food down, and according to Erik yesterday I "look like hell." In my defense he didn't look any better, but I didn't tell him that.

— — —

It's 7:00 and we are at Central Park for the vigil. Mom and I drove here, and the rest of AO was told to get here around the same time. We wanted to be the first ones, aside from the police.

The Sheriff mentioned that they like to see who attends these things, sometimes if a person is kidnapped, the kidnapper will show up and try to get involved in some way.

I'm sitting in a folding chair next to the AO guys, none of us talking. All of us wishing we were in a different situation.

Mom told dad, Brandon, and Amanda to come as well. They are talking to a couple of the officers now.

Amanda keeps coming up and giving me hugs. Every time she does, I can't stand seeing the miserable look in her eyes, and I know it's just a reflection of me. I keep looking away.

People are starting to gather, cars are filling in from every direction, and before we know it, the park is packed. I look out in the crowd but all I see is a blur of faces. Some of Olivia's family, the AO boys, and my family and I are sitting in a white gazebo in the middle of the park. There are lights on and everyone in the crowd is staring at us. I try to look at them, but the pain of it all is burning into me.

Sheriff Hayden approaches a microphone on a podium in the front of the gazebo, giving it a tap to make sure it's on. He's standing next to a large picture of Olivia on a metal pedestal. It's her Facebook profile picture. When I look at it, my heart feels like it could explode.

What if this is all I have left of her now too? Just pictures. It will be just like Casey. I can't go through that much loss again, especially not with her.

"Good evening, folks. For those of you who don't know me, my name is Sheriff Terry Hayden. First off, thank you to everyone for coming out tonight and showing your support for Olivia Dunne and her beloved family and friends. We want everyone to know where we are at in our investigation. We have searched Olivia's property and have also run a multitude of different search parties in the vicinity. Currently, we have not turned up any trace of her. We will be continuing to do two search parties each day. You can sign up to participate in them, at the website listed at the bottom of this poster next to me. We are investigating all tips that are reported to us, so if you have any information on her whereabouts, please report it to our office. We are doing everything in our power to bring Olivia home safe, and soon. Let's bow our heads in a moment of prayer."

I lean my head down into my hands and sob uncontrollably. I don't care if anyone sees or hears me. Mom puts her arm around my shoulders and brings me in for a hug.

I don't think there is a dry eye in the entire park.

CHAPTER 57

LIV

JOHN TELLS ME IT'S SATURDAY morning. I can't even calculate how many days I've been here; my brain is so foggy. I've lost the ability to move my limbs, and I can no longer formulate a sentence.

John says it's time to see "the rest of my new home". He rolls a wheelchair into the bedroom, and places it next to the bed. He removes the handcuff keys from his pocket and unlocks me. My wrists are raw and burning with pain. I can't even turn my head to look and see how deep the cuts are.

He moves my arms down to my sides, my joints cracking as he does so. I take a sharp breath as the pain hits me, but I can't do anything about it. I feel like my muscles are completely gone.

He picks me up and sets me in the wheelchair. He's trying to adjust me so I sit up, but I can't, I keep falling forward.

"Shit," he spits out in frustration. "This won't work, I'll be right back."

He grabs a handcuff and the key and attaches me to the wheelchair. It doesn't matter, I don't have the strength to go anywhere.

He leaves the room, coming back a couple minutes later. He has a tie strap in his hand. He runs the tie strap around my chest, and tightens it around the chair, latching it so it keeps me sitting up straight. I can feel it digging into my chest as it pulls me tight into the seat. He starts to unlock the handcuff, then stops, deciding to leave it on.

"Better safe than sorry," he says, giving me a dark look. His looks toward me seem to be getting more sinister, or at least that's how it feels to me. I've learned to accept the times when I am unconscious now, so I don't have to witness him touching me and giving me these dark looks. He bathes with me every night now. I haven't bothered to fight back since I can't, and I don't want him to drown me in the tub.

He turns and rolls the chair out of the room. I don't think I've ever left this room, other than to go into the bathroom. My head lolls as the wheelchair goes down the hall.

From my first and fuzzy impressions the house seems well kept and clean, but almost sterile feeling, as if it's staged. All white walls, wood floors, and furniture that looks like it's never been used. I'm sure I won't be sitting on the furniture; I'll be confined to my chair and tie strap during my first field trip.

"I bet you didn't know this about me, but I love to paint. You and I are going to paint a picture today." He says, sounding pleased with himself. I'm just confused. Maybe I didn't hear him right, but I thought he said we are going to paint.

We keep crossing the house slowly, passing the living room, dining room and kitchen.

The kitchen. I want food. And water. I need water. I haven't eaten a meal since I've been here. If I had energy I would jump out of this chair and sprint into the kitchen, like my life depends on it. *My life does depend on it*, I think to myself.

We turn into a room with double doors. Looks like it's meant to be an office. It has light blue walls and hardwood floors, he has carboard duck taped over this window too.

There is a drop cloth on the floor. *Fuck, is this where I get murdered?* He brings me to a stop in the middle of the room, locking the wheels on the chair.

In front of me there is an easel with a large white canvas on it and a table with paint brushes next to it. The only other thing in the room is a blown-up photograph hanging on the wall. It's the picture we took together at Tim and Tina's wedding.

"You and I are going to create a beautiful picture together Olivia," he says as he turns away for a moment and picks up a knife. My eyes widen in shock, and I try to move in my chair, which turns into almost unnoticeable movement.

"The more you move the more it will hurt. You must trust me and let me do what I need to."

He removes his gray T-shirt and tosses it on the floor.

"Do you know what my favorite color is, honey? You should know from my letters. It's *red*. I love red." His eyes gleam something dark when he says it.

"And by the way, this is my favorite lingerie on you yet." It's a white bra and panty set made of lace. "I picked this out for today, but tonight you will be wearing red. Tonight will be our first night making love."

A groan escapes my throat and I try and move in my chair. I need to get out of here.

"Hey!" He screams in my face, spitting on me. "You will cooperate today; you know there will be consequences if you don't."

Tears are rolling down my cheeks, my eyes burning. I think they might be the last ones I have left in me. I can't do this much longer. I miss Jay. I miss my parents. I am so alone and I'm terrified.

He turns to the side, inhaling and exhaling a couple deep breaths, and drags the knife across his chest, below his collarbone, blood seeping out in its wake.

He sets the knife back on the table, takes another deep breath, puts on a frightening smile, and grabs a paintbrush. He slowly smears it in his blood, and streaks it across the blank white canvas, making the left half of a heart. What. The. Fuck.

He keeps painting, moving his brush slowly around on the canvas, humming as he does it. He sets it down, picks up the knife, and makes another slice in his chest, more blood flowing out of him, he groans in pain. It's antagonizing to watch. He fills in the outline of the heart on the canvas as blood drips down his chest. He takes it off the easel and lays it on the table, frustrated with how much blood is dripping down the canvas.

Once he's done with it, he grabs some bandages and rubbing alcohol and cleans and dresses his wounds. He cut deep from the look of it. There is a lot of blood on that canvas. Blood has run down his chest and on to his pants, and tiny drops have splattered on the drop cloth.

He faces away from me for a minute, taking deep breaths, I can see his shoulders moving as he inhales and exhales.

He turns back to me, stone-faced, and picks the knife back up, turning it in his hand a couple times.

"Alright honey, now it's your turn." There is an unsettling look on his face, with a sinister smile. He seems like a completely different person than the man I previously knew, with a completely different personality.

He comes toward me, and I suck in as deep of a breath as I can, trying to steel myself. I feel the sharp piercing of the knife dig in below my collarbone. It drags slowly to the center of my chest, with a burning sharpness of the blade. I can feel the blood running down the front of me. I start to let my head bob, not wishing to be conscious anymore.

"Wake up. You are part of this, you need to watch," he's shouting in my face.

He sets the knife down and picks up the blood-filled paintbrush. He swipes it over my chest, coating it with my blood.

He swoops it over the canvas and makes the outline of the right half of the heart.

My head feels so heavy, and I can barely keep my eyes open. Every time he comes back for more blood, he wakes me back up. I hear him let out a frustrated groan, and he picks up the knife again.

"We need more," he says, his brow furrowing.

"Let's try a new spot, just for fun." He leans down and begins to slice at my stomach, by my belly button. I can't tell how deep it is, but it's the same sharp burning pain as in my chest, this one might hurt worse. I try to scream but I'm so weak all I can do is sob, shaking violently in the wheelchair.

"That was good, much better, this should be enough to finish."

I can feel blood running down my stomach and onto my thighs. My eyes are so heavy, and I can't hold my neck up anymore.

I let the blackness consume me.

CHAPTER 58

JAY

IT'S SATURDAY AFTERNOON ABOUT 4:30.
I've participated in all the search parties. Every time we come back empty handed; I get more discouraged. Mom, dad, Brandon, and Amanda are here too and have been going with me to all of them.

I'm sitting on the couch, hands at my sides, limp. Mom walks over from my kitchen and hands me a hot cup of coffee. "Here Jay, have some of this," she says in a quiet voice. I'm not sure how many more days I can take of this. "Jay, what do you need? How can I help?" She is rubbing my arm, but it all feels so numb.

"I need her mom. I just need to see her."

"Let's see. Do you have any pictures of her?" She's trying to sound optimistic, trying to cheer me up, but I can see right through it.

"On my phone. And, well, I have some in print too I guess." Instantly I feel a pang of guilt that I still have the box of photos under my bed.

I set down the cup of coffee and head slowly toward my bed, kneeling and grabbing the box. I walk back to the couch and sit down, holding it in my lap.

"These are all of her. I took them. I shouldn't have taken them." I break down in sobs, mom rubs my back, trying to calm me down.

I let the tears fall for a minute before opening the box. I remove the lid and pull each picture out slowly, examining each one as if it's saving my life.

I get about halfway through the pile, mom is looking at them after I set them down next to me.

"You must love her so much, Jay." I hear her say it, but something catches my eye. I don't respond.

I pick the pile of pictures up that sits between mom and me. I start at the beginning, filtering through them. I set a couple aside. Quickly I scramble, going through the entire box.

"What's going on? Is everything okay?" Mom sounds concerned. Dad, Brandon, and Amanda walk over to where we are sitting on the couch.

"These pictures. He's in some. Oh my God. It's him, I know who has her!" I jump up, pictures flying everywhere, a small stack still in my hands.

My family looks startled and confused. "It's John, John, the pharmacist. He was stalking her, and I have proof. I've captured him in the background of some of these pictures!"

My dad grabs the stack from me and starts filtering through them. He holds one up in front of him, confused.

"This guy here," I point to a man standing outside a silver car across a parking lot, holding a camera. In another I see him at her concert, right in the front of the stage where she is. Another one I can see him at the end of the aisle at Target, holding up his phone like he's taking a picture of her.

"Wait, were you also following her?" Brandon asks, confused by the pictures.

"Yes. She found out and we got in a fight." I'm speaking so fast they probably can't understand me. "We need to call Sheriff Hayden." I bend over and grab my phone, quickly pulling up his number.

I pace away from them and Sheriff Hayden answers after a couple rings.

"Hello Jay. How can I help?" His deep voice rumbling through the phone.

"I know who has Olivia!" I'm almost shouting at him, the words coming out quickly.

"What? Slow down. Are you sure? Who is it? Tell me what you know."

"I have pictures, he's in multiple of them. He follows her. Oh my God, he stopped at her house on her birthday, so he knows where she lives. We need to get to his house right now!"

"Jay, who are you talking about?"

"John. His name is John. He's...he's, her pharmacist."

"Do you know his last name?"

"No, just that it's John, and that he's her pharmacist, and he was kind of friends with her dad."

I'm pacing around like a maniac.

"Okay, Jay, stay where you are. Keep calm. I'm going to call this in, and we are on it. Thank you, son. We will let you know what we can find out." He hangs up.

I'm fidgety and can't sit still. I know where he works. I grab my keys off the kitchen counter and run downstairs. I hear my family calling after me, but I let it all dissipate behind me.

I jump in my truck, peeling away out of my spot in front of the studio. I head across town to the pharmacy. This was where I got my sleeping medicine. That creep was there that day.

I pull up to a jerky stop in front of the pharmacy. I'm in handicapped parking but don't give a shit. I run inside, hoping someone will help me.

I reach the back and see the older woman from the other day. "Hey, can you help me?" She looks up, startled.

"Um, I hope so. We are about to close. What do you need?"

"The pharmacist that works here, his name is John, right?"

"Yes."

"What is his last name and where does he live?"

She is giving me a skeptical look. "Well, his name is John DeMarcus, but I can't tell you where he lives, that's private information," she says with a tight-lipped look on her face.

I run out of the pharmacy and back to my truck, grabbing my phone and pull up Google.

I do a search to find the property tax listings for our county. I get the website pulled up, and type in his last name. I find his listing and his address flashes on to my phone. Jackpot. I type the address into my phone for the directions.

I call Sheriff Hayden back. He answers immediately.

"Sheriff, Jay here again. It's John DeMarcus. I have his address." I start telling him the address and he stops me.

"Jay, we just figured it out too, we are on our way there now. Do not attempt to get there before us, do you hear me? Stay where you are."

"Yes sir," I say, but I'm already pulling out of my spot. I'll at least get almost all the way there.

I immediately call Erik. He answers right away, and before he can even say "hello", I'm filling him in on the details.

"I know where she is. John DeMarcus has her. Look up his address and meet me there. Police are on their way. Call the rest of the guys." I don't even let him say anything before I hang up, I just need them to know right now.

I follow my GPS directions, and it's taking me out in the direction of Olivia's place. I'm confused, are they neighbors? I go past the left turn for her road, and go about a half mile more, and it's telling me to turn left. *Holy shit, he lives right near her. That's how he could watch her through the trees, he walked over there.* It all makes so much sense now.

I can see flashing lights coming up fast behind me, so I pull over to the side of the road to let them pass.

Five squad cars and the Sheriff's SUV fly by me, turning in. I go in slowly behind them, following the road to the second driveway, where they've come to a stop.

I turn the truck off and get out, not getting far away from it. I don't want to interfere, but I need to know what's happening. They have a huge white stucco house surrounded. One of the officers tries the lock on the door. It doesn't budge, so he steels himself and kicks it open. They file in and now I have no idea what's going on. My hands begin to shake; I'm so nervous.

A couple minutes pass and I'm worried, but I will myself to stay where I am. I don't want anything I do to jeopardize Olivia being rescued, hopefully alive. Hopefully I'm right that John has her. It just all seems to fit.

An ambulance pulls up into the yard, getting as close to the front door as possible.

I hear voices on the road behind me. One by one the AO boys show up, each in their own vehicles, they run up to me.

"What's going on?" Erik says breathlessly.

"They busted the door open a couple minutes ago. I haven't seen or heard anything yet."

The guy's filter in around me, anxiousness bubbling from all of us. Tears are starting to fall.

"What if she's dead," Darren is taking shallow breaths, bent down on the ground.

I hear tires. I see a white van pull up at the bottom of the driveway.

A female reporter and a guy with a camera get out and set up by the van. The local news. Neighbors are starting to filter in next to them, looks of concern cover their faces.

My phone keeps ringing, a combination of dad, mom, Brandon, and Amanda. This time it's Amanda. I decide to answer.

"Hey, can't talk long. At John's house. Police are here, they got in. Don't have any updates yet."

"Okay thanks, call us the second you know *anything*. Love you." She hangs up.

"Look, there's movement in there," Joe says, pointing to the house.

I look up and see two police officers escorting John out of the house in handcuffs. He has no shirt on, and there are two bandages on his chest. He's screaming at them and kicking his legs, trying to get away. One officer opens the back door of a squad car and the other shoves him into the back. One of the officers gets in the driver's seat and pulls away, the other one getting in a second car and follows behind them.

As he passes by, I see him in the back of the car. His eyes are menacing and he's lashing out screaming something. We make eye contact, and he yells something at me through the glass.

I go back to focusing on the front door, waiting to see Olivia. Every second feels like an hour. Finally, one of the police officers runs to the front door from the inside. "We need a stretcher," he tells the paramedic. My hearts sinks and I kneel on the ground, trying to steady myself.

"A stretcher? Is she alive?" Waylon asks out loud.

I get up and start walking toward the front door. I'm not standing by anymore. The guys are right behind me. We stand on the sidewalk, next to the back of the ambulance. From this point we can see inside the house a little but aren't in the way.

The paramedic has the stretcher ready to go and pulls it in through the front door. Our eyes follow him. He turns a corner, and I've lost him. I can hear muffled voices from inside the house. This is killing me.

"I'm going in. Wait here, I need to see what's going on." The guys look at me, nodding their heads in agreement.

I step inside, unsure of where I'm going or what I'm going to see. I listen and follow the voices. It's coming from the right, down a hallway.

I'm outside the door. I take a deep breath before looking into what appears to be a bedroom.

Staying against the wall, I peer in. Two police officers are scouring the room, looking for something. Sheriff Hayden is next to the bed, and two paramedics are on the other side, one prepping the stretcher, and one checking on Olivia.

Olivia. My heart is pounding inside my chest.

She is on the bed, her arms spread out and handcuffed to metal poles on the walls. There is blood running down her arms, chest, and legs. She has white lingerie on, and most of it's covered in blood. There is a cut by her collarbone and one on her stomach. She looks pale and gray, like she could be dead.

Sheriff Hayden looks up, noticing me, scrambling over.

"What the hell are you doing in here? Get out!"

"With all due respect sir, no way. What can I do?"

"We are looking for keys, we can't get the handcuffs undone."

"Found it." A young officer holds up keys, finding them in the pocket of some sweatpants on the floor.

"Thank God," the Sheriff says as he moves toward the officer, grabbing the keys from him.

He quickly releases the cuffs, Olivia's arms falling slightly slack, but not much.

"Move her as little as possible, we don't know if anything is broken yet," the paramedic directs.

They lay a small orange stretcher on the bed next to her, the two paramedics pick her up and slide her over onto it gently. She doesn't seem very responsive. I haven't seen her eyes open yet.

They move her on to the main stretcher and get her strapped in.

"We can't go outside with her like this, cover her with a blanket," one of them says. An officer grabs the comforter off the bed and lays it over her.

I step out of the way as they begin to roll her through the house and toward the front door.

Tears are flowing out of me. I just want my baby to breathe and be okay.

I follow them out the door, and the guys have moved to the side of the ambulance, letting them get through. Pain is ripping through the group, and I know exactly how it feels.

They get her into the back of the ambulance. Sheriff Hayden is still in the house, and the other officers are outside, directing the reporter and neighbors to stay off the property.

"Can I ride with her to the hospital?" I ask one of the paramedics.

"Are you family?"

"Well, no," I say.

"Then no, we can't let you. Sorry."

He turns back around and is hooking Olivia up to a machine, things beeping and flashing. They have pulled the comforter off the top half of her body. I can hear them saying things to each other, but none of it makes sense to me.

The ambulance driver comes to the back and shuts the doors. They begin to pull away, lights and sirens piercing the silence of the early evening.

"I'm following that ambulance," I say as I turn and run back to my truck.

CHAPTER 59

JAY

THEY WON'T LET ANY OF us see her.

She is still in the emergency wing of the Pine Lake Hospital, and the time is dragging on painstakingly slow.

The AO boys and I sit in the hallway outside of her operating room, this was as close as they would let us get. My family is in the waiting room, along with Tim, Tina, Lexie, and some other friends of Olivia's. Some of her aunts, uncles and cousins have shown up too, but now is not the time for me meet any of them. I need to be here for her, even if it means just sitting here in a hallway.

Finally, the emergency room door opens, and we all stand. I can see her on a bed, but there are white blankets all around her, I can't see what she looks like. Nurses are prepping her and rearranging things, and a doctor is washing his hands in a sink with his back to us.

It takes them about a minute, but they finally start to wheel her out into the hall, slowly. The nurses glance up at us, and exchange looks with each other.

They pass her by us, stopping. I look down at Olivia, she has no color in her face. The rest of her is covered in the white sheet.

"Is she okay? Is she going to make it?" I barely choke it out.

"She will make it. It will take some time to recover. We are bringing her to a permanent room now." They start walking away with her, not willing to give us any more time.

I didn't even get to touch her. I just want her to know I'm here. We all quietly follow the nurses and Olivia through the halls. I'm not sure if we're supposed to but I don't care.

We turn a corner in one of the hospital wings and Sheriff Hayden is sitting on a chair outside a room with a door and a small window. He nods and gives a small smile as the nurses approach. We stay back a little bit, and he speaks to them for a minute before they bring her into her room.

"Hey guys." He says to us, a somber look on his face.

"Sounds like everything went okay in there. She will be in here during recovery. We will have an officer sitting outside, to ensure nobody bothers her while she's here."

"Can we go in?" I ask with trepidation.

"I don't mind if you do, but you will have to wait and see what the doctor says, he has the final say in everything from here on out. Stay in the hall here until he comes in. Hopefully it won't be long."

"Thank you. Thank you for everything," I lean in and give him a hug. He hugs me back, pulling away with tears in his eyes.

"I'm so glad she's okay, and that she has all of you," he says, looking around to the group. "You boys really care about her."

He places his hat back on his head and starts down the hallway. "And you know, Jay, good job on figuring this out. She might not have made it if it weren't for you."

Heavy tears are falling down my cheeks and I feel like I'm choking on my breath. I don't know what to say, so I just give him a smile and wave goodbye.

About ten minutes later, we are still congregating in the hallway when the doctor walks up. "Hello, I'm Doctor Monson, I'll be looking over Ms. Dunne."

"Can we go in and see her?" Erik asks quickly.

"You can go in. Only this group though. She has been through a lot. She has two lacerations, one on her chest, and one on her stomach. I was able to stitch them up and hopefully they will heal just fine. She has been severely dehydrated and starved for a week now. We have also run toxicology tests on her, as we saw that she has many needle pricks in her arms that were not doctor administered. Once we know what he was injecting into her, that will help immensely. She has also been contained by handcuffs for a week and has some pretty bad damage on her wrists. I did have to stitch multiple places on both, and we have them wrapped now. We are not sure yet if she was sexually assaulted but have run a rape kit on her. We have lots to follow up on, but things could have been a lot worse. She will be okay."

I let out my breath. I think I was holding it the entire time he was talking.

"Thank you doctor," Erik tells him.

"You can be in there but leave enough space around her so we can move around. I want you to remain quiet, so that she stays relaxed." He motions for us to step inside the room.

Two nurses are working in tandem to get her situated in the bed with all the things she needs. Her eyes still aren't open.

"She will be sedated for a while, you can speak to her quietly, she shouldn't wake up. We need her to rest as much as possible, do not try and wake her." He says and starts looking at charts on the computer next to her bed.

— — —

The guys stay in her room with her for about twenty more minutes. An officer has shown up and is taking his post in the chair across the hallway from her door.

"Well, we are going to head out. Darren and Lexie are going to work on packing up a bag of things for her at her place and they will bring it in tomorrow morning," Erik tells me.

"Sounds good. Hey, will you guys do me a favor?"

"Absolutely, what do you need?" Waylon says right away.

"Can you update everyone in the waiting room? And tell one of my family members to go to my place and pack me a bag? I want to stay here with her."

"Sure," Waylon brings me in for a hug. Everyone joins in and we group together, tears of both sadness and joy pouring out of us. They say goodbye and head out the door as a group. I'm finally alone with my girl.

I approach her bed on her right side. Her monitors are making a slow and continuous beeping sound. She looks pale, and I can hear a little hiss sound at the breathing tube blowing air into her nose.

I pull up a chair next to her bed. I grab her right hand and hold it in mine, gently kissing it.

"I love you." I tell her quietly and lay my head down on the bed next to her.

CHAPTER 60

LIV

I SEE JOHN'S FACE. DISTORTED, angry, glaring at me. He isn't impressed with the picture of the heart. I hear beeping. *What is it?* It makes me nervous. He makes me nervous. The beeping is getting louder, faster. My eyelids still feel heavy, but they want to open. *Why won't they open?* The beeping is loud now, quick.

I feel a hand on my shoulder, its warm and soft. I still can't open my eyes. I try to open my mouth, but I have forgotten how to speak. *What's wrong with me?*

The hand is squeezing me harder now, the beeping is still loud in my head. I open my eyes a little. Everything is fuzzy. I start to make out a shape. Hair. I think it's a woman, standing over me. *Where am I?*

I open my eyes more and hear a voice. A woman's voice. "Olivia, my name is Jen. I'm your nurse. You are safe in the hospital." The words sound like mush in my brain, running together in one long sound.

I keep trying to open my eyes, it's all so blurry. Something touches my other side. My hand. I know this feeling.

"Hey babe, its Jay. I'm right here next to you." His words are smoother in my head, a familiar sound that I've been waiting to hear.

I give his hand a squeeze. I have barely any strength, he probably didn't even feel it.

"I think she just tried to squeeze my hand," I hear him tell the woman.

"Good. That's a good sign."

He squeezes mine back and I do it again. I want to see him. I keep trying to open my eyes. Finally, I get them all the way open, blinking once. My eyelids are still so heavy they don't stay open long, but I keep trying.

I get them open enough to see Jay. He's crying, holding my hand. He leans down and kisses it. I wish I could wrap my arms around him. I wish I could talk.

I try to speak but nothing comes out except a little groan.

"Hey, it's okay. Just keep resting. I'm right here."

I give his hand one more squeeze and drift off to sleep. The beeping is much quieter now.

CHAPTER 61

JAY

AFTER OLIVIA TRIED TO WAKE up, I called the guys. And my parents. And Brandon and Amanda. And Sheriff Hayden. I wanted to tell the whole world she tried to wake up.

She is still under heavy sedation. But each day I can see she has a little more color in her face. She slept the rest of Saturday night, all day Sunday, and now its Monday morning.

I have yet to leave. Darren was able to drop off a bag for me yesterday that my mom packed, and a bag for her in case she needs anything, which Lexie packed.

The officer let her come in this morning with Darren. Lexie held her hand and talked to her while I took a shower in her bathroom. I feel like a new person.

I'm sitting on my phone, the late morning sun shining in on my back. I'm still so wound up; all I want to do is talk to her. Until then though, I will happily take the fact that I know she is safe.

A nurse walks in, this one is new. She introduces herself as Sara and proceeds to check her charts. As she's working on getting acclimated, Dr. Monson steps in the doorway. "Jay, how are you doing today?"

"Pretty good. Finally got a shower in. I feel like a brand-new person."

"That's good news. Don't hesitate to ask any of us if there is anything you need, we're happy to help."

"Thank you."

"So, good news for you today. Since she did try and wake up a little more yesterday, I feel comfortable pulling her off the sedation medication. Once we do that, we will adjust things so that she can get up and move and will be able to use the restroom and things like that on her own without the use of medical equipment. I think moving a little bit will be good for her. She will have some pain, but at least we can get her functioning and talking. I know the police are anxious to get her statement, which I understand. But I also don't want to rush her into this."

"Thank God," I say, as I put my head in my hands and rub my face. "I'll let the others know too."

"I'm fine with you being here when she wakes up, I think we can plan on possibly later today that others can come and see her, depending on how she's feeling. I just don't know how overwhelming it could get for her, we will need to take this slow."

"Makes sense. I'll hold off on saying anything for now."

He gets to work checking her over. He and the nurse go over different bags of fluids and change out IV's. She never moved or flinched through any of it.

They wrap things up and tell me that as sedation wears off, she might start moving or talking, and to just stay calm with her, and to hit the call button as needed.

About two hours later, I'm sitting in the chair next to her bed, with my head on the edge. I feel her fingers wiggle just the tiniest amount. I lift my head up and give her hand a squeeze. I hear her take in a tiny breath, and a little groan comes out of her.

Her eyelids are starting to flutter a little and her fingers are moving slightly.

"Hey baby, it's me, Jay. I'm right here with you. You are safe in the hospital." She groans a little in response.

Finally, her eyes open very slowly, blinking away days of sleep and unrest. She finally looks over, finding and focusing on me.

"Hey gorgeous. I've missed you." Tears are falling down my face. I give her hand a squeeze and don't let go.

"Jay." She tries to say my name, it came out as a squeak. Still, I knew what it was.

Her eyes start moving around the room. She looks nervous. "You are in the Pine Lake Hospital. John is in custody." The second I say the name I see anxiety cross her face. Her monitor starts beeping faster.

"It's okay babe, he can't get you, he's in jail. You are safe. You've been sleeping the last couple of days." I kiss her hand, feeling bad I made her anxious.

Nurse Sara comes in a minute later. She turns the monitor off with the fast-paced beeping. "Hello Olivia, I see you are awake. My name is Sara. I'm your nurse today. I am so glad to see you have your eyes open." She says the words softly and kindly and she grabs her left hand gently.

"Dr. Monson will be in here in a couple minutes to check on you too. He is your main doctor; you will like him."

Her eyes flash from the nurse to me. I can tell she's unsure what to believe.

"Once you are good and awake and comfortable, we will let your family and friends come in and see you. You should know, this guy has been here the whole time taking good care of you," she nods her head in my direction, and I give her a smile.

Dr. Monson walks in slowly. He keeps a short distance away from the bed, behind nurse Sara.

"Hello Olivia, I'm Doctor Monson. Or you can call me Tim. We are just going to check on you, is that okay? Can you shake or nod your head for me?" He has slowly started moving closer to her, I'm guessing he's trying to make sure she stays comfortable around this stranger, who, unbeknownst to her, has been here the whole time.

She gives a barely visible nod that it's okay.

"Great. If anything bothers you, I want you to squeeze Jay's hand. Okay?" She nods again.

He runs through different checks, looking over her lacerations. He changes out the bandages, cleaning them up. I hate seeing them up this close, it's upsetting.

"They both look to be doing well."

He moves on to unwrap the bandages around her wrists. I see her eyes widen as the wrapping comes off. Tears well up in her eyes, I wipe them away for her.

"I bet all these cuts hurt pretty bad, don't they." He states, looking at her. She gives him a small nod.

"Well, the good news is that everything is looking good. It's only been a couple of days, but we are making progress."

"We are going to let you have water and ice chips now. I'm guessing your throat is in pain." She nods again in agreement. Her eyes light up, she must be so thirsty.

"That will help a lot. And once you hold down water for a while, we will start to introduce food. Right now, you have supplements coming to you through your IV's. But I think you will want solid foods sooner than later. It's been a long time since you've had a meal. Have as much water as you want, and if you need the restroom hit the call button and the nurse will come and help you. Do not try and walk over there by yourself."

He has her new bandages on, and new IV's secured.

For the next couple hours, she chews on ice chips and drinks lots of water. I can see the color coming back to her, it's amazing the difference it's making. She is trying so hard, I'm so proud of her.

She still can't really talk, her voice is so hoarse, but she is trying. Occasionally, she says my name, just to see if she can do it. She's getting there.

I turned the TV on for her. Nothing local, as the news has had her story on full blast since she went missing. I've seen the news vans off and on outside the hospital the last couple days. They can't get in here, so I couldn't care less.

I sit with her as she rests, already feeling more relaxed knowing she is awake. I let myself doze off.

I feel her scratching my head. I'm resting it next to her on the bed. I wake up, startled, immediately my eyes find hers. I check my watch; I was sleeping for almost two hours.

She looks different. Her eyes look clearer than before, and she has more color in her face. I can see her moving her hands and arms a little more now. The red call button is lit up next to her.

"Sorry to wake you, but I have to get up." I smile at her, not because of what she said, but because she talked. She got out a whole sentence.

"Hi." She clears her throat. "Thank you for staying with me. I missed you." She's speaking very slowly, but I'm so excited to hear her talk.

"Liv, I need to tell you, I'm so sorry I took those pictures. I just...I just couldn't help myself. If I had ever lost you, I'd at least have pictures. I don't have that many of Casey and I always wish I had more. I know that's weird, but I'm so, so sorry. I've been wanting to say that to you for so many days now."

"Jay, its fine. You don't need to apologize."

I stand up, leaning over her and cup her cheek in my hand. I give her the softest kiss imaginable. It's perfect.

I have my girl back.

CHAPTER 62

LIV

I OPEN MY EYES AND the sunlight from the narrow window in my room is pouring in. It feels good, warm.

I look over and see Jay sleeping on the small couch, covered by a thin white hospital blanket. He doesn't look very comfortable. I wonder how long he's been here.

I slept through the night last night, and according to the TV it's Tuesday morning.

I move my head and neck side to side, it feels a lot better, but still really tense. I wiggle my fingers, then raise my arms up and back down and side to side. I can feel my shoulders tensing and straining too hard. A week of being cuffed to a bed in a terrible position apparently does this to you.

I grab the electronic box with the bed controls, its right next to my left hand where my IV is. I twist my wrist to get to it, and wince with pain as the IV digs deeper into my skin. I'll be sure to remember to not do that again.

I reach over and use my right hand to use the control instead, wanting to raise up my head rest so that I'm not laying totally flat. All I've been doing recently is lying flat, I can't handle it anymore.

I put the control box down and look around my room. There must be at least thirty different bouquets of flowers in here. I wonder who they are all from and when they got here. Up until now, my head was in a complete fog.

I need to pee. Like now. I don't want to wake up Jay, but I won't be able to wait.

I hit the call button by my shoulder to get the nurse in here. A minute later a middle-aged woman with short hair opens the door. I put my right hand up to make the "shh" face at her and point at Jay sleeping.

She tiptoes over to me with a smile.

"You look so much better today. I was in here Sunday and have been so worried about you."

"Right now, I'm worried about my bladder, I have to pee so bad." I tell her in a whisper.

She nods and gets to work unhooking some things, hitting a button so there is no beeping or noise.

She swings my legs off the bed slowly, then steadies my shoulders. She wraps her arm around my back, holding me up. I'm wondering why she thinks I'm so fragile. I make to stand up, but my legs give out from under me. She catches me before I end up on the floor, and I'll give her credit, she is stronger than she looks. Now I understand why she was holding me like that, I feel like an idiot.

We walk quietly to the bathroom, closing the door behind us. I go pee, finally, and feel so much better. She helps me back up and I stand unsteadily at the sink to wash my hands.

As I'm drying them, I look into the mirror and see myself for the first time. I look horrible. My cheeks are sunken in, and I look like I haven't slept in a month. My skin is ashy and dry. I can see a bandage sticking out of the neckline on my hospital gown. I pull it down and peel back the tape on the bandage, revealing a red scar with stitches, about six to eight inches long. The memory of John cutting me comes flooding back.

I start to collapse over the sink, sobs escaping me without control. The nurse is rubbing my back, still holding me up. I'm shaking. I don't want these memories: the cutting, the pushing of my head under the water in the tub, the way he was putting different lingerie on me... I can't handle it, I throw up in the sink, nothing but bile and stomach acid. It burns so bad that I can't breathe and I'm hyperventilating.

"Nurse Station One, I'm going to need back up in room 114, immediately. Help with a patient getting back to bed. Send Nick. Olivia, it's okay sweetie. We are going to get you back in bed, okay? I have someone coming to assist."

I hear a knock on the bathroom door. Jay's voice is on the other side. Shit, I woke him up.

"Liv, what's going on in there? Are you okay?"

"Jay, we're fine. It's me, nurse Jen. I have someone else coming to help us."

I feel so bad I woke him up. I hear voices on the other side of the door.

"Jen, it's Nick. Can I come in?"

Jen opens the door, and a young muscular man comes in. He grabs me around my waist and carries me back to my hospital bed. I feel limp and useless in his arms.

Jen gets me hooked back up to my IV, and the machines start beeping again. Tears are rolling down my face, I can't stop them. Jay comes around to my right side and grabs my hand.

"Hey Liv, it's Jay. You are okay. We are all here to help you."

I squeeze his hand; I can't get any words out.

"Olivia, we need you to remain calm, okay?" She starts rubbing my shoulder.

After a few minutes my breathing returns to normal. Nick has left, and Jay still has my hand in his.

Jen leans closer, grabbing my left hand gently.

"I was told that if you are doing well enough today that Sheriff Hayden will come in this afternoon, and they will be taking your official statement on what happened. Do you think you will be up to it? If you have any doubt at all, I will let them know we need to push it back. It's all up to you."

I clear my throat a few times. Talking still hurts.

"It's fine. Just keep giving me water so my throat doesn't hurt. I want to get all of that over with."

"Okay dear. I will let the officer outside know. If anything changes you tell me right away, just ring the call button." She gives me a reassuring smile.

"Thank you." I tell her as she walks out the door. She stops and talks to a young officer sitting in a chair across the hall. I had no idea he was even there.

Jay and I sit quietly for a couple minutes. Then something hits me. I look over to him. "You called me *Liv* instead of *Olivia*. Why?"

"Well, John called you Olivia, it bothered me that I did too. I didn't want that to remind you of him. So, from now on, you are my *Liv*." He pauses, chewing nervously on his bottom lip. "You are my *Liv,* and my *love*."

He leans over and gives me a kiss. The butterflies in my stomach are doing summersaults over the fact that he just called me his *love*.

CHAPTER 63

JAY

SHERIFF HAYDEN HAS BEEN IN Liv's room for a little over an hour now.

I started off sitting in the chair next to the window. As she started retelling the details of what happened, I ended up standing next to her bed, holding her hand, and helping to calm her down.

The Sheriff has a chair and small side table pulled up next to her bed, opposite of me. He has a notepad and pen out, and a voice recorder, so everything is on tape.

Liv has been insistent that I be there as she retold it. She has also been insistent that the rest of AO listens in. She said that she didn't want to have to repeat the story over and over, that once was enough. At first, I wasn't a fan of the idea, but now I get why she wants it this way. I wouldn't want to have to retell it either if I were her.

All six of us have been in tears off and on through the whole thing. At one point Waylon had so much tension he looked like he was going to punch a hole in the wall with his fist.

A few minutes ago, when she talked about him cutting her and putting her blood on a canvas, I had to step into the bathroom and vomit. If I ever see that mother fucker again, I will wring his neck with my bare hands until there is nothing left of him.

All the details are done. Sheriff Hayden doesn't shut off the voice recorder yet though.

"Olivia, I want you to know some other details before I go. First, John is in custody. He cannot get to you. You can go home and feel safe. This will go to trial, and he will pay the consequences for his actions. I want you to start mentally preparing yourself for that. Second, from our investigation, we found out that your Methotrexate medication for arthritis was tampered with, he filled the bottle with rohypnol, or commonly known in its street name of "roofies". After getting your toxicology report back, we found them in your system and believe you were receiving those while you were at his house. We also found muscle relaxers in your system along with multiple other things. Your doctor can fill you in more on those details when you speak to him. Third, we have lots of evidence from his house to help account for what happened. We have a little from your house as well. Your house is back in order, so once the hospital discharges you, you can go home, and won't notice a difference, well, except you will have to bring back a whole flower shop of flowers with you," he says as he points to the back of the room and all the colorful arrangements.

"Thank you so much. I appreciate everything you and your team have done."

"In all honesty, you should be thanking Jay. He's the one who figured out it was John," he says with a smile in Jay's direction, shutting off his voice recorder and getting out of his chair, stretching.

I look at Jay in shock. "Seriously? Why didn't you tell me that before?"

"Um, well, I found evidence of him stalking you…in my pictures. The ones in the shoe box." He's tiptoeing around the words and having a hard time looking me in the eye.

That Friday night comes flooding back into my head. I had thought Jay was my stalker. The pieces seemed to fit at the time. He was taking pictures of me, and John had sent me pictures. I shake my head and brush it off. None of that matters anymore.

"I hope you forgive me for thinking you were the one stalking me," I say quietly, embarrassed.

"Babe, I was never mad at you. Just mad at myself." He kisses my hand again.

There is a light knock at the door. It's Dr. Monson.

"Hello Olivia, everyone. I have good news. I think you are doing well enough that we can discharge you tomorrow, along with all those flowers," he says with a smile.

"Thank God. No offense, but I want to get out of here." Laughter erupts around the room.

"Great. Today and tomorrow morning we need to get you up and walking and doing things like showering, to make sure you can function safely enough at home alone. Nurse Jen will be in and out helping you with that. We are also going to start drawing down some of the things we are giving you in your IV's, so that it isn't such a huge difference tomorrow when you leave. Does that make sense?"

"Yes. Thank you." I'm so excited to be able to get up and move. It probably won't be pretty, but I don't care.

Jay and the guys are in the back in a hushed discussion. I furrow my brow, wondering what they are talking about.

Sheriff Hayden and Dr. Monson exit the room, leaving the six of us. I shift and sit up a little higher in bed.

"Hey, what are we talking about over there?" I ask them quizzically in my small voice.

Their eyes turn to me, but none of them say anything. Jay walks over to the side of my bed, slowly, grabbing my hand.

"Liv, we have an idea. We all think I should just stay with you at your place until you are fully functioning. We don't want anything to happen to you when no one is around."

"Jay just wants to move in with you sooner than later," Darren says laughing, and Waylon jabs him in the gut, doubling him over.

"They will bring all your stuff from the hospital over today, so we don't have to worry about anything tomorrow when you leave. And then tomorrow I will bring you home. What do you think about that idea?"

Well, I wasn't expecting this. But I'm not opposed to it, the butterflies are in a frenzy in my stomach.

"Okay. I like that idea. This is just for a few days until I'm back to normal though, right?" I'm biting my lip, nervous. A big grin spreads across his face. He leans down and pulls on my lip teasingly and kisses me.

"Sure babe," Jay says in between kisses.

The peanut gallery in the back of the room hoot and holler like little kids.

CHAPTER 64

LIV

IT'S FINALLY TIME TO LEAVE the hospital.

I've been up and walking around, doing my best to stabilize myself.

Jay left for a little bit this morning, just long enough to run to his house and pack some things to bring to my place. I'm getting nervous about having him in my house. He might decide I'm a pain to live with and pull the rip cord on everything. God, I hope not.

The boys gathered up all my flowers and brought them to my house. I wonder how many people have been in and out of my house since I've been gone. It makes my stomach uneasy; I don't like that.

Lexie, Tina, and Jenna are all in my hospital room now. Lots of hugs and tears are being shed.

"Thankfully, Jay has been so good about messaging all of us on how you are doing, otherwise I would have lost my mind," Lexie tells me with tears in her eyes.

"And I do have to say, not everything the news has been reporting has been helpful, or correct," Tina adds.

"The news? What do you mean?"

"I mean, they suck at their jobs and will make up any bullshit just to get people to watch their stories. There was so much crazy speculation when you were missing. The only thing I *didn't* hear was that bigfoot kidnapped you," she says with an eye roll.

"Wait, this has been on the news? I guess I haven't watched it in a while."

The girls all share an odd look.

"Liv, the Midwest *region* has been talking about you. There are reporters outside right now, anticipating your discharge from the hospital. The police had to barricade the road to your house. People started a memorial by your mailbox. There were so many search parties out looking for you. And then AO went on their website and said shows are canceled until further notice. The band has been getting bombarded with questions from reporters." I feel like Jenna could keep going, but she stops short.

"Wow, I had no idea. Now I just feel bad."

"No, Liv, don't feel bad about anything. You are safe and that asshole is sitting in jail, all is good in the world now." Lexie leans over and hugs me.

Two nurses come in, one is Nick, he helped me out of the bathroom. The other one I don't know.

"Alright, are you ready to get out of here Olivia," the unfamiliar nurse says with a smile.

"Um, I need to wait for Jay, he's coming home with me." I had already filled the girls in on our situation for the next few days, they all bounced and squealed with delight.

"I'm here baby," Jay says, jogging into the room, out of breath.

"Hey," I stand up and take a few slow steps toward him, wrapping my arms tight around his waist.

"The reporters outside wouldn't leave me alone. I parked my car in the pickup zone, and they were on me like a herd of starving cats." Everyone laughs.

Nick rolls a wheelchair between us and motions for me to sit down.

"Oh no, I can walk Nick, I don't need that. But thank you."

"It's the hospital policy that upon discharge, patients must leave in a wheelchair. So, one of us gets the honor of rolling you out of here."

"Oh," I say, thinking it's weird they would do that when I've been working so hard to function on my own.

"I've got you babe." Jay stands behind it and holds it in place for me, and I sit down uncomfortably.

The last time I was in one of these was in John's house with a tie strap around me. It makes me shiver.

Jay wheels me out of the room and into the hallway. We get to the entrance of the hospital, and I can see Jay's truck, along with a group of reporters.

"Call us later," Lexie yells out and I wave goodbye to them, dreading the reporters and cameras outside.

"You ready babe?" Jay whispers in my ear.

"Ready as I'll ever be."

The automatic doors open, and cameras and lights are on us. We barely make it to the side of the truck to get my door open.

"Everybody back off, right now," a booming voice comes from behind me. I turn and see a hospital security guard immobilizing people to move away.

"Thank you," I say to him with a smile. He gives me a smile and nod in return.

Jay helps me into the truck, giving me a kiss before closing the door. He wheels the chair back to the automatic door and comes back. He then gets in on the driver's side.

"Let's get out of here," he says, putting the truck into drive. I never want to come back here again.

CHAPTER 65

LIV

IT FEELS SURREAL TO HAVE Jay in my house. We've been extremely lazy since we've been home together. We've watched so many movies and spent countless hours cuddling on the couch. The Jay cuddles will never get old. My job told me to take as much time off as I need. I asked if I could have the coming week off and they said 'yes'. They even said they would pay me for it, so I don't come up short. I told them they didn't need to do that, but they insisted. I'm never taking my job for granted ever again after this.

It's Sunday night, eight days after I was rescued from John's house. I get a text from the AO group on my phone.

> Erik: Hey guys. Can we meet up tonight? We
> have a lot to discuss.
> Darren: Yep.
> Waylon: What time?
> Erik: 6:30?
> Liv: Works for me.
> Joe: I'm in.
> Erik: Bring Jay with you.
> Waylon: See you at the shed. I'll bring the beer.

I walk into the bedroom to find Jay. He's sitting on the bed talking on the phone. I sit down on the bed across from him and wait for him to finish up.

He finally hangs up, scooting closer to me on the bed.

"So that was my dad. He was asking questions about the trial. Since he's a judge he has connections, and he wants to pay for a lawyer for you."

"What? No, I won't let him. He doesn't need to do that."

"Apparently, he knows a younger guy that has been doing a really good job, his name is Michael something-or-other. He says since it is a high-profile case, he will do it for next to nothing. He just wants the publicity of a big win. Dad already asked him. Sorry I had told him you didn't have a lawyer yet and he was all over it."

"To be honest, I didn't know I needed a lawyer," I twist up my face in confusion.

"Never hurts."

"Well, that is sweet of your dad. I'll find a way to pay him back. Oh hey, on another note, do you want to come with me to the AO shed tonight at 6:30?"

"Sure. What's going on?"

"Not sure. Erik texted us and said that we have *a lot to discuss*. I don't know what that means. And then he told me to bring you."

He smiles. I know he likes the fact that the guys think the world of him.

"Sounds good babe. We'll be there."

He leans in and kisses me. It sends a surge of passion through me. It's been way too long since we've had sex, and I don't think I'll make it past tonight without it. He keeps saying he doesn't want to rush things, but my hormones can't handle it anymore.

CHAPTER 66

LIV

WE PULL UP TO THE shed in my Tahoe. Erik and Darren are already here. I guarantee Waylon will pull up after us, and Joe will be the last, like usual.

We get out and Jay grabs my hand, pulling it up to his mouth and giving it a kiss. There is a sparkle in his eye when he looks at me. It warms me from the inside out.

We step in the door and grab some spots on one of the couches. Jay wraps his arm around my shoulders, and I lean into him.

Eventually the rest of the crew filters in. For once Joe wasn't the last one there.

"Holy shit, you beat me here?" Waylon booms as he walks in the door, a case of beer in his hands.

"There's a first for everything!" Darren says, and we all laugh. Joe rolls his eyes at us.

"Okay, since this is clearly a day of firsts — first time Joe isn't the last one to show, Jay's first beer in the shed, and drumroll please...." He stops, and we all start doing terrible impressions of a drum roll, laughing.

"And, most importantly, the first time a record label is interested in American Obsession." He has a huge smile on his face. Our jaws are on the floor, everyone is silent for a second.

"Wait, are you serious or are you fucking with us?" Darren asks hesitantly.

"Yeah, that's a mean joke if that's not true," Joe chimes in, giving Erik a sideways look.

Erik pulls a piece of paper out of his back pocket, unfolding it. He reads it aloud to us.

Dear Mr. Pierson,

My name is Mark Stevens, I am the A&R (Artists & Repertoire) Director for Anthem Records. I am responsible for the artistic development of recording artists and songwriters.

Recently we received your demo of three original songs, written and performed by American Obsession. We are interested in learning more about the band, and what your future aspirations are.

I do want to address that one of your members, Ms. Olivia Dunne, recently went through a very traumatic experience. I have been following you and did note that you have canceled shows during this time. Please reach out to me at your earliest convenience to let me know how you see yourselves proceeding.

Before we pursue you further for consideration at Anthem Records, I will need to see these three original songs performed in a public setting, AKA a show. Please respond to me as soon as possible at the email in the signature line below.

Thank you,
Mr. Mark Stevens

We sit in silence for a few seconds, all of us in shock. I look around the room and I'm stunned this is even happening.

"Holy shit. Anthem Records?" Even as I say it out loud, it sounds crazy.

"Yeah. I think we need to discuss this as a group tonight and respond to him immediately." Erik says, taking charge of the conversation. He's not in shock like we are, he's the only one that already knew about this.

"We canceled our shows for the time being. I think we need to work on getting things back up and scheduled, and then decide which show would be the best one to have him come out to." Waylon says, and he's right.

"Okay, let's divide the list of our upcoming shows up, each of us take one and call them. See if we can get our schedule back on track." Erik says as he brings the computer screen to life with our show information on it.

"Hang on. Which one do we see being the most opportune for this? Garden Park?" Joe says to all of us.

"I think we need to call there first if that is our top pick, and get that one set up, then Erik can email him back immediately. The more time we have for prep the better," Joe says.

"Perfect, I'll call them right now," Erik says.

We spend the next fifteen minutes making phone calls and getting our shows set back up.

All but one came back into the schedule. It was a wedding, and we didn't blame them for finding someone else, we had no idea when things would be back to normal.

Garden Park immediately said they wanted to keep our show, so Erik got to work right away emailing Mark back.

The case of beer Waylon brought is already half gone.

"Hey, if you're bored, you can take my vehicle home. Someone else can drive me." I say quietly, leaning over Jay, my hands resting on his thighs.

"I'm fine babe, it's fun watching you guys' work. I'm happy for you." He leans in, kissing me. We're totally making up for lost time tonight when we get home.

I stand back up, and Jay slaps my ass playfully. I turn and wink at him.

"Gross, she's like our sister, keep it in your pants," Waylon teases Jay, and we all laugh.

"Hey, quiet!" Erik shouts above us. We all stop. He's staring at his screen, and then looks up at us, a smile spreading on his face.

"Mr. Mark Stevens just responded to my email; he is coming to the Garden Park show."

We erupt into smiles, hugs, tears, and dance around the shitty old shed like we were kids. Erik stops and turns to the freezer, grabbing a bottle of champagne out of it.

"I was hoping we would be drinking this tonight." And he pops the top on it, cheap champagne spilling out on the floor.

We grab plastic cups and fill them up, all six of us making a toast to American Obsession.

CHAPTER 67

LIV

JAY AND I GET BACK to my place after the exciting night at the shed. I doubt I'll be able to sleep tonight. Thank God I don't have to get up to work in the morning.

I set my purse down in the kitchen, and lean back on the counter, letting out a deep breath.

Jay comes up and stands in front of me, closing the space in between us, his hands resting on the counter on either side of me. "I'm so proud of you Liv. I can't believe you are going to be a huge rockstar."

"Maybe. Who knows, the guy might not like us." I'm trying to be reasonably optimistic here.

"He will love you. *Everybody* loves you." He winks at me, and I smile.

Is it the right time for me to tell him I've fallen in love with him? I don't say it, I want it to be perfect when I finally tell him.

He leans in closer to me, kissing my neck. "I want you so bad, you have no idea," he says, kissing me between his words.

"Oh, trust me, I know how you feel," and I pull him to me, kissing him hard.

He picks me up and sets me on the counter, pulling my cream-colored cowl neck sweater over my head and throws it on the floor. I start unbuttoning his jeans. His hands grab mine to stop them.

"Wait, are you sure you're ready? I don't want to do anything that will make you uncomfortable."

"Oh, I'm ready. The only uncomfortable thing here is all these clothes." I keep undoing his jeans.

I get them undone and he slides them down his legs, pulling his T-shirt off afterwards. He picks me up by my ass and lifts me off the counter, walking me to the bedroom. He lays me on the bed on my back, flipping on one of the nightstand lamps.

I'm already unbuttoning my jeans, but he finishes the task, dragging them down my legs and tossing them on the floor.

I have on a matching pink bra and panty set, mostly lace, a little see-through.

"God, you're sexy," he says, bending down, trailing kisses all over me. My whole body is shivering with pleasure.

I stand up, turn him around and push him back on the bed.

He lays down with a smile on his face. I start pulling the pink panties slowly down my legs, antagonizing him. His eyes are watching me the entire time.

After I have them off, I move toward him. He slides back on to the middle of the bed, a pillow under his head. I climb toward him slowly, taking his huge erection into my mouth and sucking on him for a minute. I can feel him trembling beneath me.

I lift my head up and position myself on top of him. Before I let him enter me, I grab the front clasp of my bra, undo it, and wait a second to remove it from my breasts, a smile on my face. I know he loves this.

He groans with desire, and I can see the heat in his eyes.

"Take it off for me, baby," his breathing is ragged.

I slowly let it fall behind me. His hands reach up and grasp on to my breasts, just as I lower myself down on to him, letting him fill me.

I let him pulse inside of me, slowly moving up and down on him. He has no idea the affect he has on me. It's not just what I feel for him, it's what I don't feel for anyone but him.

I'm moving quicker on him, and his hands are clawing at the sheets now, moaning my name.

He moves his hand to my hair and pulls my head back gently, my mouth open releasing uninterrupted moans. I have no thoughts; in that moment I can only feel. His other hand moves from the sheets to grab my ass, pulling me down on him fervently.

I start to clench myself around his erection, knowing I will climax soon.

"Baby, come with me," his breathing is ragged and sexy.

We release together, and I relax myself around him, feeling him pour into me. Its exquisite.

I bend over and lay my head on his chest, our breathing is rough, our sweaty bodies tangled up in each other.

This is the happiness I've always longed for.

CHAPTER 68

LIV

THE BIG NIGHT IS FINALLY here, our show at Garden Park. It's been almost a week since Mark at Anthem Records emailed us.

I have been working so hard to get my voice back in to shape and am doing everything I can to get the deep cuts on my wrists healed enough to play tonight. I have them wrapped up with bandages and put some big chunky bracelets on each wrist, so they aren't as noticeable. I still need to be careful with them, but they seem to be healing fine.

I contacted the owners and told them that Anthem Records would be here watching us, and that we wanted the place to be packed. They decided to do a cheap beer special to help draw people in, and we posted all over our website and social media that we will be debuting three original songs tonight. It's an hour before the show starts and the place is already packed.

We got Mark Stevens a special pass with security, so he can stand backstage, side stage, or out in the crowd. We wanted him to have the best possible time at this show, hopefully without getting light beer dumped all over him by the rowdy crowd.

I looked him up on LinkedIn ahead of time and shared his photo with the group, so we all know what he looks like. Middle aged man, tan, silver-gray hair, nice smile.

Now it's right before show start. The five of us are standing backstage. Everything is ready.

We are all warmed up, now we are just trying to rid ourselves of our worked-up nerves. I keep adjusting my outfit. Handmade leggings with cut out horizontal slits in the front that are braided, running up and down the entirety of both my legs. I have on the T-shirt that Jay gave me that says, "SORRY BOYS, I'M TAKEN". I threw on some black and white Converse and put my hair in a ponytail with fishtail braids running through it, teased up like crazy. Going for the total rocker chick look tonight.

"We need to just pretend that this is a normal show. We don't get nervous for normal shows," Joe says, and we nod our heads.

"Hey guys," Jay says as he walks up to us with a smile. I got him a special backstage pass too.

"Don't look so nervous. You guys' kick ass, just do your normal level of kick ass and you'll be fine." He says it so levelheaded like it's obvious, he's lucky he doesn't know how stressful this is.

"Thank you," I say, giving him a smile, biting my lip.

"What did I tell you about this lip? Biting it is my job," he says as he pulls my lip out with his teeth, kissing me hard.

"Knock 'em dead baby. Oh, and I like the shirt," he winks and gives my ass a slap and turns to head back to the crowd.

I peek my head through the thick black curtains and see that Brandon and Amanda and his parents are standing there in the front row, in his usual area. He rejoins them and they all wave at me. I wave back with a smile.

He has the best family. I look over at my AO boys and realize that I do too. Jay's right. We are going to knock them dead.

The owners of Garden Park give us a nod and head up on to the stage, the crowd is already cheering and pulsing.

"Alright ladies and gentlemen, let's give a big Garden Park welcome to your favorite band – American Obsession!"

Audioslave's "Cochise" starts playing over the speakers as we walk on to the stage, the crowd going ballistic. This is exactly the entrance we needed to get us pumped up and excited.

We let the song fade out and we greet the crowd. Erik announces we will be performing three original songs tonight for the first time.

As he talks, we get our bottle of tequila out and pass it to each other, each taking a pull. We've never told anyone but it's just water. It's our own private joke. We launch right into our set list once we've all had a fake pull. We are bringing out all our favorites tonight to go along with our new original songs.

<u>Set 1 –</u>
Queen – We Will Rock You *(with me singing lead)*
Ted Nugent – Stranglehold
Billy Squier – Lonely Is the Night
Theory of a Deadman – Lowlife
Dorothy – Rest in Peace
Linkin Park – New Divide
Guns N' Roses – Paradise City
American Obsession – Let Down
Buckcherry – Lit Up
Eva Under Fire – Every Time You Leave

(Break)

<u>Set 2 –</u>
American Obsession – Shame
I Prevail – Deep End
The Rolling Stones – Paint it Black
Lilith Czar – 100 Little Deaths
Eve 6 – Here's to The Night
Nickelback – San Quentin
Halestorm – The Steeple
AC/DC – Money Talks
American Obsession – If You Leave Me

Sum 41 – Fat Lip
The Warning – More

Encore –

Glorious Sons – S.O.S.
Dorothy – Black Sheep

We finish our set and come back out for two encore songs. Normally we only do one, but tonight is special so we're giving them a little extra. The crowd has been amazing; I've never seen energy quite like this from them at a previous show. They screamed so loud. When we played our originals, they just didn't stop. The flashes of pictures, and people holding up their phones taking videos was overwhelming.

I finish the last of Black Sheep, and let the microphone drop to my side. The boys come up to the front of the stage with me. We stand in line and bow for the crowd, screams and cheers coming at us in waves.

"Thank you. We are American Obsession. Goodnight!" I say into the microphone as I wave my hand to the crowd.

I'm drenched in sweat. We all are. Erik and Joe gave up their shirts a long time ago.

We turn away from the crowd, exiting off the side of the stage, and go behind the curtains. We have a folding chair for each of us back here. We all collapse on our chairs, grabbing our waters and try to cool off.

"Fuck, we rocked that. I love you guys." Erik tells us, before squirting cold water over his head.

We sit for a few minutes and there is a commotion behind us. I turn to see a security guard walking with Jay.

"Liv, this guy is wondering if he can bring four other people back here."

"Yep, he sure can, let them back." I'm guessing he is bringing Brandon and Amanda and his parents back. I told him earlier he could do that if he wanted. I forgot to tell security.

"Oh my God that was amazing." I can hear Amanda from behind me. I get up, turn, and she wraps her arms around me, bouncing up and down.

"Oh my God Liv, you are so sweaty," she says as she peels away from me.

I start laughing. "Yeah, it's a hazard of the job."

"Good job baby," Jay says as he gives me a kiss. He leans in closer, "we'll have to shower together later, you *are* sweaty," he whispers in my ear. I can feel my cheeks redden.

I look over at Brandon, Amanda, and Jay's parents, about to talk to them, just as Mark Stevens walks backstage. I freeze. The band is beside me, not saying a word.

"Hey there! Great show you guys, that was fantastic. I'm Mark Stevens, A&R for Anthem Records. Do you have a minute to talk?"

"Absolutely, sorry we're so sweaty," Erik says as he gets up to shake his hand. "I'm Erik Pierson, we were emailing back and forth."

"Yes, thank you for the prompt responses and information. I'm glad it worked out that I could be here."

He turns toward me and grabs my hands. "And you Ms. Dunne, I am so happy to hear things are okay, and that you are back to safety."

I'm almost speechless, all I can get out is, "thank you," and a smile.

We are all still just standing there stunned, unsure what to do or say, along with Jay and his family. Mark lets go of my hands and faces the band.

"Well, I'm not going to beat around the bush here. Anthem Records would like to sign American Obsession to their label. Your original songs are fantastic."

We look around at each other in complete shock. Suddenly, we collide in a huge group hug, jumping up and down. We finally calm down after a minute and turn to face Mark again.

"I'm sorry, we didn't mean to be rude," I tell him, red in the face.

"No worries, I'm used to getting that reaction out of people. Or they end up begging me for a second chance," he says with a chuckle.

"Listen, keep checking your email, we are going to be sending contracts, documents, and a ton of information for you to look over and sign as a group. These items will be coming to you within the next week. If you have any questions, you simply reach out to me. I'm here to help you with anything you need." He hands us each a business card. "Any questions for me?"

"Um, not that I can think of. Thank you for this opportunity. This is everything we've ever dreamed of," Erik says with a huge smile, shaking his hand again.

"Not a problem. Nice to meet you all. We will be in touch." He turns and walks back out to the crowd.

Time to pop another bottle of champagne.

CHAPTER 69

LIV

LAST NIGHT'S SHOW AT GARDEN Park still plays in my mind. It seems surreal that Mark was even there, and that Anthem Records wants American Obsession on their label.

I'm still drifting off in my thoughts as Jay's hand touches my thigh. We are driving out to his uncle's land for another date night in the back of the truck.

"What are you thinking about babe?"

"Last night," I say with a smile that I absolutely cannot contain.

"I figured so," and he squeezes my thigh and gives me a smile.

We back into the thick CRP grass in our usual spot, the back of the truck facing west, so we can watch the sunset in each other's arms.

It's early November and the cold of winter is setting in. There isn't any snow yet, but the chill is in the air like it could snow any day. I'm already missing summer, along with the tanks tops, shorts, and flip flops. But this will be okay, at least I have a handsome man to cuddle up to when I get cold.

We flip up the cover on the back of the truck, everything is inside already. This is, without a doubt, my favorite of all our date night things to do.

We settle in on the air mattress, the pillows and blankets flowing around us.

We grab a thicker blanket and throw it over top of us. I tuck myself in right next to Jay, his right arm draped around my shoulders.

James Stapleton's "Tennessee Whiskey" is playing. I love this song; Jay does too.

"Liv," Jay says, turning his body towards me. I do the same.

"What is it?"

Jay is looking into my eyes. His left hand reaches up and holds my neck, his thumb gently brushing my cheek. I just melt every time he does this.

"I've wanted to tell you for a while now but…" he trails off. He looks nervous.

He looks back at me, into my eyes, "I love you Liv. I love you so much. You were worth the wait, and you always will be. I knew it the first time I set my eyes on you."

My breath catches in my throat. I can feel my heart swelling inside of me.

"I love you too Jay. I want to be the first and last one you love."

He pulls my face into his, kissing me passionately, yet still holding my neck and cheek. We spend the rest of the evening wrapped in each other's arms, it's the only place I want to be.

The sunset is beautiful tonight. Lots of mixed mellowed and radiant blues, and bold streaks of red. It reminds me of our lives, usually peaceful and constant, are like the blue of the sky, with splashes of vibrant reds mixed in, reminding us that there will always be chaos and change.

But if Jay is by my side, *Obsession Olivia* can handle anything.

Made in the USA
Monee, IL
31 January 2024

52617616R00177